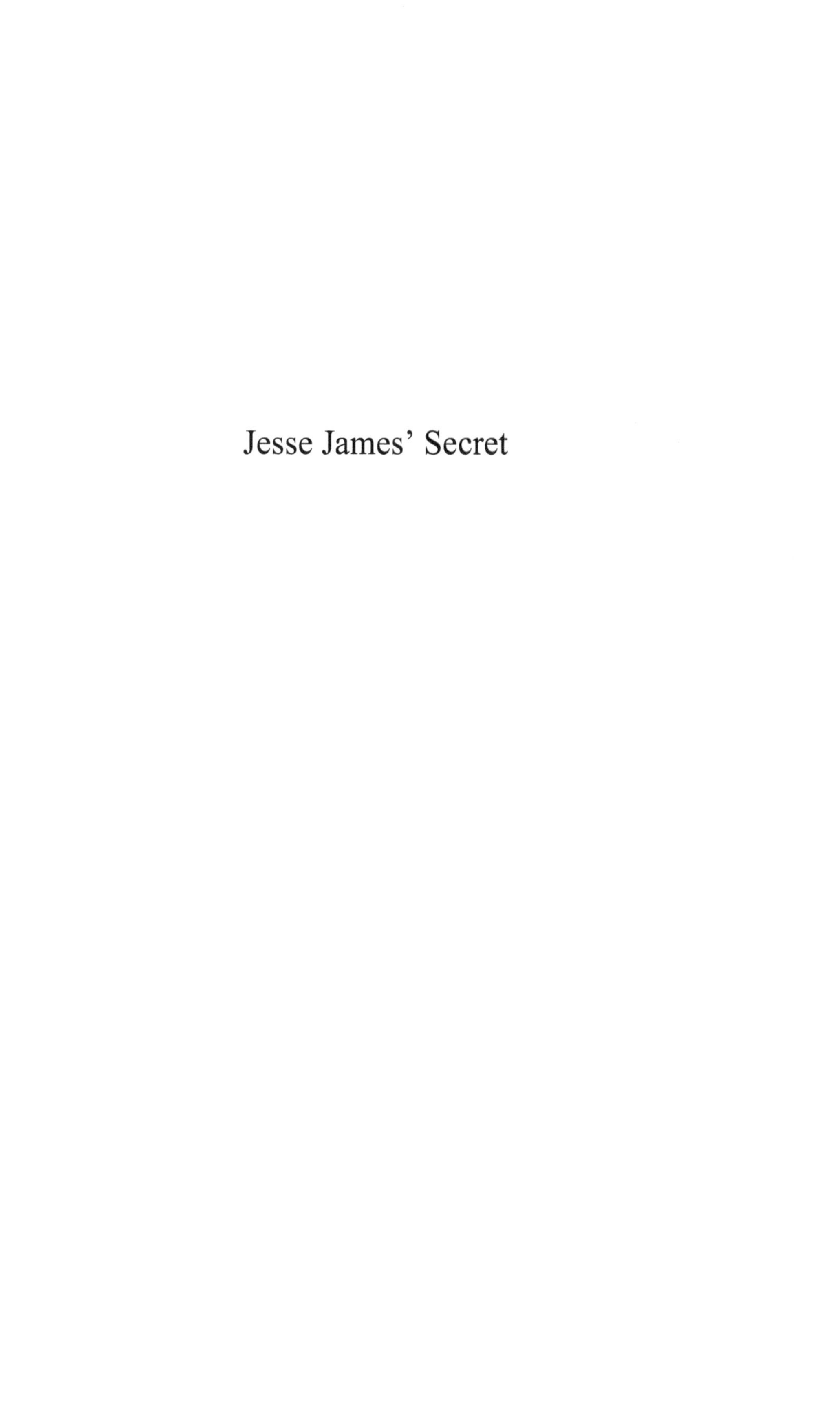

Jesse James' Secret

Other books by John O'Melveny Woods

Return to Treasure Island

Lost Tomb of Alexander

Jesse James Secret

The Crusaders

A Stroke of Hope

Also Available with Co-Author Frank Kelso

California Gold

Juan's Revenge

Now Available at

amazon.com

Jesse James' Secret

Codes, Cover-Ups
&
Hidden Treasure

Ronald J. Pastore
John O'Melveny Woods

ISBN: 978-1945190131

Cover design and artwork by Craig Attebery
www.craigattebery.com

First Edition: 2011
Second Edition 2014
Third Edition 2017
Fourth Edition 2023

FV-1

To contact the author please write to:

Author
P.O. Box 1195
Point clear, AL 36564

John@JohnWoodsAuthor.com

Contents

CONTENTS

Jesse Woodson James (September 5, 1847 – April 3, 1882) was an American outlaw, gang leader, bank and train robber from the state of Missouri and the most famous member of the James-Younger Gang. Already a celebrity when he was alive, he became a legendary figure of the Wild West after his death. Some recent scholars place him in the context of regional insurgencies of ex-Confederates following the American Civil War rather than a manifestation of frontier lawlessness or economic justice.

Jesse and his older brother Frank James were Confederate guerrillas during the Civil War. They were accused of participating in atrocities committed against Union soldiers. After the war, as members of one gang or another, they robbed banks and murdered bank employees or bystanders. They also waylaid stagecoaches and trains. Despite popular portrayals of James as a kind of Robin Hood, robbing from the rich and giving to the poor, there is no evidence that he and his gang used their robbery gains for anyone but themselves.

The James brothers were most active with their gang from about 1866 to 1876, when their attempted robbery of a bank in Northfield, Minnesota resulted in the capture or deaths of several gang members. They continued in crime for several more years, recruiting new members, but were under increasing pressure from law enforcement. On April 3, 1882, Jesse James was killed by Robert Ford, a member of the gang living in the James house who was hoping to collect a state reward on James' head.

(Wikipedia.org)

Foreword

This book could be more aptly subtitled, *How I solved a 120-year-old cold case murder mystery.* The ultimate truth surrounding Jesse James' secret life can finally be revealed. Although the previous Wikipedia blurb encapsulates what is widely written on the subject, it is far from reality.

In spite of the secretive life he led, there are numerous pieces of the puzzle that speak volumes about Jesse James. The clues came in various forms. Once enough information was amassed, I was able to process it down to a new and clear understanding of the man and his motives. What emerged was the picture of someone completely misunderstood by history.

This research project became both a lesson on investigative techniques and an amazing personal adventure. I followed the evidence even when the trail seemed contrary to the existing *facts*. Suddenly, new clues would emerge that put me back on track. Just when I thought the mystery was solved, another deeper story would come to light. It has truly been a life changing experience. And it appears that I am as yet, still only at the beginning.

My hope for this book is that the story will finally get out to the public and the truth will prevail.

My hope for the reader is that they enjoy the adventure…and that it may inspire others to inquire.

Ron Pastore
2010

www.JesseJamesSecret.com

Jesse James' Secret

Jesse James' Secret

Codes, Cover-Ups
&
Hidden Treasure

Jesse James' Secret

Birth of a Conspiracy

The following dramatization is based on books and news accounts found in archives and sets the stage for the evidence that follows.

Friday, January 7, 1881

A particularly harsh cold front had battered Denver for the previous week. As temperatures dipped below freezing, a heavy snow fell for several days. Figuring to beat the weather, Jesse and Frank James arrived by train a week earlier, a calculation that paid off well.

The gathering was set for five p.m. at the Dorchester Hotel on Virginia Street, in the plush private suite of rooms normally reserved for dignitaries. The proprietor of the Dorchester had no idea of his patron's fame, nor of the fortune in cash on hand. A discreet tip of a five dollar gold piece assured anonymity with no questions asked.

The meeting had been planned six months earlier and critically hinged on all parties being present—there was no room for error. The James boys' cousin, who went by the alias of J. Frank Dalton, arrived that morning. Jesse was growing anxious over the other guests' arrival, as the Raton Pass might close at any time due to heavy snow drifts. Not much was moving and supplies that normally arrived by wagon were running low.

"Any word on the whereabouts of Crittenden?" Jesse asked Dalton as the three men settled into the room.

"I checked the stage line and the train depot before supper. No one has seen or heard from the Governor or Timberlake," Dalton responded. "But there's word a train could still make it in before sundown."

"That'll make for a big problem if they don't show," Jesse said.

"We'll deal with it, like we do with everything else," replied Frank.

"Yes we will, brother." Jesse took a slow sip from his glass of water, concerned thoughts racing through his mind.

As the cowboys waited for the rest of their guests to arrive, supper was brought into the room along with whiskey and cigars. After consuming their beefsteak with buttermilk biscuits and gravy, the group retired to the parlor within the enclave of rooms. They filled the air with cigar smoke as they stoked the fireplace, bringing the room to a tolerable temperature.

A sudden knock on the door silenced the group. Years of reflex response caused their guns to smartly un-holster as they took deadly aim at the door. All that could be heard was the jingle of a spur.

"Come on in," Jesse said flatly. The door slowly opened. The hotel manager sheepishly poked around the door and announced that two gentlemen were there to see them. As the manager stood there, the door was shouldered open. In burst Sheriff Timberlake with Governor Crittenden, their whiskers full of ice, their faces and lips raw from the storm.

"Out of the way," Timberlake commanded as he darted straight for the fire, followed closely by Crittenden.

"Nice of you two to drop in," Jesse quipped as the weapons discretely disappeared under the cowboys' jackets.

The manager quickly backed out, gently closing the door.

"Nice of us, huh?" retorted Crittenden as he eyed the others, shivering. "Do you have any idea how blasted cold it is out there? We had to move God, the archangels and a few demons to get here, for Christ's sake. My train car was delayed for hours clearing the pass. Nice of us to—"

"Okay gents, I get it," Jesse interrupted. "Warm yourselves and have a drink. Y'all know why we've had to call a meeting at this ungodly time of year."

The sheriff and governor nodded as they settled into the plush couches and poured themselves a brandy.

"First order of business, gentleman. We've been preparing for years hiding treasures all across the country for the time when the South would rise again. By God, by now we have more hidden in the earth than there is in the whole damn Yankee economy," chuckled Jesse. "The time has come to make the caches ready." Jesse motioned to his cousin. "Fill them in on the details, Dalton."

"Sure Jesse. The Supreme Commander has ordered that we record the exact whereabouts of the hordes using the new coding system," Dalton began. "We'll send the codex along with the amounts to him come spring. As you know, a lot has to do with getting an early thaw. We have the mining gear ready, but whether conditions will cooperate is a different story. All of the earlier caches will be recovered and included in the master plan. If it goes well, the whole project can wrap up by June." His eyes furled as he made a calculation. "July at the latest."

"Will that be quick enough for 'em?" Jesse asked. "You know we've been hearing rumors…"

"I received a telegraph just before I left Missouri," Dalton continued. "The generals want access to the money for the latest armaments and recruiting. The North keeps tightenin' its grip on us by pressuring state and local governments, and it ain't likely to change anytime soon. It doesn't affect our long term goals, but in the short run, things could get tricky. So our best bet is to take control from within the Yankee gov'ment. Our Southern allies all agree.

"However, we're havin' trouble controlling those damn Tehanos. Poncho Villa is bein' all kinds of troublesome. He still believes we're the ones who 'absconded' with Maximilian's fortune."

Jesse started laughing as Dalton winked and smiled.

"Poncho ain't gonna see one peso," Frank chimed in, a slight smile gracing his steely gaze. "Make sure that old Maxi's 'treasure' is on the top of the manifest we send, so they can get at it first."

Dalton and Jesse laughed even harder.

"On a positive note, we know the cause is alive and doing well," Dalton said. "Our fellow Knights have filled all the vital offices, and the ones who ain't "with us" can be controlled. Or eliminated. We're continuing to build lodges and temples in damn near every small town across the West. Someday soon we can even announce the Knights of the Golden Circle has disbanded. We'll be able to operate freely in the open after that."

"A day I know we're all anxiously awaiting," Jesse noted.

"Here, here's" were uttered by all.

"Are you going to handle the coding?" Frank asked Jesse.

"Yeah, I'll do it," Jesse replied. "We'll mark up them caves with the code 'round May, while Dalton supervises shippin' the caches."

"Good," said Dalton as he took a long look around at everyone present. "I've staked out all the best locations, and we built our own cargo rail line through the backcountry. We'll move it by night undetected."

"We've got to deal with those damn Pinkerton agents," Frank said. "Hell, they been closin' in on us for the past year. Seems like they're startin' to figure out what we're up to before we do, and it's cost us dearly. Especially after what they did to our Ma and young Archie, fire bombing our home."

"I'm mighty sorry 'bout your family, boys," Timberlake said. "Them Pinkertons got no shame, going about thinkin' they're above the law."

"Above the law?" Dalton responded. "That's a hoot, considering what we're about to pull off in St. Joe, Sheriff."

"Anyways," Jesse continued, "they're offerin' so much reward money on us now, I'm not sure we can trust *anyone* not to turn us in. It could wind up puttin' the cause in danger. We always knew this was a possibility, but I reckon the circumstances force us to move up our time frame. Which brings us to the second point of business. I think you'll all agree the time is right. If we wait much longer, we'll miss our shot."

"I have orders from the President to use every last State Militia troop to find and capture you and your boys, Jesse," Crittenden announced. "It seems the Pinkerton boys reach goes pretty high."

"Not only that, but now they're calling the James Gang *terrorists*," added Timberlake. "They know about your connection with the KGC and they'll never let up."

"That's for sure," said Crittenden.

"That's why we gotta act now," Dalton stated matter-of-factly. "We have to take the heat off once and for all. There's a lot more at stake here than our lives."

"Agreed," said Crittenden. He stood and started pacing about the smoke filled room, stopping in front of the roaring fire.

"So what is the latest plan?" he asked.

"The way I see it," Jesse said, "we gotta pull this off right after the spring thaw. That way, we can get the body in the ground lickety-split. Besides, we'll need that much time to tie up all the loose ends."

"Has the Supreme Commander approved of all this?" asked Timberlake.

"Yep," replied Dalton. "He's fully aware and gave us a free hand to expedite the plan. He also wants us to keep makin' deposits to the coffers. But with the St. Louis gold, we'll be set for now."

Jesse turned to Timberlake and asked, "Are you prepared on your end in St. Joe?"

"They'll be no problems, Jesse, although I could use a couple of deputies to help keep the local folks away and distract everyone."

"How about Dick Liddell and Jim Reed?" suggested Frank. "They're clever boys and will pretty much do anything they're told. We've seen that plenty of times."

"Good idea, brother," Jesse added. "That okay with you, Sheriff?"

"Fine by me. Makes no never-mind who they are, as long as they're loyal."

"Loyal Knights they are," Jesse replied.

"I might point out, gentleman," Crittenden mentioned, "that this has to happen before the next election. Although I am running the best re-election campaign money can buy," he said winking at the group, "we can't assume that some honest citizen won't see through the ruse and expose our whole scheme. I can only intervene to help you if I'm still in the governor's office."

"Then we'll make it the day before the elections," said Jesse. "By the bye, if you need any more than the thirty grand we already gave you, talk to Dalton after the meetin'. We brought some cash with us."

Crittenden nodded and smiled.

"I've got one question," Timberlake interjected. "Don't we need a body? And a fresh one at that. The coroner's no idiot and he can't be bought."

"I've been thinkin' about that very item," Jesse stated with a stern resolve, "and I think I know the perfect candidate. He's been causing a lot of problems posin' as me for the past few years, and this is the most direct way to take care of it. He's such a bad seed, not even his own kinfolk will miss him. Two birds with one stone, if you catch my drift."

"We oughta map out the details right now and make sure there are no holes in the plan," Dalton suggested. "You know how I am about planning, boys. This is no different. A well thought out plan and enough manpower will always succeed."

"Agreed, cousin," said Jesse. "Let's get on with it."

Timberlake stood up as he hoisted his brandy-filled glass into the air.

"Gentleman," he said, his eyes demanding they join him. The rest stood up and raised their glasses in unison.

"To the tragic death of Jesse James."

Based in part on a period article in the *Sedalia Daily Democrat*, Beacon Montgomery reporting.

Section I

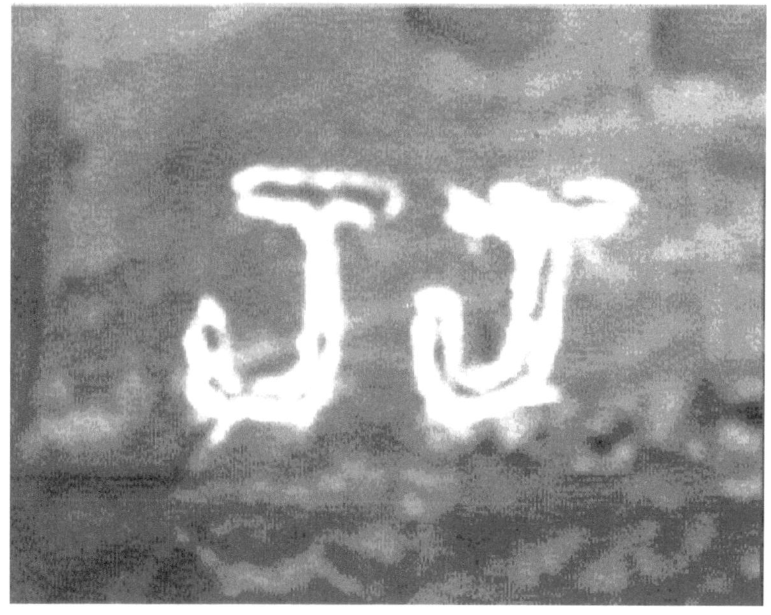

Rendezvous with Destiny

Spelunking

Wichita, Kansas, 1996

Some of the most beautiful days in the world occur during the early spring in Kansas. The rich azure hues of the midday sky frame the white wisps of clouds that paint the horizon, while warm breezes caress the rolling hills that surround the interstate highways. A perfect distraction from the seemingly endless array of seventy miles per hour cement roads that were originally built during the Great Depression era public works programs.

Heading east along US 54, the ghostly ruins of former settlers' farmhouses and barns littering the lonesome hillsides raced passed my peripheral vision; dreams that were finally beaten down by nature and time itself. I wondered what had become of those settlers and where their descendents might be that day.

The distraction was a welcome relief. The previous two years' events were relentlessly swimming around in my mind and I had yet to make sense of it. All of the stressful days and sleepless nights caused by not knowing what would happen next. Everything I had experienced was still somewhat blurred together making it difficult to get an objective read. I needed perspective, as my Dad would say.

"Ron, you've got to get the big picture before you can make sense of the minutia." I heard Dad's words. "Don't sweat the small stuff." Although he used a word other than stuff.

The big picture? I was hoping the spring air would clear my mind and allow me to catch a glimpse of it.

Easier said than done, Dad, I thought.

Besides the obvious events that everyone else saw, I had encountered seemingly endless intrigues, double-crosses and layer upon layer of personal agendas. All the while, I was constantly being faced with treacherous events that, in hindsight, I should have seen coming, but simply did not. So, there I found myself again driving down that desolate highway, the same highway that was the starting point of this adventure. Only now, I was questioning why I had allowed myself to become involved in this quest surrounding the enigmatic outlaw known as Jesse Woodson James.

As if I really ever had a choice.

Two Years Earlier, 1994

"How long until we get to the cave sites, Ron?" Dave would ask about every five minutes. Not that I minded. Even though he was goofing on me and knew full well when we would get there, I let him keep it up. I was pretty excited too.

It was our inaugural weekend in the field, our first adventure after weeks of researching, visualizing, planning and procuring all the supplies we would need. The 1987 Ford F-150 conversion van was fully stocked in preparation for the journey. We were on our way to find and explore our first set of caves.

I had recently completed my undergraduate degree in Cultural Studies after years of intensive research. I was burned out. So an opportunity like that, driving down the open road with nothing but hope and anticipation filling my thoughts, was pure freedom.

David Sampson had been a trusted friend since high school. We decided to explore caves as an exciting pastime. I had spent months investigating the facts, figures and descriptions of various caves in the region, but finding the locations quickly became a major challenge. Most were on private property, and landowners didn't want the liability of hapless city folk injuring themselves and getting sued. I had heard about some pretty outrageous court rulings of late, one in particular that literally cost the owner his farm when a hunter shot himself while trespassing over a fence line. So, finding the locations *and* getting permission to explore them proved a bigger obstacle than I had anticipated. However, on that day, the first day of exploration, I was sure of what we were looking for and the hunt was on.

Caves, it turns out, are a fairly common occurrence in Kansas; there are over eight hundred known caves in the state. Many are unusual in a major way: they emanate from what are called sinkholes. These types of caves are much more difficult to find. In fact, you can literally walk right past one in the fields. The rock outcroppings and depressions in the earth are often obscured by brush and trees. The rocky sinkholes can range anywhere from a few feet to over fifty feet in diameter. This was quite different from looking for the more traditional types of caves nestled within limestone cliffs.

We were heading for an area east of Wichita in the Tall Grass Prairie region known as the Flint Hills. It was close to our home base in Wichita and some interesting stories were attached to the region.

Legend had it that late one night back in the 1870s, a stagecoach was overdue and failed to arrive. Folks figured since it was a dark moonless night it may have wrecked, so a search party was sent out the next morning. When they arrived in an area called Seltzer Springs, about ten miles east of the town, they discovered, among the savannah grass and native elms, the burned out smoldering carcass of the stagecoach. No men, no horses and most importantly, no strongbox. It, along with the fifty thousand dollars in gold inside, was missing and never found. The story faded into legend and is known locally as the "Seltzer Springs Stagecoach Mystery."

This was the stuff archeologists and treasure hunters thrived on.

"Should be up here another mile or so, Ron," Dave reported. He had the map open in his lap and was the official navigator for this first adventure.

We found a place to park and took along the old metal detector given to us by a friend. Hiking through the tall grease grass, the same grass that provided Native Americans with a means to make red colored paint, we finally reached the Seltzer Spring area.

"This place is gorgeous," I muttered. "Hard to believe such a troubling incident happened here."

Dave heard me and concurred. Our naiveté aside, we couldn't help but hope to find the strongbox and maybe even an undiscovered cave or two.

During this initial expedition, we started creating routines and exploration strategies that would become our *modus operandi* when locating and exploring new sites. We created and defined a search pattern and then expanded it concentrically outward. I dutifully logged all the data in my field journal and maps.

That day was not the best test however, since the metal detector wasn't working properly. We learned our first two lessons in artifact and treasure hunting. The first is test the equipment thoroughly before you get in the field, and the second is called "ground effect," which is caused by the mineral content of the soil bouncing back false readings to the detector, rendering it essentially useless.

Although the expedition was basically a bust, the exhilaration of being "on the hunt", as Dave said, was more than enough to compensate for our less than stellar results. We continued to explore for a couple of hours and found the namesake spring, a beautiful thirty foot aqua blue pool gushing ice cold water. We packed our gear and planned to return someday when more advanced technology became available that would overcome the false readings.

We got back on the highway and continued traveling east toward Butler County in search of caves. After all, we had come this far and wanted to at least make a "find" of some sort. We started noticing rock outcroppings, technically known as the Karst limestone topography. This was truly beautiful terrain. It looked as if something pushed the huge boulders straight out of the ground without regard for the surrounding landscape. The Karst topography extends all the way to Nebraska and is a classic limestone formation. Formed by a vast inland two hundred million-year-old sea, it was exposed by glacial runoff fifteen thousand years ago.

We were looking for sinkholes, which are formed by rain hitting limestone and releasing carbon dioxide (CO_2). The water collects in the stone, and the chemical action of the CO_2 combined with water erosion enhances the dissolution of the limestone, forming caves over the course of millions of years. Often, when one finds a sinkhole, it portends a cave formation below. Every so often, I pulled over and checked for caves as we drove along remote secondary roads. Unfortunately, the sinks were either filled with the sediments from modern era farming runoff or had become dumps for old barbed wire and other debris. Local farmers did this to eliminate habitat for predators like bobcats and cougars and to keep curious livestock from falling in. None of these sinkholes led to the caves we had expected to find.

In addition to everything else we were doing, we stuck to our earlier commitment, which was to treat this as a research project as well as just plain having fun. So, I studiously charted every sink we found on a topological map of the area. A pattern seemed to be emerging.

"You realize this is probably how Indiana Jones started out, don't you?" Dave asked as a condolence on the long drive home.

"I doubt it," I retorted. "He started in the mind of George Lucas. And I don't think he would try to find and study caves in Kansas," I added. Ironically, I later discovered that an archeologist from Wichita named Schuyler Jones was the model for that iconic character. Looking over at Dave, I saw his familiar grin and realized he was yanking my chain again, as he'd done ever since high school when we were both flower power kids.

"More likely we're closer to being like Cyrus Thomas from the late nineteenth century," I continued. "He created the model of scholarly integrity for studying archeological sites in the late 1800s that still perseveres to this day. That's who I'd like to emulate."

Another quick glance at Dave confirmed that he had no clue who I was speaking about. Gotcha back, I thought, smiling to myself. We arrived home, called it a day and began planning for our next trip.

The following weekend our target was even bigger. This site was much further east than the Seltzer Springs area and held its own mysterious legend. I had heard the tale in bits and pieces since I was a teenager. It was on a par with those spooky stories that were designed to scare us around campfires as scouts.

I coined it the "Towanda Cave Mystery" and that's the only way to describe it. Towanda is an Osage Indian word meaning rushing water. Early settlers set up trading posts at the springs which

Jesse James had come to visit on several occasions. Soon after, a small town sprung up complete with a beautiful two story limestone Masonic Lodge in its center. Today, the building is home to a historical museum.

As the legend goes, in the late 1880s, a couple of children failed to return home one evening. Because the nearby Towanda cave was known to the locals, a search party was formed consisting of two adults. They entered the cave with lanterns in hand, searching for the youngsters. This cave system, by the way, was reported by local accounts to be so big that it had its own lake over two hundred yards long.

The two adult rescuers never returned. So another search party, this time consisting of four adults, set out with lanterns into the cave system. They failed to return as well. The next morning, a search party of twenty men was organized. Every member had a lantern, and they were all tethered together by twenty foot lengths of rope. Searching the cave system all through the day and night, they found no one.

However, when they exited the caves, the last two members of the search party were missing, their length of rope having been cut. The town folk were aghast, giving up all hope of finding either the children or the others rescuers.

They decided to seal off all of the entrances so nothing like that would ever happen again. However, one of the entrances was on a farmer's property and rumored to have been left open. The farmer was secretive by nature and would not reveal the location of the cave or even let anyone set foot on his property.

One more bit of trivia related to the story. Supposedly, inside the primary cave was an old medicine man's teepee full of artifacts. Apparently, it looked like he just up and left on a moment's notice, leaving everything behind, never to return.

Over several years of research, I deduced that two of the five entrances might still be open. I noticed that because of the way the water flowed in the area, the openings were more than likely located *opposite* each other, one north of town and the other directly south.

We scouted the area to the north, hoping to glimpse some rock formations that would give a hint as to the location of the entrance. We hiked to the area where we thought we would most likely find the cave system. A farmhouse nearby matched the description in the folktales, so we decided to give it a shot.

We searched for those illusive sinkholes or some other clues that could lead to an entrance. Dave and I noticed something peculiar at the same time. It looked like we were walking in the debris path that a tornado must have traveled. There was an old round bale frame used for holding large thousand pound bales of hay to feed cattle. It had obviously been picked up and hurled a great distance and then fell from the sky, landing right on top of a cow. The skeleton was still pinned beneath the large metal frame.

But it was what we noticed under the bones that caught our interest: a large checkerboard pattern within the limestone. We didn't learn until later just how important this observation was. At the time it was simply an interesting anomaly. It turns out this pattern is indicative of a cave system below, with the upper layer exposed.

Caves generally have three layers: the sponge form rock layer, the cavern layer and the passageway. Had I known this at that time, we would have continued our search in a different way. But we were still neophyte spelunkers. Experience matters.

We started our standard search pattern, moving in larger and larger outward circles looking for sinkholes. We checked near the mulberry and cedar trees, which were another indication of a possible cave entrance because of the water source below.

Nothing.

Okay, plan "A" didn't pan out, but we still had plan "B". So, off we headed to the south of the little town. We were starting to get a bit tired at that point. However, I still held out hope that luck would be with us and that we'd find the cave where the disappearing medicine man had lived. Our last resort now was to find the sole remaining entrance to this potentially fantastic cave system. Little did we know that we had just passed within a few yards of an obscured cave entrance.

We took off in the van, still undaunted. And then it happened—BOOM! A tire blew out as we swerved down the rough gravel road. Dave was cursing everyone except the Pope about having to change the tire. It was getting late, the temperature was dropping precipitously and we were cold, tired and hungry. After an hour, the deed was done, and our energy levels were spent. We decided to pack it in for the day, which was almost nightfall by then, and headed on back toward home.

This might have discouraged much less adamant searchers, but not us. "It's just another spot we don't have to check again," Dave observed. "One less wrong place to look means we're that much closer to finding what we're looking for."

I felt the same way. What we were doing was creating a discipline and teamwork that would come to pay off many times over the next couple of years. What else would we be doing…it was Kansas after all!

Thanks to meeting some local teenagers who were talking about their secret party hangout, we ended up finding the entrance we missed to that cave system almost two years later. It was a sinkhole no more than three feet around, dropping straight down twenty-five feet to the first level. The cave opened up into a large room that dropped off to another level. It seemed to go on but was silted in from farm runoff. We did notice a nearly imperceptible hole in the floor in one corner. When I looked down inside the hole with my light, I found another level below. The hole was very small, but I managed to slip through.

"Spectacular!" I shouted up to the guys. Huge boulders hung from the ceiling of the thirty-foot around room with nothing supporting them, as though poised to fall if you so much as touched them. I heard a strange ticking sound that I mistook for my watch until I remembered it was quartz. I tracked the sound to a small pool of water atop a flowstone formation. Once there, I noticed something else: my sensor going off. It was natural gas seeping into the cave. That silent killer is virtually undetectable without a sensor.

"Hey man, don't light a match. We're in a natural gas dome and we gotta get outta here fast!" I shouted.

I was already starting to get a headache from the odorless gas, and when I tried to climb back out of the hole it was too tight. I had to peel off all but one layer of clothes to squeeze back through the hole. By the time we got out of the cave, we all had major headaches and sat under the starry sky for an hour to recover. That must have been what happened to the victims lost down there back in the 1880s, I thought. Asphyxiation from natural gas.

Except… I still couldn't explain the severed rope of the last two victims. As I said, it was a mystery.

Over the next few months, we went out every weekend, searching for caves by chasing down any lead we could find. Clues came from books, old newspapers and from local yarn tellers who hung out in the quaint cafes and bars of the historic small towns we passed through on our travels.

One weekend, we headed further east toward a cave system in the El Dorado area, which was said to have over two hundred caves. We stopped along the way as usual, checking every sinkhole we found.

Since my divorce years earlier and the demand of completing my college courses, I had difficulty seeing my two girls as often as I wanted. But we managed to get every other weekend together. Abby was seven and Veronica was nine that first year in the field. Both were equally bright and energetic, always asking questions that kept me on my toes.

"What does El Dorado mean? Where are the seven cities of Cibola? Who was Coronado? Did he come through here to see the caves too, Dad?"

I would research the archives, find out the answers and we would discuss it at length the next time we got together.

Then, one of those strange coincidences that often happen in life occurred. I could find no other explanation except that it was meant to be.

We had traveled a lot further east than originally planned, constantly stopping and checking for sinkholes along the way there—"there" being the key word. We weren't exactly sure where "there" was at that point.

Dave was first to notice the old abandoned farmstead. We decided to stop, take a break, get some snacks from our picnic basket and rest for a while. While there, we figured we could putter around and look for something interesting.

Even though most of the people I've run into in Kansas are pretty friendly folks, I always had some trepidation when looking for caves on other people's land. As a matter of protocol, we would try and seek out the landowner and get permission every time a house was in the area we were exploring. But most of the areas we were in had been abandoned decades before, and there wasn't much chance of running into anyone.

Except that day.

One of the girls noticed a plume of dust on an old farm road coming straight toward us. Within minutes, a dusty Chevy pickup slowed to a stop in front of us and out stepped the owner. He was of medium height, sporting a traditional wiry farmer's build and faded blue overalls. He broke out in an infectious smile, and in a baritone voice belying his diminutive stature, greeted us.

"My name's George Wence. How y'all doing today?"

"Fine thanks. Is this your land?" I asked.

"'Tis now. Homesteaded by my great grandfather."

"It's really a beautiful place," Veronica said.

"Why thank you dearie," he responded kindly. "This here was the original farmstead. New one's back south about a mile. Couldn't bring myself to burn it down like most of the neighbors did theirs, but then vandals did it last year."

"We just stopped to take a rest here," I told him.

"Not to worry; glad you like the place." He eyed our metal detector and equipment and gave a slight smile. "Expecting to find anything valuable today?"

I decided to come clean.

"Actually, we've been searching for caves for the past few weeks." I motioned with my thumb toward the detector. "We use that to try and find old metal objects once we get in them."

"Seems like a good idea," he offered.

A moment of silence passed while his eyes sized us up.

He then proceeded to tell us, in his Kansas accent, about how there were caves all over Butler County. The area used to be called the "Kingdom of Butler" because of the beauty of the Flint Hills. It turned out old George was a direct descendent of King Wenceslas, Emperor of the Holy Roman Empire. (The King was known for his benevolence and support for the Knights Templar.) If George felt any pretension because of this connection to royal lineage, it certainly didn't show. Finally, he stopped with the good ol' boy stories and got pensive for a moment.

"You boys ever been over to Cave Springs?"

"Nope," I replied. "In fact, I've never even heard of it."

"Oh," he said, seeming genuinely surprised. "You oughta head on over there and check out the cave. It's the largest natural cave in the whole area. You can walk right in it. Once inside, you can go back at least a couple hundred yards. Dandiest thing you ever seen."

This information was a complete surprise to me, and by the look on Dave's face, he was caught off guard too. We thanked George for the suggestion as he wrote down directions to the cave.

Life has a funny way of getting you to where you ultimately need to be. Good ol' George Wence turned out to be my guide to the beginning of a new, life-changing rendezvous with destiny.

Cave of Wonders

We excitedly traveled down the highway to the farm in Butler County where this mysterious cave was supposedly located, following the directions George had given us. Once we arrived, it was a bit of a let down. The place was quite dilapidated, and for the life of me, I couldn't see, at least from my vantage point, where such a wondrous cave as he described could possibly be hiding.

The past week seemed interminably long. Both Dave and I had day jobs, so we had to wait until then before we could hunt for the cave system George Wence had described the previous week. In the meantime, I had searched through books and the Internet for clues. But up to that point, we had not been able to find much in any of the literature we had researched regarding this particular cave.

Those fleeting thoughts of discouragement were soon interrupted by the sight of a woman heading down the driveway toward us from the farmhouse. Did I say heading? More like barreling—jumping full of animated energy, her smile already visible even from where we were stopped.

I wondered about the cryptic warning George had given us about "watching out for that cantankerous woman who owns and runs the place."

We waited in the van as Ms. Enthusiasm met up with us.

What a character she was. I knew then that George was pulling our legs. The best way of describing Robin is a bundle of charged wires in a Mama Cass sort of body—vivacious, friendly, always seeming like wherever she was at the moment was just the most fun place to be. She was the antithesis of a stylish dresser—frumpy, dumpy and wearing perhaps seven layers of dresses and sweaters.

Large round coke bottle glasses and a long cigarette hanging from her lips finished off her "look".

"You here to see the cave?" she asked enthusiastically.

We all excitedly said yes! She had us park by the closest of two, of what my daughter Abby charitably referred to them as, "barns". She then whipped out release forms for us to sign. I liked her instantly because she really took to my girls, constantly paying attention to them as she talked.

And talk she did. With a certain liberal misuse of the English language—what my parents used to refer to as "Crosby-isms", after the comedian Norm Crosby. She always spoke in a rhythmic staccato of iambic pentameter, somewhat like how a rooster crows.

She explained, while motioning for us to follow her, how this area was once an old stagecoach stop in the 1800's. The local Indians considered it a mystical place, journeying here for spiritual rejuvenation. She also said that the caves still contained many secrets yet undiscovered. Truth be told, I wasn't sure at this point if this was just a plain old Kansas yarn or if she really believed it. Didn't matter to me though, as we were hooked like trout on a wooly bugger fly.

We snaked our way past the one hundred-year-old barn, then up and over a hill. When we reached the top, we could see a beautiful cave opening at the bottom on the opposite side of the hill. Dave and I looked at each other—you would have thought we were Lewis and Clark. I felt like a kid again and wanted to run down to it. In the meantime, my daughters did just that, breaking into a joyous dash for the entrance.

Robin went on about how the entrance to the cave was called the "Hall of Autographs", being covered with the signatures of people who have visited that dated all the way back to the 1700s.

We hurried down the hill, doing our best to keep up with the girls. The six feet tall by four feet wide entrance was framed in limestone, with the opening fading into the darkness. Once inside, the first thing I noticed was the marked change in temperature. It felt cool and invigorating. I later learned it stayed a constant fifty-five degrees all year round. The passageway continued back about forty feet until it hit an intersecting stream where you could go either straight ahead, left or right. As promised by Robin, the signatures, initials and symbols covering the walls continued the entire length of the long passageway and beyond the intersection.

The sweet, pungent, musky smell of the cave—earth, water and time—poured into my nostrils, spreading throughout me like an electrical current. This is exactly what I had always envisioned; exploring caves, looking for archeological remnants and seeing and experiencing what others had seen hundreds of years ago. It was a real sense of connection with the past.

Once we reached the four-way junction, we decided to explore the main passageway straight ahead. My daughter Abby, riding on my shoulders, pointed high above to where there were two capital "J"s chiseled into the wall near the ceiling, which had risen dramatically to over twelve feet in height at that point. I guessed those letters were about ten feet from the ground. I remember wondering how whoever wrote them got that high. Must have ridden a horse in here, I surmised.

"Daddy, what are those marks?" Abby asked, pointing.

I said, rather nonchalantly, that they must belong to someone like Jesse James, although I literally made it up on the spot, not having a clue if he had ever been here. That seemed to satisfy her curiosity, and we continued further into the cave. Little did I know that this was a foreshadowing moment of things to come.

After traversing another four hundred feet, the cave became a muddy mess. We stopped and turned back toward the dim light of the distant entrance.

I emerged supremely satisfied after an hour of exploration, even though the mud in the cave had reached the tops of my shoes. Robin was sitting on a rock waiting for us, puffing away on her long generic cigarette. She let out a cackle akin to the wicked witch in the Wizard of Oz. Her smile was infectious. We were smitten and she knew it.

Over the next couple of months, we came out regularly and explored more and more of the cave system. On one excursion, Dave and I traveled so deeply into the interior that we were inside for over eight hours. It was the perfect grounding to my life. Every week I had somewhere amazing to go for the purpose of research and exploration.

We also started taking pity on Robin and wound up splitting our time between spelunking and helping her clean up the place. It made me feel good. In addition to helping her, I was able to help return the land to its original beauty. One day, Robin mentioned her "psychic guides" told her we were doing a good thing, although that was a little weird for me.

Over the next few months, we hauled more than twenty-five trailer loads of about two tons each to the dump. It felt great to see the natural beauty of the landscape reemerge from beneath all the debris obscuring its view.

Tale of the Crazy Cowboy

One of the many folktales I learned about the cave was especially intriguing. Back in the 1870s, three cowboys were said to be camping outside the entrance, huddled in front of their campfire. One of them went to explore the cave where he suddenly heard the sound of children's voices echoing from deeper inside one of the passageways. Arriving at the intersection where he heard the voices, torch in hand, he saw two children dressed in Native American attire, frolicking as if they had not a care in the world.

They appeared to be a boy and girl around ten years old. Suddenly, a man materialized out of the side of the rock wall, admonishing the children in some unknown language. He grabbed their hands and they all disappeared right into the wall. There were no other passageways anywhere nearby.

Utterly amazed and quite shaken by what he had just witnessed, the cowboy ran to tell his two compadres. They simply dismissed his claim, knowing there were no other entrances for miles, and told him so.

Unable to calm him down, they thought he must have lost his mind. This evolved into a raging argument, resulting in the shooting death of the man who had seen the kids by one of his buddies. Legend has it he was buried somewhere on the property near the cave entrance.

The weird part is, even today, people going into the cave experience hearing what they think are little children's voices, although I've never personally heard them. Others say they felt someone tapping them on the shoulder, only to turn around and find no one standing there.

Eerily enough, I experienced that sensation on several occasions.

An Unexpected Offer

"Ron, I got me something to speak with you about," Robin said one day, energy and smile abounding.

We walked toward the now clean barn area and she started in.

"I've always had this vision of turning the place into a non-profit nature preserve, and I was wondering if you would help 'fracelate' me doing that?"

"What did you have in mind?" I asked.

"Well, maybe we could create us some sort of agreement whereby you boys take over like a trustee or like that. I'm a wantin' this here land to give up its secrets. This was once part of the underground railroad, smuggling slaves and all to the north, don't cha know?"

"I recall hearing that story once or twice," I said.

"Right." Her eyes searched for her next thought. "I was thinking that, with your continued research, you can take over the place as caretakers. I've been told by my guides that you would be the best suited to do that sort a thing."

Well, that was a surprise. And then again, maybe it wasn't. I was feeling more and more connected to the land each weekend I visited. I had occasionally harbored thoughts about what I would do, if ever given control.

I also wondered what she meant by her "guides", but let it pass.

"You don't have to give me your answer right now," she continued, interrupting my thoughts. "You can 'mentiate' on it. See if it feels right for you. And I'd understand if you weren't up to wanting to do it."

But I knew in a heartbeat I didn't need to think about it, nor "mentiate" on it as she put it. No, I knew that I needed to be there. In a fleeting second, I caught a glimpse of what I wanted to turn this place into and how I would do it. It all made sense at that point.

They say the universe tries to give you what you want. If you close a door on it one way, it finds a different door to open for you another way. This was my door opening to living the life I'd always wanted and to create the place I'd often dreamt about—offered to me all in one package.

"Okay, I'll think about it and get back with you," I quietly replied, not wanting her to get too much of an idea just how badly I wanted to do this. "I'll let you know by next week."

During the next few weeks, I wrapped up a few business deals and made inquiries about how to pull this off. I met with Robin a number of times, negotiating contracts, liability issues and plans for what was to become of the place. It turned out not to be such an easy decision for me after all. I had to give up a career as a financial planner, move outside of Wichita and learn to run the place. Once I got my head around that, it all seemed doable. I made her an offer to lease the place for five years. She accepted, still using her cryptic, creative and yet totally out-of-place vocabulary.

The transition period was a great time. My excitement grew as the days passed waiting to take over operations. Finally, the day arrived when Robin packed up her family in the old Ford pickup truck and trailer, bound for who knew where. As the smoke from the exhaust pipe rose from the "Beverly Hillbilly" mobile (complete with spare tire tied to the roof) and it headed down the road, I finally felt relief. After a few minutes, the truck disappeared over the top of an asphalt hill and they were gone.

That's when an immense wave of gratitude overcame me and something else I'm not sure I'm able to describe. I knelt down and kissed the ground, thanking God for the opportunity to take care of this wondrous place.

I brought a little camper onto the property and lived in it until the house was habitable. Within a couple of weeks, I managed to clean out the old farmhouse, fix the roof and put a few coats of paint on the interior and exterior. Soon enough, I had a nice place to live and a headquarters. Then, it was on to the hundred-year-old barn and out buildings. I cleared the cave entrance area of debris and made a pathway smooth enough for small children and elderly visitors.

The work was joyous and arduous at the same time. I recalled my Dad's comment about the project being akin to inserting a wet noodle into a certain part of a tiger's anatomy. Not altogether impossible, yet requiring considerable finesse. It didn't matter nor discourage me.

The old farm was gradually transformed into a private nature retreat and working ranch. Friends and volunteers started helping out. I acquired quite a menagerie for the visitors to interact with: peacocks, ducks, rabbits, chickens, big Tom turkeys, goats, dogs, cats and a beautiful black wolf.

In a word, all was working perfectly according to the inner vision I had for the place in that split second when Robin made the initial suggestion.

I bought some horses from an old-timer named John Hogoboom, founder of the Flint Hills Wagon Train and the man who ran the Butterfield Overland Stagecoach Company. He took a liking to our projects and helped a lot, in spite of being in his late eighties.

John was the first to tell me stories of Jesse James having close friends in the area. I have since confirmed that Jesse was well acquainted with Dan Cupps, an early settler of Towanda, Kansas. The legends and lore of local history were starting to come alive for me, yet another foreshadowing of my future.

Among my discoveries in and around the Cave Springs cave were a number of artifacts and various bone specimens. I called the Anthropology Department at Wichita State University. They connected me with Dr. Peer Moore-Jansen to evaluate the bone matter I had uncovered.

Congress had recently passed the Native American Graves Protection and Repatriation Act (NAGPR), which calls for the return and re-interment of all Indian remains. The first step was to find out if any of the bones were human and then define whether they were Native American.

A few weeks later I received a call from Dr. Moore-Jansen. He told me that one of the specimens was in fact human skull fragments from a young adult Mongoloid male. He dated the specimen, based on the mineralization content of the bones, at about one thousand years old. The left front tooth was of the pan-ridge shovel form, confirming its native origin. Peer advised me to contact Dr. John Reynolds, Ph.D., chief archaeologist for the Kansas State Historical Society to report an unmarked human burial.

Dr. Reynolds came to the cave site with his assistant to conduct an archaeological site survey. After showing them where I found the bones and filling out some forms, I took them up the hill above the cave and showed them a foundation I was excavating with Roger Ward, our staff archaeology expert. Dr. Reynolds agreed that this was the site of the old Cave Springs Post Office, circa 1874 - 1898. He filled out a second set of forms submitting two previously unknown archaeological sites. He asked me to call him with any other findings and he would register them.

"You know you can become a state certified archaeologist site registrar once you've submitted fifteen unknown sites," he said. "I think you can do that, Ron."

I thanked him for the encouragement and dreamed of the future discoveries I might make. The first step in that journey came in a most unexpected way.

Chance Encounter

During the next year, I made substantial changes to the Cave Springs property, not the least of which was to finish cleaning it up. After yet another twenty-five large horse trailer loads to the dump and at least thirty gallons of paint, we were ready to share the place with the public.

We created tours and started getting the word out about this wonderful cave system that was visitor friendly. Schools responded by the bus load. I would guide them through the Hall of Autographs and then talk about the history of the area. I was doing what I loved, spending lots of time with my daughters and living a pretty stress free life. Life was very unchallenging in many ways at that point. But, be careful what you wish for.

One warm summer day, a young man arrived at the ranch. Tall, lanky, well spoken, he looked a little out of place in his blue jeans and sport shirt, as if his Brook Brothers suit was waiting in his car for him to return. He was affable enough, although right from the start he seemed to have an ulterior motive for his visit.

After the standard "pitch" I gave on how wonderful this cave was, he looked straight at me with his piecing dark eyes and asked, "Are there any double J initials in that cave of yours?"

"Matter of fact, there are," I replied. "Would you like to see them?"

It was a moot question. He was already heading for the cave entrance halfway through my response. I quickly caught up with him and in we went.

He studied the initials for a few moments while he carefully took out a piece of paper. His eyes darted between the two, and he then he slowly replaced the paper in his pocket. I could make out through his dark burly mustache that his lips were mouthing something to the effect of "it's true".

Okay, so now I was caught up in this little mini intrigue. "What's true?" I spontaneously asked, forgetting that he hadn't verbalized the comment. Startled, he became a bit embarrassed and sheepish about my having read his personal thoughts through reading his lips. After my interruption, he smiled awkwardly.

"Do you know of any other caves around here that have these initials?" he asked.

"Not really. This is the only one I've explored that's had them. So what are they?"

His eyes sized me up for a few moments, and then, as if an internal voice released him from some secret oath, he stated they were Jesse James' initials.

"The outlaw?" I asked.

He nodded.

Suddenly, I went back to the first time I was in this cave with Abby riding piggyback and remembered telling her the same thing. The chills spiraled up my spine—kinda' spooky.

"Are you sure?"

"Pretty much. I've been talking directly with the James family," he replied, as he turned and walked back out toward the entrance of the cave. We continued walking in silence up the hill together to the grassy knoll where he had parked his car.

"Have *you* seen other caves with those initials?" I asked. I was fishing for information, mainly so I could tie this all in to the tours I gave, the marketer in me coming through.

"A few," he replied. But he was clearly wrapped up in thoughts about something else and wasn't about to lose whatever train of thought he was on to answer any more of my questions.

When we got to the car, I decided to take a chance.

"Can you tell me anything more about those initials? The reason I'm asking is I'm really interested in historical information, especially if it's local. If Jesse James was here, that would be pretty cool information to follow up on."

My question jarred him from his inner thoughts. I'm really not able to fully explain the next few moments. The best I can say is there appeared to be a battle going on within him, such as a person might appear to be if they were sizing up an offer to help get them out of a jam, yet not knowing whether to trust the person or not. He seemed to be tossing about in milliseconds all the possible outcomes. I almost wished I hadn't asked the question, when he turned toward the car's door, opened it and pulled out a large briefcase.

"I've been working with the James family to see if I can validate their claims of being related to the famous Jesse James," he stated. "It involves a collection of pictures and documents they found hidden away for the past hundred years."

He opened up his briefcase. It was full of photos, along with broaches, jewelry and artifacts.

"You're not going to believe what I'm about to tell you," he continued. "What do you know about Jeremiah Woodson James?"

"Who?"

Section II

A Traditional Historical Account

of

Jeremiah "Jesse" Woodson James

(1847 – 1882)

Innocent Years

The James family history has a pedigree that goes back to King James, the Scottish ruler of England. Jesse's father, the Reverend Robert Sallee James, was a Baptist preacher. He was twenty-three and Zerelda Cole was seventeen when they married on December 28, 1841 in Lexington, Kentucky. The next August they packed a Schoonover covered wagon manufactured by Robert's uncle and headed for Missouri to visit his mother. Robert's father was said to have died on a Buffalo hunting trip to the Indian Territory in what is now Kansas. Robert's mother had remarried after the death of her husband and moved to Clay County, Missouri.

Reverend James

Zerelda James

Jesse's mother's family, the Coles, ran an alehouse back in Lexington, Kentucky called the Black Horse Tavern. A popular spot, it hosted many famous figures of the time. As a girl, Zerelda worked in the kitchen and served hot meals to the guests. Some of the regular visitors included candidates of the 1824 presidential elections, John

Quincy Adams, Henry Clay, William H. Crawford and Andrew Jackson.

The purpose of the newlyweds' trip to Missouri was to introduce Robert's bride to the family and begin scouting for a piece of fertile farmland to homestead. Many of the James and Cole family relations were moving West to "Misery" (Missouri). After visiting Robert's mother, the couple returned to Kentucky where they lived for a couple years. Robert's duties as a minister kept him away from home much of the time. He was busy setting up the North Liberty Baptist Association and the William Jewell College.

Zerelda was an imposing woman, six feet tall and two hundred pounds, with a strong willful spirit. They argued frequently, and she insisted that Robert start being more helpful around the place.

In the Reverend's absence, there was never a shortage of male suitors around the territory, and the further West a gal went, the more attention she got, married or not. Historical accounts report that not all Jesse's brothers and sisters were the product of Zerelda's marriage to Robert James. No doubt this was part legend mired within a hint of fact.

The political climate had been deteriorating in the East since 1835. That was the year a newspaper editor from Ohio was murdered for his abolitionist views, which he regularly published. The growing population and political unrest made the idea of moving West ever more appealing to the Jameses.

Robert and Zerelda loaded up the Prairie Schooner wagon and headed for their new Missouri home in April, 1843. Travel by wagon was arduous and slow on the rough trails, making four miles an hour on a good day. In spite of the many hardships of living on the trail, the promise of a different life far from the strife in the East drove them happily westward.

Once there, Zerelda spent time looking for the perfect place to homestead. She stayed with various relatives, including her sister Sara Ann, who was married to Robert Mimms, the owner of a large prosperous farm. The Jameses found a fine piece of land in Clay County near Kearney, Missouri. They took clear title to the farm and built an earthen sod shelter to live in until they could afford to build a house. Robert James was still busy with the ministry in Kentucky and traveled back and forth quite often.

They chose to homestead in Missouri because of the success of other James relatives who had tried their luck on the fertile river valleys and made a comfortable life of it. The James Farm was located in the northwest corner of the state, which was lush and hilly. Wild game and elk were plentiful.

Zerelda was soon pregnant with her first son, John Thomas James. He is not recorded in common accounts, but independent corroboration of this claim from several separate sources have been found. I have seen their family photos and genealogy to support their claims, but have not delved too heavily into the topic since my research was about Jesse.

Alexander Franklin "Frank" James, born on January 10, 1844, was Zerelda's second child. She was soon pregnant again with Robert R. James, who was born July 19, 1845. She named him after her husband Robert and her brother in-law Robert Mimms. However, he is said to have died five days later. (It is possible that since they remain out of all accounts of the family, John and Robert lived with Robert's sister Sara Mimms to be raised as her own.)

Baby Jesse James

Jeremiah "Jesse" Woodson James was Zerelda's next child, born on September 5, 1847. His first name was in honor of Zerelda's brother, Jesse R. Cole, who died in 1840. Jesse's middle name was after Robert's brother Drury Woodson James. Uncle "Woody" ran a fancy health spa resort in Paso Robles' hot sulfur springs near San

Luis Obispo, California, and he became very successful during the gold rush.

Zerelda was not aware until later that her in-laws back in Kentucky, John and Matilda James, had borne a son on October 11, 1846. They also named their son Jeremiah "Jesse" Robert James after Zerelda's brother Jesse Cole. Hence there were two Jeremiah "Jesse" James, with their middle name being the sole difference.

On November 25, 1849, Susan Lavenia James came along. Susan had a tough time as the first daughter. As soon as she was old enough, she was taught to cook, clean and sew. Later, during the Civil War, this sweet, hard-working girl was treated with indignation by Northern troops. She even went to jail with her mother for over a month under Union General Sherman's anti-Rebel strategy. As the other children were born, Susan became a second mother to them.

Frank and Jesse James

Frank and Jesse had as normal an upbringing as could be expected for rural life in the mid-1800s. The brothers lived carefree, concerned only with the daily chores of the farm, school and play. Because of accusations and gossip, their parents' relationship was not the same after Jesse was born, and they subsequently grew apart.

Robert was drawn by the lure of the gold fields in California, no doubt to minister to the miners. He headed out West on April 12, 1851. He first went to visit his brother Woody in the San Francisco area. Months later on the first of August, he arrived at the gold fields and started mining. It wasn't long before Zerelda got a letter explaining how her husband had become ill and died. It said that within eighteen days of his arrival, he had gotten food poisoning, developed pneumonia and passed away. He was buried in an unmarked grave in California. She had received two letters from Robert prior to his death which hinted at his dismay with their marriage. Questions and doubt still linger on the matter of his "death", and in later years Jesse would head West to learn more about his father's fate.

After the passing of Rev. James, the family attorney administered his estate which was in probate court. During this time, Jesse suffered a severely abscessed lower left front tooth. The matter of the dental treatment was recorded in the court files as a payment disbursed by the lawyer. This is a significant clue in future attempts in identifying his remains.

Overwhelmed with the duties of family, a two hundred seventy-five acre farm, thirty sheep, six cows, dozens of chickens, several pigs and seven slaves, Zerelda sought the help of a man by remarrying.

Benjamin Simms, also known as Robert Mimms, came into the picture hoping to gain ownership of the James family farm. Unsuspecting of his motives, Zerelda accepted a marriage proposal.

Simms was a difficult man and had trouble getting along with the kids, especially Frank and Jesse. Just a few months into the marriage, Ben was tending one of the horses in his typically harsh manner. The stallion was strong willed and swung around, knocking Ben against the corral fence. The horse began kicking at Ben who was pinned in a corner with nowhere to go. A hoof caught him in the temple and cracked his skull. When Jesse came out of the barn to see what all the ruckus was about, Ben lay slumped over in a heap, limp and lifeless.

Dr. Reuben Samuel arrived in good time, but Ben had long since slipped away. Doc Samuel was a kind, caring man and took a personal interest in the family after the accident. Over time, he began to court Zerelda, and in 1855 they married. During their marriage, they had several children as well.

Sarah L. Samuel was born the day after Christmas, December 26, 1858 and was named after Zerelda's sister Sara Mimms. John Thomas Samuels was born May 25, 1861. Fannie Quantrill Samuels followed on October 18, 1863. She got her middle name from Frank James' Commanding Officer in the Civil War. The next child in the family was Archie Payton Samuel, born on July 26, 1866 who met a tragic and untimely death at only nine years old.

Frank and Jesse were the closest siblings and spent a lot of time with their cousins from the Younger family who lived on a nearby farm. The Youngers' five boys were Cole, James, John, Robert and Grat, whose namesakes were from their close relations, the Cole and James families. Frank and Jesse explored the wild, hunted, fished and gigged for frogs.

The boys loved to fish, and one of their favorite "tricks" was to fill a gunnysack with fresh walnuts that still had the green husks, beat the sack against a rock until the tannic acid juices started to ooze out, then tie a rope to the sack and throw it into a pond. The oil from the walnut hulls would coat the surface of the water shutting off the oxygen supply. The fish couldn't breathe and were rendered unconscious for a few minutes. As the fish came floating to the surface, Jesse would swim around and throw them up on the bank. Frank would pull in the sack, dump the walnuts and fill it with all the fish they could carry.

Jesse didn't care much for farm chores, but he loved horses and he named his favorite steed Stonewall. Each time the horse came to his whistle call, Jesse rewarded him, and it didn't take long to condition him to come on command. He didn't need to keep Stonewall in the corral after that, so he let the horse roam the pasture freely and graze to his heart's content. With three quick blasts of a two-fingered whistle, the tall, handsome, black stallion would come running from a half mile away.

Daily chores on the farm consisted of tending to the horses, milking the cows and goats, collecting eggs, weeding the garden and picking produce. Frank didn't mind his chores, but Jesse would rather sit under the shady caster bean tree, draw pictures, read history books and dream of faraway places. He memorized historical facts and shared them with Frank. Together they made plans to someday see the wonders of the world.

The dream of travel to exotic places was preempted one day when a group of horseman showed up at the James farm.

DRAWING BY JESSE JAMES

Innocence Lost

The War Between the States was the nation's bloodiest conflict. The battles claimed over half a million American lives. The main cause of the conflict out West, in what became known as the "Border Wars", was largely due to Northern army regulars. The 7th Kansas Volunteer Cavalry of Union troops was under the command of James Lane, Charles Jennison and James Montgomery. The Regiments from New York that were stationed in Kansas to "keep the peace" became known as Jennison's Jayhawkers. These Pro- Union raiding parties would ride into neighboring Missouri to confiscate livestock, grain and property from the local farmers and burn their homes. The indiscriminate attacks turned many Pro-Union Missouri farmers to support the South. The only ones spared the thievery were Northern sympathizers who had formed groups of Home Guards and State Militias to protect themselves. Eventually, the victimized Missouri farmers banded together in a loose confederation to resist the "Red Leg" raiders. These federal troops got their name from the red pant leggings of the uniforms worn by this merciless outfit of Mounted Dragoon soldiers.

Zerelda was concerned that the raiding parties might come to steal their meager possessions and family heirlooms, so she loaded up two camel back trunks and hid them under the floorboards of the porch. Even though the thunder of cannons was far from home, rumors of recruitment had spread like wildfire. Kansas had stayed neutral in the conflict, but that didn't keep the Jayhawker Red Leg raiders from crossing into Missouri.

One day, the dust cloud of distant riders delivered Northern desperados at the James' doorstep. A company of soldiers from

Kansas rode in and read a proclamation claiming all usable material and personnel for the Union cause. The James boys were still young enough that Zerelda managed to convince the Army that she couldn't run the farm without them.

- - - - - - -

A young man named William Clark Quantrill had moved to Stanton, Kansas at age twenty to live with the oldest of three brothers. He had been a teacher at the Union School in Dover Canal, Ohio where his father was the principal. Extremely bright in mathematics, history and geography, he became a qualified surveyor before leaving home in 1857.

He was peaceable unless provoked, loved to fish and hunt and was an excellent hand with a gun. He went by the name Bill Clark and later used the name Charlie Hart to avoid the law over some cattle he had stolen. He moved to Lawrence, Kansas for a while and took various jobs from teamster to farming and ranching. Due to the political unrest, he decided to move to Pike's Peak and prospect for gold until things settled down. He and his brother packed their belongings and headed out with a free negro female cook.

Quantrill found himself in trouble again in Colorado for killing a man over a gambling quarrel and barely escaped a lynch mob. He then made his way back to Lawrence. Once again, he was indicted this time for burglary, arson and kidnapping. He escaped and went on the lamb living with the son of the Delaware Indian Chief.

While camped along the Little Cottonwood River one night, thirty armed Jayhawk raiders rode in and shot the Quantrill brothers. After stealing all their supplies and "freeing" their female Negro cook, they left the men for dead. William lay mortally wounded for three days occupying himself with keeping the coyotes and buzzards away from his brother's body. He managed to pull the bullet slug out of a cartridge and pour the gunpowder on his wounds. When he lit the powder it cauterized the wound, but the pain was so intense it rendered him unconscious.

An Indian Chief named Go-Lightly Spy-Buck came along and found Quantrill in a feverish fit. The Chief put Quantrill on his horse and took him to a remote camp. There, he was treated with snakeroot to fight the infection and native ginseng and goldenseal tea to cleanse the blood. While the natives nursed him back to health, Quantrill devised a plan of revenge.

Once he had regained his strength and by then sporting a full beard, Quantrill set out to find the Jayhawk band that attacked them and killed his brother. He vowed to avenge his death and joined up to infiltrate the group. Once he was mustered into this group, he set upon his plan. On each of the successive raids, the group started losing men from their ranks. Quantrill had shot thirty of them before he was found out and fled for his life to Missouri. Tales of his vendetta spread among the Southern sympathizers and persecuted farmers began to join Quantrill's band of Rebels.

Chief Go-Lightly Spy-Buck

Federal raiding parties hit the James farm several times attempting to take the James boys into their ranks, but each time a tense standoff kept them out of the fighting. One day, while Frank and Jesse were away from home, the Federals started rounding up all the women in the families of Southern sympathizers. Brigadier General Thomas Ewings suspected the women of the Cole, Younger and James families of giving aid and comfort to the Rebels. Consequently, Federal troops came and took Zerelda and her daughters Susan, who was then fourteen, and five-year-old Sara to jail in Kansas City, solely for their political views. They were held without charges for nearly a month under severe and filthy conditions with barely any food and little water. Emaciated and gaunt, Zerelda agreed to sign a loyalty oath, and they were set free on June 5, 1863. This was the last straw for her son Frank. He left the farm to join Quantrill's guerillas.

On August 14, 1863, a heavy rainstorm caused the building that Zerelda and her daughters had been held in Kansas City to suddenly collapse, killing fourteen women and injuring dozens more. One of Rebel Captain William Anderson's sisters was killed and another was severely maimed. He vowed to brutally avenge the death and injury of his sisters. From then on, he never took another prisoner, earning him the name, "Bloody Bill". An investigation later revealed that the collapse was deliberate, caused by undermining the foundation.

Cole Younger's father had also been murdered by one of the Jayhawker raiding parties, and Cole left with Frank to join Captain Quantrill. When the federal troops returned, they were harsher still in their determination to locate Frank and the various guerilla bands.

One day while Jesse was working in the cornfield, Federals came to their farm and hanged his stepfather, Dr. Rueben Samuel, from the caster bean tree in the front yard.

Hearing his mother pleading to spare her husband's life, Jesse ran to the house. He was apprehended by soldiers and bull whipped until he could no longer stand. The troops demanded to know where Frank and Quantrill's gang were hiding out. They lassoed Jesse around his neck and dragged him about the farm, but he was finally able to escape. When all their efforts to persuade him had failed, they left to torture other Southern sympathizers. Dr. Samuel was cut down before he died, but the lack of oxygen caused severe brain damage and he was permanently disabled. He could do little more than sit in a chair from that day on.

The brutal attack on his family by soldiers from the Federal government deeply affected Jesse's psyche. It was the last straw for Jesse, and he rode off to Quantrill's hideout to join up with the gang in spite of his mother's protests. Quantrill would not allow Jesse to join as he was only sixteen, but Captain William "Bloody Bill" Anderson took him into his Rebel squad. Captain Anderson, whose antics against the Jayhawks were by then well known, outfitted Jesse with a war shirt, pistols, cross-draw holsters and cartridge belt. Frank always kept an eye on his little brother, staying in close touch by volunteering for many of the missions that Jesse went on.

Jesse was often the target of practical jokes being the "young 'un" and his tenacity only encouraged the men to ranker him more. Having been raised the son of a Baptist minister, Jesse didn't use profanity, tobacco or alcohol. When something did rile him, he would just say "dingus!" It wasn't long before the men started calling him Dingus.

Jesse was said to have had an injured or missing fingertip. One story is that some of the Rebels were in a mood for some fun and they had Jesse clean a rifle. They said it was unloaded, and he set about job of reaming the barrel. This set off the powder load, firing the ball and damaging the tip of his left index finger. The Rebels laughed loud and hard as he writhed in pain on the ground. Frank heard the commotion and hauled him over to the medic at the field infirmary where he got his first taste of laudanum, a tincture of opium dissolved in alcohol. It would become a frequent friend in his times of pain and suffering. Once the bleeding stopped, the field surgeon sewed up the fingertip.

Another version states that when Jesse was a boy he was playing gun fighter games with his friends. While practicing quick drawing and fanning the trigger hammer, he accidentally shot the tip off his left middle finger.

Yet another tale says that it was chewed off during a knife fight with a Mexican.

The events of the previous year caused Jesse James to cross the line and become a full-fledged member of the Rebels and soon Quantrill's resistance.

The innocence of his youth was shattered.

No more fishing.

No more lazy days sitting beneath the caster bean tree, drawing and dreaming of faraway places.

The War Years

Jesse was physically agile and very courageous in the field. He vented his anger over Yankee abuses by volunteering for scouting, recon and special missions. He learned to track and trail from their Indian scouts and forward lookouts. His talent for disguises allowed him to cross Union lines, sometimes even dressing as a woman. Occasionally, their missions involved stealing into enemy camps unnoticed. He learned how to sneak up on a sentry and quietly slit his throat so the escaping air did not gurgle in the victim's blood.

Rebels were always looking for caves, not just as hideouts, but also as a source of gunpowder made from bat guano collected from the cavern floors. Once again Jesse's age and size suited him well for the job. At times, Union soldiers occupied the caves and Jesse would have to slip into a sinkhole and work silently in the night as the enemy slept, often while bats flew around his head as he worked. He also became skilled in rappelling and rope climbing.

Quantrill's Cave

By far, the Rebels' specialty as guerilla fighters was the pistol charge. A small group of forty men could take on two hundred or more Union Infantry soldiers and inflict severe damage upon the opposing rifle brigade.

Their first advantage over the Bluecoats was that the fight was personal and the Rebels had a score to settle. Nearly all of them were avenging crimes against their own family and property. The Bluecoats, on the other hand, were there for a job and fighting to free slaves. Many of the young Union recruits were recent immigrants from Europe. Most of them had never even seen a black man and had no idea what they would do once they were freed. The Yankees needed the meager pay and just wanted to live long enough to make it through another day.

The Rebels were using six shot pistols against the single shot rifles of the North. Guerilla fighters practiced intensely for these charges, learning how to ride with their horses' reins in their teeth. Having both hands free, they could lay down a field of fire in all directions. Each man carried four to six pistols and extra cylinders that were also pre-loaded. It was unconventional warfare and extremely effective. The other advantage was that they would bring the battle to the enemy. They rode down on the Union troops in a wave of fury and confusion, firing with both hands as the enemy tried to defend their line and reload at the same time. The Rebels would overrun the battle lines and ride among the confused and frightened Bluecoats.

Rebel kill ratios were significantly higher since they had two to three dozen shots to every one shot of Northern troops. These hit and run skirmishes wiped out entire companies, and survivors that tried to escape were run down to the ground. For the Rebel guerilla, prisoners were given no quarter. Wounded soldiers could only expect a merciful bullet to send them to their maker. With no survivors, their tactics would remain safe and indefensible.

Their mission as Rebels was to defend and avenge crimes against the citizens of the Western territory. The Rebels covered a lot of ground, from Nebraska to Texas and all points in between. They believed there was no choice but to strike back for the awful things done to their loved ones. Many combat exploits were recorded during the time Frank and Jesse rode under Quantrill's Black Flag. The Rebels had become very skillful at their craft.

With all of the events happening in the East, the War continued to rage in the West. On the morning of September 27, 1864, Captain William "Bloody Bill" Anderson and his Rebel troops intercepted a passenger train arriving in Centralia, Missouri. There were twenty-four newly trained Bluecoats on board including their unit commander. The men were taken off the train and forced to remove their uniforms, for which the Rebels had other plans. After this humiliation, they were interrogated as to troop movement and strength of forces in the area. They treated these soldiers with no more regard than the Jayhawkers had treated innocent Southern farmers. In the end, they were all shot dead on the railway platform.

When word of the executions got to Major Johnson of the Union Army, he was outraged. He called out three hundred of his finest soldiers and rode for Bloody Bill Anderson's Rebel camp. Three miles south of Centralia, the Bluecoats came upon their Rebel encampment off in the timber. Major Johnson ordered his men to dismount and form a battle line. He then called out a challenge to combat Captain Anderson and his men, two hundred and sixty-two strong. Bloody Bill swiftly took up the gauntlet and mustered his men to a charge on the Union soldiers with his typical battle cry, "No survivors!"

The well-trained Rebel horsemen rode down on the Union battle line like hell's fury, holding fire until they could see the "whites of the enemy's eyeballs". The Union soldiers eagerly fired their single shot rifles as the Rebels charged onward. With the Union guns emptied, the Rebels leveled the Bluecoats in close quarters combat. Jesse rode his horse straight into the battle line picking out the one he thought was in command. There, behind the column standing next to the flag-bearer and bugler, was an officer with sword in hand. Jesse made him out as the CO and the target of his attack. With reins in his teeth, a 45-caliber Colt in his right hand and a 36- caliber Smith & Wesson in his left hand, he rode up within five feet of the man. The first shot struck Major Johnson in the brain and he hit the ground a corpse. With the remaining eleven rounds, Jesse shot the lieutenant, company sergeant, flag bearer, bugler and a half dozen infantrymen.

The Rebels overran the panicked troopers and continued on to the rear of the battle lines. They shoved the spent weapons into their holsters, pulled a second set of pistols from their belts and immediately attacked again. With their weapons discharged, the Bluecoats clumsily tried to reload as the Rebels returned, attacking from the rear of their defensive battle line.

Bloody Bill Anderson assessed the damage to find he had only lost nine men. Yet, when he looked back upon the ranks of the Union troops, he saw that they had been annihilated. Only sixty of the original three hundred troops remained alive. They were desperately attempting to reload, regroup and remount their horses in a flurry of confusion. The final Rebel charge met little resistance and was nothing more than keeping the mandate of no survivors. A few dozen Bluecoats attempted to flee via the road to the town of Sturgeon, but to no avail. They were swept away by pursuing Rebels littering the three-mile trail with bodies. Out of three hundred Federal soldiers who set out that afternoon, only eighteen escaped with their lives. Major Johnson and his men had been wiped out by a new style of military confrontation for which they were unprepared.

Three days later, Jesse was among a squad of one hundred seventy-three men sent to rout a company of German federal military soldiers. The Rebels rode from their camp on the Blackwater River toward Lafayette County. Jesse rode point, ahead of the squad in a ten-man patrol to scout the trail. They encountered an opposing patrol of fourteen U.S. infantrymen, and the Rebels quickly gave chase. They didn't know that the Federals had laid an ambush of one hundred troopers hiding in the hazel brush. When the rest of Jesse's company heard the gunfire, they rushed headlong into the ambush.

Upon realizing the situation, the Rebel company dismounted and charged upon their ambushers in the brush, killing all but twenty-two Bluecoats. Jesse's patrol was still chasing two remaining riders of the fourteen fleeing troopers when they ran full speed into U.S. Cavalry reinforcements.

Suddenly, there was a sea of blue-coated cavalry dead ahead. The column of two hundred federal troops was closing in on Jesse's squad at a gallop. The Rebel squad tore at their horses' reins to break off the chase. They turned about and ran for their lives as the troopers broke into a riot of gunfire and battle screams. Jesse went down in a hail of bullets, his horse shot from beneath him. He was shot in the left arm and in his side, as he hit the ground hard. Taking cover behind his dead horse, he killed five of the men closest to him. Again, the Rebel Company came riding in at the critical moment and forced the Bluecoats back. The Rebels killed one hundred and seventeen Bluecoats, and Jesse had taken ten of them himself.

After recovering from the wounds of the two bullets he had taken along the Blackwater River, Jesse rejoined the fighting. The guerillas had gotten word that a heavily armed federal militia of forty-six men had taken the courthouse in Plattsburg, Missouri. Jesse was among twelve Rebels sent to rout the troops.

That night, in four groups of three men, they attacked the courthouse from all sides in the face of heavy gunfire from every window. They rushed across the three hundred yards to the Courthouse Square in a barrage of musket balls and captured the federal militia. The Northern troopers surrendered, and in a rare gesture of benevolence, their lives were spared if they swore an oath of mercy toward Southerners in the future. The Rebels destroyed two hundred rifles and confiscated ten thousand dollars in Missouri defense bonds.

Upon leaving Plattsburg, the Rebels crossed the Missouri River making their way to Independence, Missouri. They were headed to what was known as a "disorderly house" about four miles from town. The young woman who ran the brothel catered to Union officers. Jesse, with his smooth boyish skin and blue eyes, disguised himself as a woman and approached the Madame. He said there were several ladies who were seeking to entertain officers from the garrison at Independence. Word was sent to the officers that there would be four new women at the bordello that night. Jesse was among ten guerillas to sneak up on the house after dark and peer in the windows. He saw twelve officers inside with five working women. On a prearranged signal, they all fired on their targets in unison through two of the windows. Nine of the officers were killed on the first volley, and the remainder died seconds later. Leaving the women unharmed, the Rebels rode off into the darkness.

The war continued until General Lee formally surrendered on April 9th, 1865 to Northern General Grant at Appomattox south of the James River. The Generals met at the McLean home. The war had begun near the McLeans' previous homestead in 1861 by the Manassas railway junction. Now, years later, the war had followed him, ending with the signing of the surrender of the Southern army in the same man's parlor at his new home in April of 1865.

But for Jesse and his Rebel band, the war was far from over.

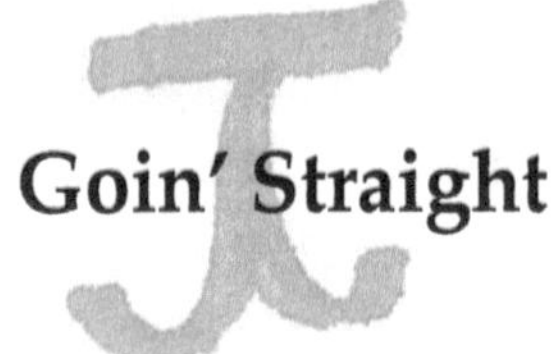

Goin' Straight

A few months after the surrender of the Confederate Army, the Union issued a general amnesty. A full year later, a special amnesty was ordered for the Rebel guerillas. Frank and Jesse rode to Lexington, Missouri and tried to surrender under a white flag of truce. However, the Union had suffered heavy losses at the hands of the Rebels that rode under Quantrill's Black Flag and still harbored a deep hatred toward anyone who served with them.

As the James boys approached, the Union soldiers fired without mercy and Jesse was shot through the chest, the bullet piercing his lung. The brothers hastily retreated and narrowly escaped. Jesse had heard the sound of a sucking chest wound many times before and knew it was his doom. Frank found a barn to hide Jesse while he went looking for a doctor. Finding none, he located a wagon and turned the horses toward Rulo, Nebraska where they met up with their mother.

Jesse was in critical condition, frequently passing in and out of consciousness. He told his mother he did not wish to die on Yankee soil. So Zerelda had Jesse's bed carried to the docks on the Missouri River where they boarded a steamer bound for Kansas City, Missouri.

They stopped over in Harlem, across the river from Kansas City at Zerelda's sister's boarding house. Jesse's cousin, Miss Zerelda (Zee) Mimms, helped run the boarding house. Zee nursed Jesse slowly back to health and they became quite close. He had not seen her since she was a young girl, and he noticed she had grown into a fine woman. Jesse told his mother he was going to marry Miss Zee, but she objected in her usual strong manner since they were first cousins. Jesse went along with her wishes and did not see Zee again for several years.

Jesse returned home to their Kearney farm for a long, slow recovery. He had left the farm as a boy and returned from war a man with a hardened edge. Soon, things started returning to normal. However, the war had brought hard times on the homestead, and many families had taken loans at the local banks. They were starting over again with almost nothing; all their livestock and property had been stolen under the illegal "Special Order Number Eleven" by Union Federals, Jayhawker Red Legs, Militias and Home Guards. Still, they were not disillusioned; they had their land and all worked together to restore their way of life.

One night, the brief tranquility was broken when six federalist patriots came to the family farm in Kearney, Missouri to arrest Jesse. Being ever vigilant, Jesse had the drop on them. He managed to disarm the men and ran them off their farm. Jesse decided that he had better not stay there any longer, as hostilities still ran high and would not blow over any time soon. He went to live with a friend, Dr. Woods, to continue his recovery.

In the spring of 1866, Jesse traveled to New York City, where he stocked up on laudanum and boarded a streamer on the Isthmus of Panama passage to San Francisco. Once in California, Jesse stayed at the hotel spa of his Uncle Drury Woodson James to recuperate. It had a hot spring for medicinal healing where Jesse could soothe his many wounds. In total, Jesse had been shot thirty- six times and it had taken a heavy toll on his health.

Jesse finally came back home to Kearney, Missouri after spending some time in California, only to find that he had been accused of robbing a bank in Gallatin, Missouri. The Marshall had connected him to the crime from a horse that was left at the scene of the robbery. Jesse had sold the horse to Captain Bill Anderson's brother James more than a year earlier. John Sheets owned the bank in Gallatin, Missouri and had been a Captain in the Union Army. It was Sheets, with the help of an informant named Charlie Bigelow, who captured Bloody Bill and dragged him around behind a horse until he was no more than a bloody log.

James Anderson walked into the bank to kill John Sheets as a vendetta. After informing him, "This is for killing my brother, Bill Anderson!" Jim shot Captain Sheets in the head and heart at point blank range. Since the Captain no longer had need of the money, the men with Anderson helped themselves to all the cash they could find.

When the Pinkerton detectives got a hold of the horse and a few descriptions, they mistakenly placed Jesse James at the scene.

Sheriff Thompson led a posse to the James farm to arrest Jesse with the motive of killing him in the process. Jesse ducked out the kitchen window and ran to the barn to mount his horse, which was always saddled and ready to go. The posse spotted Jesse riding off behind the house and gave chase. Several hundred yards out in the pasture, Jesse stopped, turned in his saddle and shot Sheriff Thompson's horse out from under him. The rest of the deputies halted in their tracks. As the sheriff picked himself up off the ground, Jesse warned the posse that the next man to take a step would die on the spot. The sheriff called off the deputies and they went back to the farmhouse. The sheriff took a horse from the barn and rode back to Gallatin.

When Jesse returned home a short time later, he found that his favorite horse, Stonewall was gone. Jesse was so upset that he rode out in a rage after the sheriff and his deputies. The posse got away, so Jesse went to Kearney and wrote a letter to Sheriff Thompson in Gallatin. Knowing he was a good confederate soldier back in the war, Jesse did not wish to kill him, so he gave him three days to return the horse. Stonewall was returned to his stable in two days, and Sheriff Thompson never attempted to arrest Jesse again.

Jesse tried to help around the farm but really wasn't cut out for the plow. The family needed money to keep the farm afloat, and Jesse heard there was work in Kansas City, Missouri. Jesse made a deal with Frank to run the farm while he would try his luck at the stockyards and railroad hub in West Bottoms, Kansas City. While there, he stayed at Zee's boarding house. Kansas City was a major crossroads and the end of the rail lines. This was the destination of cattle drives from the West. Hundreds of cowboys came to grab a bath, a shave, a bottle of whiskey and a sporting gal.

These were rough and tumble times in America's history, with killings every day in the saloons and streets.

Jesse figured a new beginning called for a new name. A common practice was to take a new handle, so Jesse chose the name Tom Howard from his Aunt Elizabeth's family.

Many former Union and Confederate soldiers were running around a cow town the size of Kansas City, all looking for work or trouble. Jesse was good at making connections and found odd jobs around town.

He volunteered to ride on a posse that turned into a major stroke of luck. His Civil War skills lent themselves well to the duties of a bounty hunter. Jesse would turn the outlaws over to the sheriff and collect his reward. Then, he sent the money home to his mother to help with the farm. He was a successful bounty hunter, and the sheriff made Jesse a job offer as a Kansas City Special Policeman.

Jesse began moonlighting in other counties under the name Tom Howard and quietly and steadily built a reputation of success as a man hunter. Among his aliases were Thomas Howard, Tom Vaughn, Tom Johnson, James Morgan, J. W. Howell, J. W. Hallel, Jim Reed and Ed Reed to name a few of more then twenty that have been uncovered. His cousin, Jesse R. James used Jesse Frank Dalton among the more than seventy aliases in his lifetime.

Jesse James sent enough money over the years to save the family farm and help their kinfolk and neighbors. That turned out to be much to the dismay of the local bankers and railroad companies who tried to gain possession of the surrounding land. The James family had settled a beautiful and fertile piece of ground. Frank poured his heart into the place clearing farmland and building up the old homestead cottage into a handsome house. He was happy on the farm, but his thoughts would sometimes stray to the exotic places he and Jesse talked about during their school days. It was not surprising that Frank would jump at the opportunity to join Jesse on an occasional job to round up escapees and thieves.

Over the war years, Jesse had become familiar with caves all across the country that gangs of outlaws and ex-Confederates used to hide out. Even fancy bordellos had been set up in caves with a stable of fillies to service local patrons. Some caves were useful hideouts for moonshiners who worked hard at keeping their location secret. Frank and Jesse were always welcomed by these various parties and given hospitality, food and a dry place to sleep. Their knowledge of these many safe havens made it difficult later on for the law to hunt Frank and Jesse down.

Jesse's guerilla war skills paid off when it came to tracking outlaws who thought they would elude capture. The rewards were good and paid in cash on the spot. However, it appears that once in a while they *may* have supplemented this income with a robbery or two.

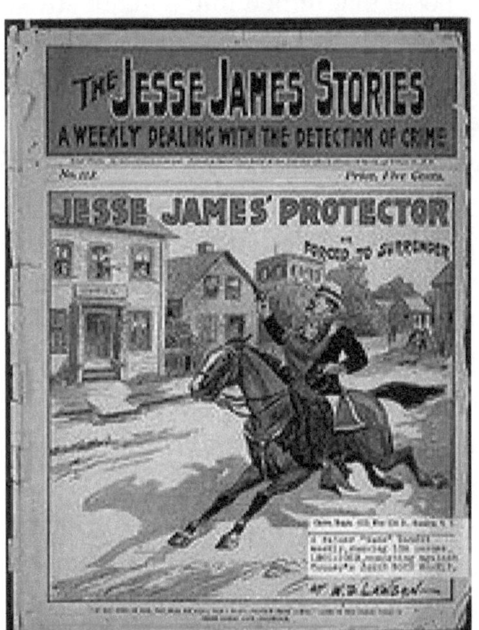

The bankers began wondering why foreclosures were down and learned of the rumors about a local Robin Hood. The stories were embellished by the newspapers and territorial sheriff. Things went from bad to worse in no time as the stories became ever more colorful. Writers from back East got wind of the tales, and they grew taller as book sales soared at the James boys' expense.

One of the more famous "Robin Hood" stories involving Jesse and Frank had them on the road to the Jackson State Fair horse races. They stopped in Tennessee to visit the widow of one of their comrades, only to find that her farm was going to foreclosure the next day. The widow needed seven hundred dollars to pay off the mortgage, which was nearly all the cash Frank and Jesse had between them. They decided to give her the money and made sure that she knew to get a formal signed receipt. The next morning, Frank and Jesse laid a trap for the banker and Sheriff who had gone to serve the foreclosure papers. To the banker's surprise, he was paid in cash the monies due and promptly gave the widow a receipt. On the road back to town, Frank and Jesse stopped the banker and sheriff, took back their money and sent them on their way empty handed.

The Outlaw

Eventually, Jesse and Frank tired of bounty hunting and decided to go full time into robbing banks and trains. The reasons were not clear at the time, although new research sheds light on their ulterior motives.

Jesse knew he needed a "gang" in order to run a successful endeavor such as he was planning. He approached many of his former Confederates in arms from his Quantrill days, as well as some relatives.

In time, the James Gang grew and consisted of close relatives Bud, Cole, Bob, Jim and Grat Younger. His former Rebel comrades consisted of Roy Baxter, Rubin Busse, Bill Chadwell, Bud Dalton, Wood Hite, Dick Liddell, Clell and Ed Miller, George and Will Overton, George Payne, Charlie Pitts, James Poole, Jim and Edd Reed, Bill Stiles, Zack Smith, George and James White and many others over the course of their 18-year crime spree.

By far, the most relentless scourge upon the James Gang were the three Pinkerton brothers and their agents. Ironically, they had similar beginnings. Alan Pinkerton was a Scottish anarchist who was wanted by the government when he fled his country. He had committed terrorist acts for the Revolutionary Proletariat movement, and the Scottish authorities found out that Pinkerton was an active member of the subversive Chartist Party. He fled from prosecution in the belly of a cargo ship bound for North America. The weeks of seasickness and diarrhea took its toll, and he deeply resented having to leave his homeland.

Pinkerton quickly found an income, having worked as a coppersmith in Scotland. He made his way to Dundee, Illinois where he set up his own copper repair shop. Enjoying a decent living, he involved himself with politics and fell in with the local counter-culture. He helped set up a network of safe houses for fleeing slaves and ran the Dundee Station of the Underground Railroad. Pinkerton became active in the Chicago abolitionist movement. Once he established himself there, he was put in charge of the major hub in the network. Pinkerton made many influential friends in Chicago and was eventually appointed to the police department. He was selected to run all the investigations and became the first detective of the Chicago Police Department. Here he built a reputation of investigative success, and the department grew to a force of half a dozen detectives under his command. However, the limitations and scrutiny of public service hampered this well-connected man and his unorthodox ways. Pinkerton left and set up his own private detective agency, taking his loyal squad with him.

His business grew due to the unusual circumstances at the time. Many Rebels found they were unable to surrender or find work after the war, so they turned to crime. And no one questioned Pinkerton's methods of apprehension.

The Pinkerton Detective Agency was hired by the railroad to find and apprehend Jesse James and his gang. The James Gang had robbed several stagecoaches and trains with such success that they quickly became America's most wanted.

Although the membership of the James Gang varied depending on where the job occurred and the manpower needed, there were simply too many robberies spread out over too large an area to attribute to Jesse and his gang. It would have been impossible for the James Gang to have covered many of the distances on horseback.

Others, including Jesse's cousins Jeremiah "Jesse" M. James and Jesse R. James, (who also went by the alias Jesse Frank Dalton), were also pulling holdups posing as the James Gang. It was common to blame every robbery in the territory on the James Gang, and the reward on Jesse's head was ever mounting.

Having failed all attempts at capture, the Pinkerton Detective Agency sent a group of agents to Jesse's mother's home to execute a diabolical plan.

On the night of January 26, 1875, they crept upon the home with a plan to fire bomb the house and shoot Jesse down as he emerged. Agents threw a surplus Army mortar through the kitchen window without a thought for who was inside. The only people at home were Jesse's stepfather, Dr. Rueben Samuel, his mother and his nine-year-old half brother, Archie Payton Samuel. The family was sitting in the parlor when they heard the kitchen window break.

Pinkerton

They ran into the kitchen to find the window sash on the floor and a round mortar wrapped in an oily cloth that was ablaze. Zerelda tried to roll it out the back door and was shot in the elbow by agents outside. Dr. Samuel used his cane to roll it into the fireplace to keep the house from catching fire. Within seconds, it exploded with such force that it threw Archie across the room. A large chunk of metal shrapnel had torn his chest open. Another large piece of the shell hit Zerelda in the right arm and severed it just below the elbow. Escaping the blaze, they quickly ran from the house, laying Archie's limp body in the snow. They could not see anyone in the surrounding darkness as they watched their home ablaze. In spite of Zerelda's amputated arm, she managed to put out the fire with buckets of water with limited help from her husband.

The next morning, Jesse got word of the incident and followed the tracks in the snow, figuring out there were eight men involved. He also found a revolver lost by one of the assailants with the Pinkerton mark stamped on the grip. The remains of the eight-inch wrought iron mortar shell were kept on the mantel as a reminder of the murder of nine-year-old Archie. There was such a public outrage over the cold-blooded crime that the newspapers even called for an all out amnesty for the James Gang. The Pinkertons never came around the James farm again.

However, that did not stop Frank and Jesse from swearing to avenge the senseless attack on their family.

- - - - - - -

Jesse focused his robberies to specifically target stage lines and express trains that were guarded by the Pinkerton Detective Agency after the firebombing. This would give Jesse a small sense of retribution for Archie's death and keep them well funded. The robberies started out by Jesse and Frank boarding a train at the station like normal passengers. They would ride quietly for a couple of miles and then split up. One would make his way to the engine and stop the train. The other would catch the guard in the freight car by surprise and force him to turn over the contents of the cash box. The rest of the gang waited for the train to stop, boarded and joined the robbery by covering the passenger cars. On a few occasions, Jesse spotted a banker or former Union officer in the passenger car and relieved them of their cash and jewelry. Jesse avoided robbing working men, and if there was ever a doubt, he was known to check a man's hands for calluses.

- - - - - - -

Committed to the pursuit of the James Gang, the Pinkertons were never going to give up until they were either caught or killed. The railroads had raised the reward on Jesse to thirty thousand dollars, dead or alive. In today's value that would be over one and one half million dollars. However, it was not the money for the Pinkertons. It had become a personal war between Alan Pinkerton and the James Gang, specifically Jesse. The gang had stolen millions of dollars, destroying property and lives. The Jameses felt the same way about the railroads. In order to lay down tracks, the railroad company had forced out hundreds of families from their land paying pennies on the dollar. If someone refused to move, other means were used to get rid of them.

- - - - - - -

After the devastating loss of life in the Northfield Bank robbery attempt (Appendix L), the James Gang laid low for a couple of years. They next scored big with the Glendale train heist, a $50,000 bonanza in 1879. In the following few years they were not especially productive, with four or five holdups netting around $35,000 all together.

Traditional accounts state that at this time Jesse needed to recruit new talent, so he set up a meeting with his cousins Charles and Robert (Bob) Ford. They met at Jesse's mother's farm in Clay County, Missouri to plan the next job. They arranged to meet again in two weeks at Jesse's home in St. Joseph, Missouri. Jesse bid his mother farewell, and she admonished him, "Be careful of those Ford boys."

Bullet hole in Jesse's house

In St. Joseph, Jesse went about day-to-day life under the alias Tom Howard where he lived with his family. He was thirty-five years old and had two children with his wife, Zee. Their six-year-old son, Jesse Jr. was raised with the name Tim Howard and their daughter, Mary Susan was nearly three years old. No one suspected that the Howard family had such an infamous patriarch living quietly among them on the edge of town.

Historical accounts say that Bob Ford had been living with Jesse and his family for several weeks. Charlie Ford showed up at the James home on the morning of April 3, 1882. Jesse invited them in to the parlor and noticed a picture frame on the wall was crooked. He first took off his jacket and gun belt, laying them on the divan. Then Jesse stepped up on a chair to straighten the picture and heard the familiar click of a gun hammer being cocked. As he began to turn and look back, he heard the report of a pistol firing. Jesse was shot from six feet away by Bob Ford with a .44-caliber pistol. Jesse fell to the floor, dead from a single shot to the back of his head.

Ford was convicted of killing Jesse Woodson James and was subsequently pardoned by Governor Crittenden. Jesse's brother Frank turned himself in and was found not guilty of any crime by a jury.

Section III

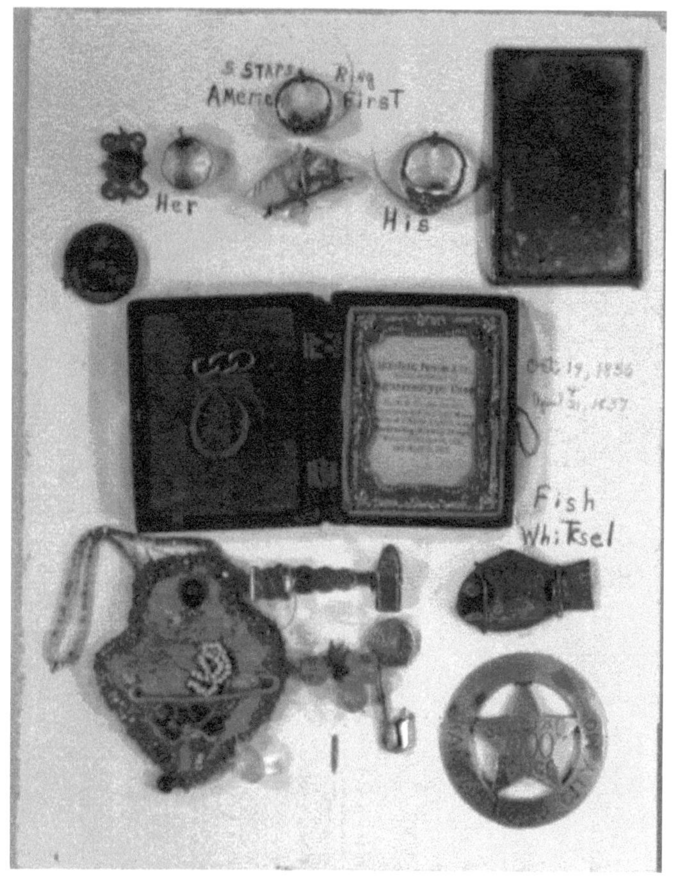

A Voice from the Past

The Discovery – June, 1985

As Chuck and his brother Bob James wound their way up the road to their great Aunt Daisy's home, they had no idea of the task that lay before them. Built in the early 1920s by Daisy's parents, she had lived in the home for the past sixty years. It was a dark, two-bedroom, four-room house constructed of local cedar and spruce wood and was a couple of miles out in the country from Neodesha, Kansas as the crow flies.

Daisy had lived alone for the previous two decades. Although Chuck had caught glimpses of the inside when he stopped by to say hello, he had really never looked around in earnest. Since he was a little boy, he liked exploring the area and hunting. He remembered Aunt Daisy always had a little desert or pie ready whenever he or his brother Bob would visit, which was usually three or four times per year.

Aunt Daisy

After Daisy's funeral, the director called Chuck, Bob and their Dad into his office and laid a bombshell on them.

"I've known your family for over forty years, and I really hate to even bring this up; but the fact of the matter is, your Aunt didn't have any money to pay for these services. So, we had to put a funeral lien on her property. If this bill isn't paid, her house and land are going to go up for auction next month. "All I want is my costs, nothing more," the funeral director said. "I know you've had this property in your family for years, and I'd hate like hell to see you lose it." He let it sink in for a few moments.

"Like I said," he continued, "I'm not looking to profit from this tragedy. All I want are my expenses and it's yours."

It was the first time the family had heard of it. They surely did not want to lose the property, so Chuck's dad worked out a payment arrangement that satisfied the funeral director, and he gave them access to Daisy's place.

Several years passed since the funeral before they did anything with the house, and by that time the mice had taken over.

It was a hot spring day, and Chuck wasn't looking forward to the task ahead. They were heading up to the house to clean it out so Bob could move in to keep an eye on it. A few weeks earlier, someone had broken in and stolen paintings and other items, although they weren't quite sure what, since the place was a disaster.

Once inside, things went from bad to worse. They found thousands of newspapers haphazardly stacked against the walls, waist high, fifty-five gallon drums full of who knew what, as well as hundreds of letters and envelopes scattered everywhere. They discussed how daunting a project it would be and realized they needed a plan.

The brothers decided to create an area near the middle of the driveway and turn it into a burn pile. They picked up stacks of papers, clothes and anything else lying around and started a fire with a bit of gasoline. Once lit, they continued feeding it until they were ready to go home that night.

This went on every week until the day Bob found an old Prince Albert can and shook it before tossing it into the pile. Cling, cling, cling. He opened it and found an old hundred-dollar bill and some coins. This presented a problem for the boys. Now, instead of throwing everything into the pile, they decided it would be more prudent to actually check the items first, in case old Auntie had squirreled away more valuables here and there.

After about three months, they only had the furniture left, having burned or given away everything else. One of the pieces was a tall wooden sideboard that held mason jars on top and the family plates and dishes in the cabinet below. They decided to move it outside while the place was being painted.

And then they found it.

Hidden behind the cabinet they discovered the door to a closet. The door handle had been removed so the sideboard could lay flat up against the wall. Chuck and Bob just stared at each other, searching their memories as to whether they had ever seen this door before.

Nothing.

Chuck ran out and returned with a screwdriver, stuck it into the square opening where the shaft that connected the door handles went through and turned it. The door popped ajar and slowly opened. It too, was full of old newspapers, letters and mason jars filled with aged fruit and vegetables. To Chuck's eye, these items looked much older than what they had been throwing away. This seemed to them like a Geraldo "Opening of Al Capone's Secret Room" moment. Yet, why would Aunt Daisy have hidden this four-foot by six-foot closet behind a piece of furniture?

The process of cleaning out that little area proved tedious. The papers were stacked high, and they wanted to go through everything before throwing it out to burn, lest they pass up another bundle of cash or coins.

When they got down to the last layer, something intriguing started to emerge. As they removed more of the papers, the prize came into view: two old, weathered, camel backed trunks. They quickly removed the rest of the *junk* next to their find, and Chuck again jimmied the lock open with his screwdriver on the trunk closest to them.

They slowly opened it and were met with some black cloth. They gingerly lifted it out, half expecting to see a reenactment of the scene out of the "Pirates of the Caribbean" with sparking jewels, pieces of eight and all other manner of treasure.

What they found next was worth even more to them.

A family secret held hostage for the past hundred years.

Camel Back Trunks

Cave Springs, Kansas

While Tim P. and I stood outside of his car near the cave where I originally found the JJ initials, he showed me photographs, newspaper clippings, clothing and various artifacts he had received from the James family, on whose behalf he was working. His narration painted the most fantastic and improbable story regarding Jesse James I had ever heard. Truth is, I was hooked. And also quite immersed in a dilemma.

There were too many obstacles and historical facts that flew in the face of these new insights. My "internal mind", the intellect that chance processes gave us to reason out and discern the truth within most any situation, was completely at a loss as to what to believe. I had this "feeling" that there really might be something to this improbable tale. But it was just that.

Then reality set in, and I resigned myself to the fact that I was too busy to take an interest in the mystery at the moment. But I did decide that as soon as I could, I would look deeper into this enigma. It shouldn't be too hard to track down the source of this information since Tim was really open to giving me all the contact info I needed. I got his card before he took off and I never met him again.

Despite the burning desire to follow up on the story, the day-to-day grind of the ranch and cave operations chipped away at all my free time. It was almost three years to the day before I was able to track down the James family and confirm a meeting with one of the nephews who cleaned out Daisy's house and found the trunks. I had an appointment to meet Chuck at his place, which was over one hundred miles away from the ranch.

An affable and stout fellow, Chuck J. was welcoming and did all he could to make me feel at home. Although the drive was long and the weather had clouded up threatening torrential downpours, the thought that I could see the original pictures and artifacts was electrifying. After a few perfunctory exchanges, I could hold back no longer.

"Do you have the *items* here that Tim P. told me about?"

"Of course I do. Hang on a minute and I'll get 'em out for ya," Chuck replied.

He disappeared into a back bedroom and rolled out a suitcase. It was packed to the gills with what looked like papers and photographs sticking out of the sides. How ironic, I thought, if this all turned out to be true and he was just walking around with the artifacts unsecured.

"Here they are," he said.

I remember my first impression very clearly. They looked, felt and *smelled* old, emitting an air of authenticity. Looking through them, Chuck relayed the story of how they were found. But to tell the truth, I was only half listening. What I was looking at floored me. Pictures, jewelry, written documents… it was a treasure trove of artifacts… again, I'm thinking, *if* they were authentic.

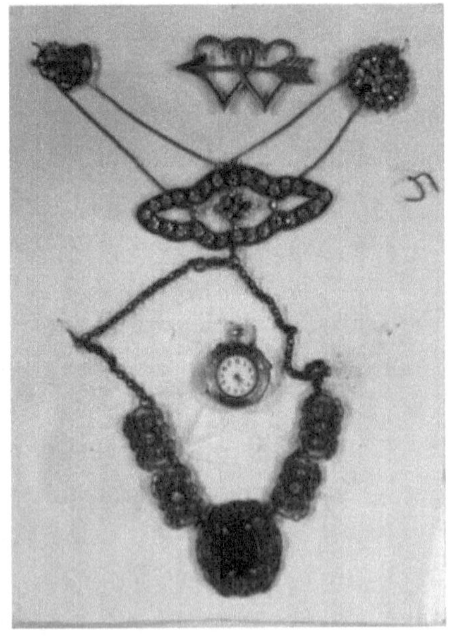

Chuck told me at first he wasn't sure about what he had. He figured some ancient relative must have left them. But then his mother started doing some research. And ever so slowly they started to look at their ancestral history in a completely new way.

Chuck's Story

"The story I've been able to put together," Chuck finally stated after a couple of hours of going over everything in the travel bag, piece by piece, "is pure and simple: Jesse James faked his death. I believe that he went to Oskaloosa, Kansas and ended up marrying my grandmother, Martha Jane Presgrove. That's why the trunks were in the closet with all of the missing James family heirlooms."

"Okay," I responded, "then why? Other than the fact he didn't want to get caught as an outlaw. Because it seems to me he went through quite an elaborate charade to convince people he was dead, when there were a hundred other simpler ways he could have done the same thing."

"That's a question we've been asking ourselves for the last twenty years," Chuck replied. "We're not exactly sure. A couple of the things in the trunk have us stumped. Maybe they'll be able to shed some light on the whole business. But it don't change the facts. This here is Jesse's stuff, and the only way it could have got here is if he wasn't killed when they say he was. He must have had his reasons."

"What about that documentary on the History Channel they aired a few years ago?" I had remembered seeing it, although it was a vague memory. "Seems to me they proved it was Jesse in that Missouri grave. Not only that but they were something like 99% certain it was him due to DNA tests that were conducted. How does that square with what you've just said?"

That created a moment of silence in the house, while a bewildered look passed between Chuck and his wife.

"To tell the truth, Ron, that did floor me when I saw it," he said. "It was like watching a trial where the evidence overwhelmingly showed you were guilty when you knew in your heart you didn't commit the crime. Almost what you would call surreal. I don't know what to tell you about that. Somehow something's not right there; I just can't tell you what it is."

If that wasn't a Perry Mason moment, I don't know what was. I can's say how many times I had been sitting in front of the old black and white TV screen when a client pleaded with Mr. Mason: "I'm not guilty, you've got to believe me!"

The small talk went on a bit more before I asked some more perfunctory questions. At the same time my mind was racing a million thoughts a second. I did get Chuck to agree to make some copies of the items for me, which I'd come back again and pick up. Also, I figured the elapsed time would give me the perfect opportunity to gather my thoughts and questions and take a second shot at getting some answers.

The drive back refreshed me and gave me a chance to form a new perspective of all that I had viewed and heard while at Chuck's place. But the majority of those thoughts and questions were greatly overshadowed by one main concern: the 1995 documentary seemed like airtight evidence that everything I had just physically seen, touched and heard was the equivalent of what the software industry called vaporware—it just didn't exist.

And yet it did.

But it was just the *main* obstacle I had to deal with. Besides the incongruous nature between what I sensed and saw and what others have said actually happened, there were a whole host of other questions. Who was buried in his grave if it wasn't Jesse? Why did he abandon his family? How did the sheriff and Jesse's friends and relatives not recognize that the body wasn't his? Who were the guys who claimed to have killed him and how were they connected? Why give up an inheritance to your family? And most importantly, a nagging question still bubbled to the surface every chance it could.

Why create such an elaborate hoax, rife with opportunities to get caught, when there were any number of other ways to disappear than to create the legend that you were killed?

No, it didn't make sense, none of it. And yet there must be an answer, *right*?

I sat down and started writing out all of these questions and more, hoping something would jump out at me and say, "here's the answer; just follow this path". But of course, that only happens in Agatha Christie mysteries, and I was right—it didn't happen.

But I did formulate a plan. A simple one, really. I would take two paths simultaneously. The first would be to track down all I could about the documentary. The second would consist of tracing back and learning all I could about this elusive Jesse James. If I could see the evidence, then perhaps I could figure out his true motives, if he had any other than saving his own skin.

I remember years back, right after the Vietnam War, I met and had drinks with an old Special Forces buddy. He was sharing with me some of the heroic and daredevil missions he and his squad went on when I decided to bend his ear about some problem or other I had at the time.

"Know what we'd do if faced with an insurmountable problem?" he asked, a serious demeanor immediately taking over.

"Kick ass and take names?"

"No, smart ass, we'd break down each aspect of the mission's problems to their simplest elements and then overcome each one individually. By the time we were finished, so was the mission. Otherwise, we'd all just be standing around with our heads up our 'you know whats' wondering how we were going to accomplish anything. That's the key, break it down."

I decided to do just that.

And I would start with the documentary.

Smoke and Mirrors

The 1995 History Channel documentary arrived in the mail a few weeks after formulating my two-part plan. Upon opening it, I realized I had almost forgotten I had ordered it. The ranch was getting busier with the chuck wagon suppers and cowboy evenings I had created to generate more income. The cave tours were rapidly gaining popularity. My thoughts were focused on the more mundane tasks of ordering enough buffalo meat and making sure we didn't run out of liability release forms for visitors.

Still, there weren't very long time spans where my mind didn't revert back to thoughts of that day and meeting with Chuck.

What was I getting myself into, I wondered.

One of the fortunate things about this whole Jesse James story was that I really didn't know much about it. Of course I'd heard the legends regarding his train robberies and that the outlaw was killed in his own home. I didn't have much more than a cursory sort of knowledge, the kind you get when you're in school or on a scouting trip. So, I was starting with a blank slate. No preconceived notions.

I was intrigued and enthused about digging into the stories—actually it was more than intriguing. And I was surprised to discover just how many books, magazine articles and periodicals had been written about the man's life. I read as much as I could of his exploits in my spare moments during the day and night. I started getting a sense of how he was truly revered in history—a sort of good old bad boy—not quite Robin Hood, but in the same vein.

As I slipped the tape of the 1995 study into the VCR and sat back to watch the show, I wasn't sure what to expect—especially how I'd feel about what I was going to see. I had dreaded the thought of sitting through it, concerned that at the end I would be no closer to understanding the disparity between the artifacts and the stories I had read up to that point. And in a purely self-delusional moment, I resigned myself to be an objective observer—a furtive attempt at impartiality, which flew out the window within the first five minutes.

I say that because what I noticed right off the bat were the words they were using. Not in a linguistic sense, but more in a clarifying sort of way. In sales they are referred to as "slippery English" types of words or phrases—things that sounded like you were saying something which in reality you weren't.

"It is thought that... It's probable this... People have come to believe that... It's an incontrovertible fact that... In all likelihood..."

Nothing I could put my finger on at that point, since I was listening with a different ear. Searching for discrepancies, contradictions and non-facts being touted as facts proved fruitful. I was actually able to hear them. Otherwise, it sounded like an objective, matter of fact, scientific examination of the remains of one Jeremiah "Jesse" Woodson James. The obvious thrust, or more precisely the show's intention, was clear: to put to bed once and for all whether it was Jesse Woodson James in the Missouri grave or someone else.

Then the bombshell hit which I already knew was contained within this documentary, but in the back of my mind I was hoping would be different.

"The DNA evidence shows conclusively, the body in this Missouri grave is indeed that of Jeremiah 'Jesse' James, and he was killed in his house as all the newspaper accounts have given. The test concluded it with a 99.7% certainty."

That's some strong medicine—99.7% certainty!

The words of the narrator, Professor James Starrs, echoed through my brain, and I must admit it affected me more than I thought it would. Only differently. I was angered. And it caught me by surprise. Angry because there was a certain amount of arrogance involved with the way he said it. And angry because this flew in the face of what my intuition and the facts I had discovered told me could not be true.

I played the tape again. Then, right after the beginning, I heard something I hadn't recognized as important the first time. Professor Starrs had opened with the following:

"My personal opinion of this whole thing is balderdash." Really?

I thought. Where is the objectivity in that? It got worse.

A little further on, he stated:

"I had to admit I was wrong... I now have to rely on scientific methodology."

Now the anger was welling up again.

What was he planning on using before this scientific approach, voodoo?

I started noting, line by spoken line, what was said. And more importantly, what was *not* said but rather merely implied.

I finally clicked the stop button on the remote and took a walk to try and make sense of the whole thing. On the one hand, the documentary had made a lot of seemingly good and plausibly valid points. Unless I was able to come up with proof of something different, an alternative possibility, those points would be very difficult to refute. Yet, on the other hand, even the minimum amount of research I had done up to that point contradicted some of their key points. And what about those trunk loads of artifacts thrown into the mix? It was hard to tell the facts from fiction at that point.

Then it hit me squarely between the eyes.

Fact from fiction.

That was the problem. I didn't have enough information. I needed more facts. Here I was lamenting about a documentary, which in its essence was merely the "opinions" of the filmmakers and people on the screen, or more to the point how *they* interpreted the facts. However, I didn't know, nor did I have access to, the underlying facts they relied upon. It could have been someone else's opinion, who relied on someone else's interpretation of what they believed the facts to be.

It's an age old problem, which is why our founding fathers did not allow "hearsay" evidence to convict someone. It was either from the source or not, simply because everyone colors what they see, read or hear with an unconscious agenda—not usually in a malicious way, but simply biased by their beliefs and experiences. I've seen it all through my life.

I needed to get to the source, not the filtered conclusions of others. I felt better. I had a plan, sort of.

The immediate problem was I hadn't a clue as to how to find the sources. Then again, that had never before stopped me from getting the scent of my prey and following through to the end. I remember feeling a calm sweep over me, as if a light had been thrown in a room where the boogeyman might be hiding. Now I could see there was nothing there. The unknown still lay ahead, and I couldn't even be sure what I would find. But I was sure I had a starting point and that was enough.

Was I being objective?

No way.

I knew what I was looking for. The difference? I was open and upfront about it. Yes, I had my agenda. However, I was also open to at least exploring the possibility that there was more to this story than what the "authorities" in the documentary were claiming as undisputed fact.

Two sides of the same coin. I was about to find out which side would win the toss.

The Search

Not everyone I wrote to or spoke with in my search was as excited as me about exploring all of the evidence to see if it supported the conclusions that were espoused on Starrs' 1995 documentary. In fact, I now look back and realize that it wasn't just a lack of enthusiasm for the truth that may have been at the core of these attitudes. It could've been much more.

My plan seemed simple enough. At least it ended up that way. First, I took all the things that bothered me about the documentary and tried to group them into columns and categories. Things like comments, innuendos and opinions. I found content analysis was rather difficult and time consuming to do. When all was said and done, I looked through it and thought: this is a nightmare.

So, let's say I prove what this or that person said here or there is not true. Then what? It's a pissing contest at that point, and the other side's "bona-fides" will end up trumping any argument I bring up from a point-by-point perspective.

That won't work.

My Dad always said, "Don't get into a pissing contest with a skunk." Alright then.

What I needed to do was present the filmmakers with base or foundational evidence of the inaccuracies of their statements—again if there were any (realizing at this point I wasn't being objective), then let the chips fall where they may. I was inwardly entertaining a hope that they would ultimately announce there was a mistake and blame it on new evidence that had been uncovered, thereby giving them academic cover for stating something as fact that turned out to be wrong. Sort of a scholarly 'Cover Your Butt' card.

Reluctantly, I tossed my "work of art" spreadsheet into the circular file and decided to narrow my search down to two major tracks. The first was the autopsy and DNA report from the 1995 documentary, and the second was to get copies of the original autopsy reports and witness statements from 1882. My thinking was simply to compare them and see if there were discrepancies.

Getting possession of the original DNA report referred to in the documentary was the higher priority of the two. So, I contacted George Washington University, where the documentary said Professor Starrs worked. I was courteously transferred to his office which, by the way, was not in the Anthropology or Forensic Science Department, but rather in the Law Department. A yellow flag immediately shot up. I let them know who I was, what I was doing (to a certain extent) and requested a copy of the report. Whoever was on the other end informed me that it was not yet available, and that when it was they would be happy to forward it to me. Now remember, the documentary was already five years old at that point. When I asked why it was not available and how they could base a documentary on it, the attitude of the woman speaking changed markedly. The first of what would seem a consistent set of roadblocks surfaced.

"When we have a copy of the report, we'll send it to you," she tersely stated.

"That's wonderful. Would you like my address as to where to send it?"

"No, just give us an email address and we'll notify you."

"Okay then. Thanks."

After months of waiting, I never received anything from them.

"So now what?" I wondered.

Going back to the video, I noted another professor named Ann C. Stone was mentioned, so I called Penn State University and was informed that she was working at the University of New Mexico. Yet another yellow flag. That didn't exactly sound like a promotion to me. But then again, maybe she had allergies and wanted a drier climate. I was able to reach her by phone, and it was a pleasant surprise.

Not only was she courteous and friendly, but she was also very helpful.

"How is it that Professor Starrs was able to state with 99.7% certainty, that the remains were actually those of Jesse James?" I asked.

"We had the preliminary forensics report and based it on that," she replied.

"Doesn't it require peer review and comparison against other variables before a conclusion can be made?" I queried.

"Usually," she replied. "But in this case, it wasn't at first. However, it subsequently did get published."

"I'm sorry, what did you say?"

"It has been published and is open for peer review."

"Do you have a copy of the DNA report that I can read?"

"Of course. Would you like me to send it to you?"

That's interesting, I thought to myself. Starrs' office said it wasn't available yet, and now Professor Stone was offering to send me a copy. I started to get a sense of the controversy and resistance of what was ultimately going to confront me during the next few years. However, pondering on the "why" of this would have to wait.

"That would be great," I responded, and promptly gave her my contact info.

I had reasoned, without any basis in fact, that getting the original autopsy report was going to be the easier of the two tracks. That assumption turned out to be wrong. When I tried to get copies of the local original newspaper articles that ran in 1882, I was floored. Turned out that all the copies of the newspapers in the local archives for St. Joseph, Missouri, on that day and the entire week after the death, were missing. There were three local newspaper publications in St. Joe at the time, *and copies of all of them were missing*! No editions were missing, as far as I could tell, before or after the shooting. Only those on the day and week after the killing were not available. That was very odd, but I had seen this before, where archives had been sanitized, although I was mystified as to why such a procedure would possibly be used for a seemingly straightforward event.

When I called the local courthouse for the actual legal documents, I was informed that they were all burned—on purpose—in the 1920s.

Wouldn't the local authorities try and save the documents on the most famous—or infamous—outlaw of all time? I asked myself.

Still another yellow flag shot up. This one higher than the rest.

I also started collecting accounts of what happened that were written years later from the supposed original witnesses to the crime, which were much easier to get copies of. I scoured libraries, museums, bookstores and historical archives in Missouri, Kansas, Oklahoma, Texas and Colorado.

After several weeks, I hit the mother lode at the Kansas State Historical Society in Topeka and the University of Kansas in Lawrence.

Back then, they took the fact that a local outlaw was killed pretty seriously, and the newspapers carried all the accounts, including a description of the autopsy report! I suspect that another reason for their existence was Jesse's possible involvement in the historic raid on Lawrence, Kansas.

The staff at the University was extremely helpful, and I had access to what I considered credible baseline, first hand information. I found a reprinted copy of the actual autopsy and it matched a partial previous version I had found. I took copies of my finds home and started scouring them, line by line.

It didn't take me long to realize why those newspaper files may have been sanitized.

Firsthand Accounts of the Newspapers

THE DAILY GAzETTE – ST. JOSEPH, MO - WEDNESDAY, APRIL 5TH, 1882.

EXTRAH

JESSE, BY JEHOVAH

JESSE, THE NOTORIOUS DESPERADO, INSTANTLY KILLED BY ROBERT FORD.

HIS ADVENTUROUS CAREER BROUGHT TO AN ABRUPT CLOSE, ON THE EVE OF ANOTHER CRIME.

FORD GETS INTO HIS CONFIDENCE AND SHOOTS HIM FROM BEHIND WHILE HIS BACK IS TURNED.

JESSE, A RESIDENT OF ST. JOE SINCE THE 8TH OF NOVEMBER LAST.

AN INTERVIEW WITH MRS. JAMES AND THE TESTIMONY DEVELOPED FOR A JURY.

One thing became obvious from the start: newspapers certainly have changed how they report stories over the past one hundred plus years. I was taken aback by how matter-of-factly and objectively those articles were written, in a style that present day newspapers mockingly emulate but never seem able to achieve. Journalism at its finest, I remember thinking.

The newspaper accounts themselves painted a rather different picture of the event than the historical lore that has reached us today. More correctly, a "conflicting" view of what happened on that fateful day in 1882, as well as the days and weeks surrounding the incident, emerged. It seemed there was a spin on the historic accounts as well.

I was reminded of when I was in the scouts and we played a game called whisper, where we all got in a circle and started with one of us saying something like "the rain in Spain falls mainly on the plain." We would whisper it to the next boy, and then he would whisper it and so on, until the last kid in the circle told us what was said, which usually ended up something like "airplanes land in trees on Wednesdays."

The firsthand accounts reported in the newspapers, although *sounding* like what I'd read and heard, differed in almost every key area. When looked at through the filter of what I knew was true, they took on a completely different meaning. Different in that they contradicted what was quoted later by news organizations and authors. It was clear that I had chosen the right path by finding the original source material.

The first thing I noticed was the utter absurdity of how Jesse was supposedly killed in his own house. Why would he remove his guns, turn his back on his friend, pull out a chair and reach up to adjust a picture? More importantly, why would this Bob Ford fellow wait until then to shoot Jesse, in his own house, when it was reported that only minutes before they were both in the barn together where he could have just as easily accomplished it with no danger to himself. How did he know Jesse's wife didn't have a gun around?

And Jesse's children were in the house. I realize the guy was supposedly heartless, but killing someone in front of his own children seemed pretty harsh, even back then.

But that was only the beginning. One of the newspaper articles gave me a clue as to the confusion that was going on at the time. It turns out that upon initial questioning, both Jesse's mother and his wife denied that the body was Jesse's. It wasn't until later that they recanted their testimony and said, yes, it was in fact, Jesse. That's very strange, since one of them supposedly gave birth to him and the other was allegedly his wife of eight years (1874-1882). It doesn't seem reasonable that they were *both* confused. There were others who knew him that were also "confused" about whether or not it was Jesse.

I decided to study the autopsy report, which was a real help, or hindrance, if you believe Jesse was killed that day. I focused my attention on the narrative regarding the condition of the body and the injuries sustained. Detailed descriptions of where his wounds and scars were found *did not fit the alleged details of the killing*. What jumped right off the page was the fact that the coroner stated unequivocally that certain bruises and trauma suggested that a struggle had ensued and that the victim, *Jesse*, had his right thumb cut off in some kind of fight.

I next read Ford's testimony at the inquest, which was quoted word for word in the newspapers. Again, his words painted a very different picture from what most people believe happened. He described in detail how he followed Jesse into the house, how Jesse had taken off his guns and then stood up on a chair to fix a crooked picture. Bob Ford stated he whipped out his brand new Smith and Wesson .44 and fired a shot right through Jesse's head and into the wall. Ford then stated that Jesse fell "relatively gently backwards to the floor". He even described in rather morbid detail the blood gushing four inches out of the hole in his forehead. Trouble was, he also gave three different descriptions for the direction the body fell in three separate interviews. In part of the testimony, he stated that he and his brother Charlie, who was present at the shooting, immediately ran from the house before Jesse's wife found him dying on the floor. Too many contradictions appeared in all those stories, and none of the versions matched the physical evidence. I had to find another version of the events.

Back to the coroner's report. He verified removing the fatal bullet from the skull and further, *there was no exit wound in the front of the skull.* Additionally, he described the bullet he removed as a round ball lead shot, which is not a .44 caliber slug, the gun Bob Ford testified he used. And, the coroner also noted an injury to the left temple shaped like a gun hammer as though the deceased were struck with the butt end of a pistol.

So, here was the question that got the hair rising on the back of my neck: How did a bullet both remain in the skull *and* end up creating a hole in the wall at the crime scene, which is still there today as part of the Jesse James museum? Especially since only one shot was supposedly fired?

It was hard to believe the coroner could make such a gross oversight. Other questions followed.

Was the coroner mistaken and had not taken a bullet out of the skull? Or was the hole in the wall and therefore the entire story related by Ford and his accomplices fabricated? How did the sheriff, judge, coroner and everyone else reading those accounts miss that?

You would almost have to purposely ignore the evidence to not have seen and questioned it.

And finally, if the entire account of his death was fabricated, and Jesse was not killed that day, who exactly is the poor guy laying in the casket in proxy for Jesse? Was he an unwillingly participant in this charade? A murder victim?

Now, I had some tangible evidence to at least hang on to; a place to start from to sort out what really might have happened. The actual forensic evidence of the 1882 murder provided the proof that Jesse Woodson James could not have been killed in the way described that fateful day. And that's why I believe the autopsy report was so hard to find.

Upon objective scrutiny, the facts themselves exposed the ruse.

DNA Report

Within a week of talking to Ann Stone at the University of New Mexico, the 1995 DNA report arrived as promised. I found that it had been submitted to the *Journal of Forensic Sciences* in January of 2001, almost *five years* from the time the documentary was made. The report seemed very technical in nature. Since I had to read it over, if only for the sake of saying I did, I plopped onto the couch and started wading through it. Plus, armed with my latest discoveries in the newspapers, I was interested in exactly how this report could possibly be true.

Okay, so it started with the explanations of the methodologies used, standards for analyzing DNA, yadda, yadda. The first two pages were, well, technically boring. I finally arrived at the last paragraph and my jaw dropped.

Do the mtDNA results prove that the exhumed remains are those of Jesse James?
The answer to this question must be no…

Must be no???

Whoa, wait a minute. I remembered without hesitation this paper's same author, James E. Starrs, stated unequivocally in the documentary that the remains were a 99.7% certainty to be those of the outlaw Jesse James. What's going on here?

I read a bit further. There, also buried among what turned out to be hyperbole and fluff was another statement:

We are left with three possibilities: (1) the exhumed remains are indeed those of Jesse James; (2) the exhumed remains are not Jesse

James, but from another maternal relative of RJ and MN (related descendants); or (3) the exhumed remains are from an unrelated individual who, by chance, happens to have the same mtDNA sequence as RJ and MN.

Again, where was the 99.7% certainty of this DNA being Jesse James? According to this paper, by my calculations, it would at the very best be only 33% (one of three possibilities). And that is before Starrs stated that those tests did not prove it was Jesse James in the first place, which now lowered the possibility to ZERO!

How could that be? What scientific evidence did he base those documentary statements upon? It couldn't be according to the DNA report I had in my hands.

Did he just make it up?

I tried calling him to get his response, but he never returned my calls.

Still hasn't.

Frankly, I didn't care at that point. I had two major pieces to the puzzle that I hadn't a clue even existed before. Had I relied on the eight hundred or so other books and accounts of the Jesse James story, or even that documentary, I would have eventually thrown in the towel and conceded that they were right, and Jesse was killed that day in 1882.

As it stood, I had scientific as well as historical eyewitness evidence to suggest he wasn't—the early accounts that disputed the way he was killed, and the present day DNA that showed it was not a certainty at all that it was Jesse James' body in that grave. More importantly, a renewed vigor to keep on searching for the answers to the myriad of questions still swirled within me. Only with more passion. With this new information completely contradicting what was popularly known, I had many questions that demanded truthful answers.

I wanted to celebrate at the local "drinking establishment" that many of my musician friends frequented. But I still had a lot more work to do. As far as I knew, I was the only one who had figured out this historical puzzle. I needed to connect more of the dots before launching the campaign that was slowly starting to form in my subconscious.

But two things were crystal clear to me: One, that Jesse James pulled off one of the greatest hoaxes in history, and two, just because someone says it's so, don't make it so.

The Plan

Okay, so I didn't really have a perfectly reasoned or thought out plan. It was more of a dynamic set of actions that I was hoping would eventually lead to more concrete directions as they gained momentum.

But I did know that taking action, any action, was something I needed to continue in order to keep *my* momentum and enthusiasm going. So, I started studying all of Chuck's materials. I also sent out copies of the DNA report to experts I had been consulting with regarding this case.

My reasoning centered on the idea that when I was asked to back up what I was saying, I would have the reports, copies of artifacts and newspaper accounts ready to send out to support my assertions.

I continued collecting evidence. In my research, I started turning up more copies of letters, pictures, old newspaper articles and obscure books that were tending to support the path I was pursuing. One of the more fascinating areas I was exploring was a bunch of copies of letters and legal documents containing Jesse's handwriting and signature, which were surprisingly plentiful. He was quite the historical document writer. I started to match these signatures to the subject I suspected was the alias that Jesse may have used after faking his death.

This will be much easier to prove than I thought it would be, my still unbruised and naïve ego chimed in. Once people see all of this objective evidence, I continued reasoning, I'll be credited with finally breaking open the entire story.

Grandiose visions of television interviews, sixty-minute background stories—even Oprah herself giving homage to my most excellent detective skills. I would become known as the man who solved a one hundred and twenty-year-old murder mystery, the ultimate cold case file.

A number of things still bothered me about this whole scenario, not the least of which was the timeline given for Jesse's life before the supposed murder. For example, how could he have covered the ground to commit all the robberies attributed to him? In one instance, his gang was credited with two robberies that were committed over two consecutive days. The first was in Mississippi and the second in Kansas, hundreds of miles apart—an amazing feat even in a swift early twentieth century car, which hadn't been invented yet.

Then we have the question of who exactly was lying in the Missouri grave. I believed that murder was still the central theme to this whole affair. But whose murder? And why?

The answer came much later as to who might be in that grave, from an unexpected source—Chuck and his suitcase full of photographs.

And then the final mystery—the cornerstone underlying all of what plagued me from the beginning: *Why go through such an elaborate charade if you only needed to elude the law?*

An interesting question that would have to wait to be answered. In the meantime, I needed to get back to the plan. I now had all of my "evidence" ready to go. And therein laid the rub. Where should I go with it?

I started making calls to the local newspapers, historical societies and organizations created around that enigmatic figure.

I also decided to go to the source of all the confusion—the History Channel, since they were the producers of the first supposedly "authoritative" documentary. I wondered if they even knew about the problems associated with the case and the outright untruths it contained. I was finally able to connect by phone with Mark F., the director of programming, a cordial and understanding person. After laying out what I had discovered, point by point, he asked me to put my thoughts onto paper and send them to him. He would then be in a position to decide how to proceed.

Surprisingly, I never heard back from him.

Now what? I thought.

Hopes of sitting on Oprah's couch were slowly fading.

First New Clue

"What do you think happened to it?" Dave asked.

It was a tough question to even think about. I guess I had never given it much thought up to that point. The last three months had been both exciting and frustrating, mainly because I started to get a glimmer that something being self-evident doesn't necessarily mean anyone is going to readily accept it. In fact, in many cases it seemed to me people and organizations started to dig in a little deeper and get angrier in defending their opinions. The facts be damned!

This caught me off guard, so I decided to take a week or two off to think through this still materializing plan of mine. I'd already decided I needed to get off the ranch, so I made arrangements to have someone else run it. The drive back and forth was taking its toll on my patience. That, coupled with the frustration of running into brick walls, was even becoming noticeable to my daughters, who on more than one occasion had asked, "what was up" with me.

The more immediate question was: Where to go from there? I had already satisfied myself that the 1995 documentary, for whatever reason, was a sham. And I believed I could prove it, if anyone would listen. The evidence I was collecting about what actually happened at the time of the killing was growing daily. The same picture kept emerging: an elaborate hoax had been orchestrated to convince the world that Jesse James had finally been laid to rest. All well and good, but what next?

"That's a great question," I replied as I remembered Dave's question and snapped back into the present.

"It doesn't really make sense, does it Dave?" I continued. "I mean, if he was such a prolific train and bank robber, why did he end up living like a dirt farmer the rest of his life? It's not like he spent a lot of money on living the high life."

"So where is all the gold he supposedly took from those trains and banks?" Dave asked.

That was weird. From all I had uncovered, Jesse was a much more prolific thief than I first suspected. Estimates ran from a few million dollars to perhaps as much as three hundred million, if you believed he had something to do with sacking the St. Louis Federal Reserve.

And then another gestalt moment happened. I remembered one story which talked about Jesse burying some of his loot—in caves. Caves! That's where this whole thing started. The initials in the cave! Tim P. asking me if I had seen any JJ initials in other caves. Why would he be interested in JJ's initials in the caves, anyway? He had copies of all the artifacts. What was his motivation? Maybe there were still clues left in a cave somewhere out there in Kansas, waiting to be discovered?

I wasn't expecting to find any treasure. I figured that the remaining members of the James Gang, in case of Jesse's disappearance, would have gone back and divided their plunder—faked death or not. What was just as interesting was the hope that there could be more documents that would help me understand the reason why he did it, and why he never used the wealth he had accumulated in his subsequent "life after death".

- - - - - - -

I had met Retired Air Force General Skelton several years earlier during my research into Native American ceremonial mounds. He was not only well informed and well read, but very obliging. I'd kept in touch through the ensuing years, checking in when I found out anything new or unusual regarding those ancient mounds. I contacted him and inquired if he knew approximately how many caves in Kansas had JJ initials carved in them. He thought he'd heard about at least half a dozen. He put me in touch with a fellow who had a list of those caves and a host of others, located mostly in Kansas.

I took the list and decided that finding and exploring these caves was my next direction. It's not like there were a lot of options available to me at the time. And I wanted to keep the momentum going.

I'd learned that looking for, finding and then exploring caves was a lot like snipe hunting. It's tedious, boring, methodical and mostly tiring work. And sometimes dangerous. Although the hunt for the quarry—the *game being afoot* as Sherlock Holmes used to say—was always a motivator. The plain truth of the matter was less glamorous: there's a lot of time, not to mention miles, of hiking rough terrain, between the hunting and the finding.

Dave and I explored two caves within the next few weeks. Although they had the JJ initials, they yielded precious little else. No artifacts, petroglyphs or further directions. Nothing.

And then we came to the third cave. It was different. Besides displaying the initials, it had something else—what I can only describe as "turkey tracks" etched into the walls in various places. Were the signs carved by Native Americans, or were they more contemporary in nature? Very curious. We took pictures of the glyphs, the initials and the cave entrance, made extensive notes in my field journal and then moved on.

We were pleasantly surprised to discover the next cave we explored contained the same type of turkey track marks. Again, it could be a coincidence—after all, the natives had known about these caves for thousands of years. Nevertheless, they interested me on some deep intuitive level. I wasn't sure why, but I was learning to trust my gut.

During that time, I frequently went back to visit Chuck and his family. At one of those visits, he remembered some other photographs of Jesse from the old trunks and brought them out.

There, among this new batch, was a photo of Frank and Jesse much older than previous photos, standing in a field. However, far off in the background, I could make out what looked like the mouth of a cave. I recognized that cave. I'd seen it somewhere before, but where? And why would Frank and Jesse meet up again in their old age to have their picture taken in front of a cave?

Bingo.

The bells started going off in my head!

Very clever, those James boys.

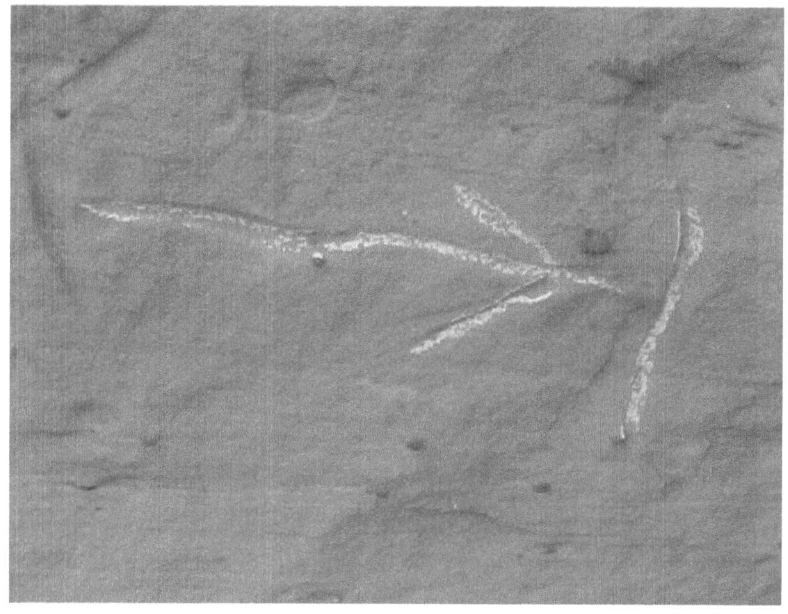

Caves and Codes

I studied that picture for hours, trying to visualize exactly where the cave was located. The photo was a relatively tight shot, which didn't afford too many landmarks, although I was sure when I found it I would know it, based on a couple of unique features in the background. I figured that we just needed to get out and look at the various areas where caves were known to exist, and then try to match it.

Chuck's son, Jeremiah "Jesse" James V (the 5th), became part of the exploration team, which now consisted of Dave, Jesse V and myself. I said became, but the more honest way of saying it is that I dragged him along whenever I could, since Dave had moved and wasn't always available to go with me on these expeditions. Jesse V and I searched various areas for almost a year before a lead came through in a most innocent and unexpected way.

We were traveling through the Flint Hills and entered a small town that couldn't have had more than eight hundred people. The historic main street stretched perhaps three blocks long. It was your typical James Dean Midwest 1880s stone building town (ala "Rebel Without a Cause"). We ended up speaking with some of the locals, asking about caves, and they suggested in a rather off-handed way a particular spot to look around. Based on that, we drove out to the general area they described.

This was an interesting part of Kansas—rolling hills, lush grassland and deep ravines with thick vegetation. The road was pretty rough: unpaved and unmaintained. We finally stopped and got out to have a look around. On this beautiful spring day, we hiked the hills around the bluffs and down into ravines, as time seemed to fly by. The only thing we found the first day were a few "potential" petroglyphs. I say potential because they were quite faint from erosion. It started to get late, so we decided to pack it in, set up camp at a state park and throw down a few brewskis while roasting some hot dogs.

The second day we were awakened by a troupe of wild turkeys, we made coffee and struck camp. We ventured further into the lush green riparian valley and were almost immediately rewarded with various cliff art and petroglyph renderings. Fantastic in their simplicity, I again wondered if they were made by Native Americans or perhaps some historical figure like Montezuma or Cortez.

Funny how your mind can go to some distant past and imagine what it would have been like to live in that area back then: hunting, gathering, enjoying life on the plains. Right then, that seemed an idyllic dream, because by the end of the second day we still hadn't located anything remotely resembling a cave. Discouragement was starting to poke its head up and dampen my enthusiasm. Jesse V, on the other hand, was getting uncharacteristically motivated. He enjoyed himself out in the wilderness and was really connecting with the land.

We both agreed one more day was all we would invest in our search of the area and came back the next morning ready to go. The underbrush was much thicker as we ventured deeper into the hills. We stopped and talked to the landowners whenever we came upon a local farmhouse. But the tracts of land were so vast, some areas covering thousands of acres, that we were not always able to locate any people. The thought crossed my mind of the consequences of running into whoever owned this land and trying to come up with some lame story about how we ended up so far out there. However, there was no way we could get that lost, I reminded myself. Maybe some other story would pop into mind if that circumstance occurred. Turned out we never did run into anyone in this particular search, even after covering over twenty miles on foot.

We encountered a slight clearing to the north and headed toward it, when suddenly we broke out of the trees and there it was—the exact cave Jesse and Frank were standing in front of in the photograph. We found out later that erosion had ripped away the cave entrance, destroying a huge petroglyph. But there was no mistaking it—Jesse James had stood in this exact same spot over one hundred years ago. It was mind blowing. We took a cursory look inside the cave, which was covered with the mother lode of petroglyphs. We decided to take advantage of the remaining daylight and check out the surrounding area.

Traveling down a ravine, we found the scrub and trees were getting thicker, slowing us down quite a bit. As the hours wore on, the excitement from the cave discovery was not giving me the expected bump in energy I needed to keep going. I noticed something to the south and motioned Jesse V to follow me toward it. I was hoping it would be a place to sit down and rest for a few minutes.

We found a large flat boulder overlooking the valley and sat down. Hungrily, we munched our nature bars while contemplating and discussing what Frank and Jesse might have been thinking if they had been sitting on that exact spot making their plans, although *what* plans, we weren't quite sure.

Rested and recharged, we continued on.

Exploring further, we noticed a huge bluff ahead with a sixty foot face protruding westerly. Although there's no scientific way to confirm this, I instantly felt a pull toward it, and the closer we trekked, the more magical it felt. As we approached the bottom of the bluff, I felt compelled to shout: "I've brought your great, great grandson, Jesse!"

A cold chill ran up the back of my neck, while the hair on my arms rose as an electric shock of excitement raced through my body. I quickly glanced at Jesse V and could see it in his eyes too.

We started scaling our way up the facade. About an eighth of a mile in, we rounded the corner of the cliff face. That's when we caught a glimpse of what we were looking for: seven caves about thirty feet above the valley floor.

The ledge leading around the cliff face started out about six inches wide, and slowly widened to about two feet by the time we made it to the first cave entrance.

We found sandstone caves recessing into the north facing bluff with moss and lichen growing over the top edge of the embankment, partially covering the overhang.

After reaching the first cave, which was only three feet high, we found it to be full of debris. The second cave was much larger with loose sand on the floor, but it only went in a few yards to a dead end.

The third cave was tall enough to stoop down and walk in. As we crept inward, we noticed a small opening to the right that didn't seem natural. Actually, none of it seemed natural. I had never seen, or even read about, any of these types of caves forming either naturally or otherwise in that area.

Peering into the small opening, I could see a large chamber that faded into the darkness.

"Are you going in?" I asked Jesse V, realizing I was already videoing his feet disappearing through the hole. Joining him, I had to take off most of my gear to fit through the opening. After some squeezing and pulling, we made our way into the cavern. Our heartbeats racing, we shined the light and video camera in every direction. We had entered a large room, and over toward the rear wall we found a passageway. It continued on for about eighty feet, gradually sloping downward. The echoing of my heart started pounding louder in my head as we continued toward the back. The ceiling was getting lower but the sand floor remained level when suddenly, after a slight turn, it abruptly ended as if filled in. I noted that there was a lot of sand on the floor.

Where did this passage go? I wondered.

We explored the rest of the caves and found no artifacts of any kind. But what we did find was even more amazing: petroglyphs and signs carved into the rock facing. And, more importantly, those same mysterious turkey tracks that showed up wherever the James boys had been.

A few moments later I discovered something I truly was not prepared for.

I remember thinking that this might be the culmination of the past year's journey—all the dead ends I had encountered, not to mention the remarks now starting to emanate in my social circles about "Ron's crazy quest" to rewrite history. I was also dealing with my own doubts as to whether or not I would ever find the original cave in the old photo of Frank and Jesse. Now I was hot on Jesse's trail. Although what would ultimately result from this discovery was, as yet, not clear to me. At that point in time, it was the quest that mattered.

We started exploring west of the last cave and moved a little of the overhanging moss to the side, *revealing three signatures*.

There was "Jeremiah" spelled out in block letters. Above that was "Frank" his brother and below was "Susan", Jesse's sister. This had to be it. There was no other explanation I could fathom. Where we stood could only be Handson's Cave—a cave that had been rumored to be a hideout for the gang, but up until now never verified!

Finally, I had a real sense of knowing that I was on the right track. From what I could tell, no one had connected this spot to the Jameses. That meant it was relatively undisturbed, and I could explore the site to possibly discover some of this Jesse's mysteries.

I made a commitment to keep meticulously accurate records of my work. I returned several times during the next couple of months and brought another buddy, Kip, who was the poster boy for techno-nerds. If we needed a gadget or remote camera, he'd invent it for us. His contributions would help keep us on track for the tasks I wanted to accomplish. I collected and recorded all the data I could in my field journal, hoping to make sense of it one day.

Detailed photographs, GPS coordinates of the carvings, renderings of the cave and relative positions on maps were all taken and categorized as we continued exploring the surrounding area for more information.

At one point, we decided to uncover the original bluff where I had shouted out my now prophetic message of meeting Jesse's great, great grandson. While up on the ledge, I removed a patch of moss, and there was the first inkling of how truly important this site might be. Incised deep into the cliff face was a Spanish cross about two feet tall and one foot wide. And not just any cross. It appeared that it could be the cross of Francisco Vasquez de Coronado, who made it to the region in 1541. Was this a spot on his failed mission to find the seven golden cities of El Dorado? They could have buried weaponry and other artifacts for a later campaign in this very area— one for which Coronado never returned.

We started to remove the overhanging growths of moss carpeting the face of the various caves. I found numerous other strange markings and codes underneath. I guessed by the amount of growth, the caves hadn't been seen by anybody for a century or more. Truly awesome!

I documented them all, hoping that, as in seemingly everything else up to this point, I would be led to someone or something that would help me understand what in the world these markings meant.

I believed that the markings must lead to something, either information or perhaps the location of artifacts. I was sure of it.

I was soon to find out what they meant through a most unexpected source.

And to learn, painfully, to what lengths men would go in order to steal what is not theirs.

Section IV

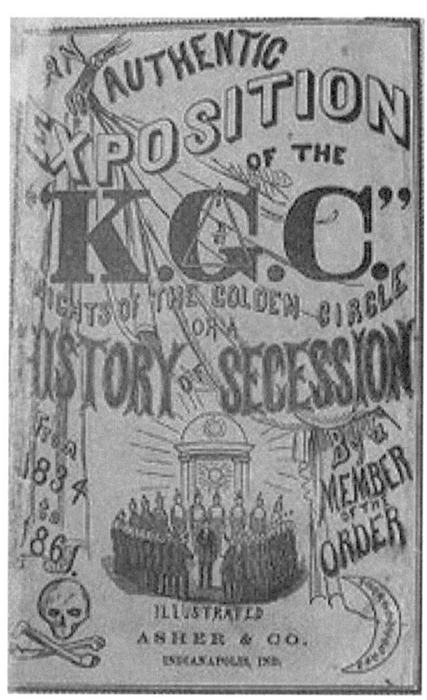

The Missing Motive

Exhumation, Texas Style

Tuesday, May 30, 2000

The entire town of Grandbury, Texas was abuzz when I arrived for the exhumation of J. Frank Dalton, an alias of Jesse James. For the past couple of years, a group of people had lobbied to exhume the remains for examination and DNA testing. I thought it highly unlikely that this man could be "the" Jesse James, especially in light of what had happened in the 1995 Missouri exhumation and the evidence I had accumulated.

A few hours earlier, Jesse V and I were at a beautiful campsite on the banks of Lake Bob Sandlin in Texas, getting ready to spend a leisurely day, watching the great blue herons make a mockery of my fishing talents, and communing with nature. This was a birthday present I had promised myself all year. However, the mood changed abruptly when I received a call from Chuck James telling me that they were moving the exhumation up a day to May 30th and I needed to get there right away.

Grandbury, Texas is located about thirty miles southwest of Dallas. The first thing you notice is it's built around a lake and is quite picturesque. As you make your way into town, you're taken back in time to the late 1800s with the quaint buildings and center town square. Signs point the way to various historic spots. During the war with Mexico, many of the men who fought at the Alamo left their families safely behind in Grandbury. Among the markers are signs pointing to the grave of Jesse James in the Grandbury cemetery. As promised, there was a grave marker for Jesse W.

James. On any other day, it would no doubt be a quiet spot to visit, but that day it was a circus. Hundreds of people and dozens of reporters with remote ENG satellite trucks blanketed the area.

Temperatures were well over one hundred degrees with the humidity up in the high double digits. As the crew prepared to locate the burial plot of J. Frank Dalton, I noticed that they were standing *behind* the headstone as they viewed the plot plan of the cemetery. I approached Dr. David Glassman, who was the physical anthropologist in charge of the dig.

"Hey, Doc," I asked, "shouldn't they be *facing* the gravestone to view the plot plan? You're gonna dig up the wrong guy if you dig there."

He explained they only had a court order to dig up the grave with the marker for Jesse James. Even if it were the wrong one, they had to go through with it. I stated for the record that I felt they should go back to the Judge right then and get approval to move over one plot to the left.

"That wouldn't be possible," he told me, "since it had taken months to get the dig approved."

The backhoe was brought in after the headstone was moved, and the dig began. Slowly, throughout the day, the dirt was carefully removed from the plot. By the end of the day, a portion of the burial vault had been uncovered. The dig stopped at sundown and security was posted to guard the plot overnight.

That evening at the hotel, I had a long talk with Dr. Glassman over several beers. Our topics ranged from DNA protocols to evidence collection. We even touched on forensic DNA cataloguing of ancient cultures. That was the in I needed to discuss my suspected subject for Jesse in Neodesha. The Doc graciously gave me a few pointers on how to proceed and what to avoid. It was close to midnight when we all turned in for an early start in the morning.

The second day was as hot, humid and miserable as the day before. By midday, three sides of the burial vault were exposed. The backhoe was brought in to dig out the last side. As we got down to the six-foot level, the bucket came up with a bucketful of wood fragments from the neighboring coffin. Once exposed, the vault was chained up and hoisted out of the hole. The backhoe strained under the weight of the vault as it was maneuvered into the coroner's van. The springs and tires of the van flattened as it took on the full weight. The van pulled away under police escort.

Bud H. had been the moving force behind making the exhumation happen and couldn't be present in the room due to the DNA evidence handling issues. I met Bud when I first arrived and his smile was immediately infectious. He had heard about what I was doing with Jesse and thought there was some kind of fit with what he had been able to set in motion that day.

After some small talk, I mentioned that I was exploring various caves in the Midwest, to which he rather nonchalantly asked me if I had seen JJ's initials around any of the caves.

"Of course," I said.

"Really?" he responded, again in that tone of voice that spoke as if he couldn't care less. "What about rock carvings?"

"We've seen all kinds of them, mostly illegible," I answered.

Someone ran over apologizing profusely for the interruption and whispered something to Bud. He smiled and off they scooted.

"Sorry about that," he said coming back a few minutes later. "It's almost time to crack the vault and see whose bones are lying in there." He looked around as if searching for someone, and while his eyes darted through the crowd, he asked nonchalantly, "You ever see anything that looked like turkey tracks?"

"As a matter of fact Bud, I just found a set of caves with a bunch of marks like that all over them."

The blood drained out of his face, coursing somewhere else through his six foot plus, two hundred and fifty pound frame. His demeanor immediately changed from the jovial car salesman that had been his career for the previous thirty years, to one of earnest compadre—almost paranoid in nature and feeling.

He leaned in and sternly said, "We need to talk!"

Another fellow came up and whisked him away to where the actual burial vault was located. Outside, the facility was being surrounded by cameras and reporters, the usual media circus waiting for a seminal moment that would get them some "face time" on the six o'clock news.

I was more concerned about what those turkey tracks could mean and why they affected Bud the way they had.

Then, the project manager for the event in Grandbury approached me with a proposal.

"Ron, we need an impartial third party observer for the opening of the vault," he stated. "You've got some great credentials, and the team agrees it should be you. Would you like to participate?"

"Would I? Hell yeah!" I said as I grabbed my camera and went to the room where the examination would take place. I remember Chuck and some of the others were asking how come I got to go in and they didn't. I felt fortunate to have been asked and my grin showed it.

After some forceful movements with the tools of the trade—in this case they looked like garden variety crowbars—the vault was opened and the excitement level in the room started to elevate. The coroner, ME, DA, police chief, anthropologist, mortician and myself looked on as the lid was raised. Two of the men stood over the vault. Once they eyed the insides, they had a rather heated discussion in monotone whispers. And then one of them turned to the rest of us in the room and ordered us out—not in an asking way, but a forceful request that left no room for objection.

I noticed right away there was an arm missing from the corpse. The public found out months later that they had disinterred the wrong body. The mystery of if J. Frank Dalton, one of Jesse's cousins and closest friends, was in that grave would have to wait for another day.

In a word, it was a bust.

Once we were ordered to leave the examination room, we milled about outside until it became obvious I would not be asked in again soon. I was considering leaving when Bud came over and pulled me aside.

"Tell me more about the glyphs you saw," he quietly implored.

"I'll tell you what," I responded, "can you tell me what they mean or why they're important first?"

A gutsy play on my part, which felt a little manipulative, but I wasn't about to give up what I found without first knowing what I was giving away.

Bud analyzed me like it was a Texas hold 'em game and he was making a river draw. Finally, he relaxed a bit and began to explain.

"This whole James Gang thing is much bigger than most people realize. It wasn't merely about the South, per se. It was much more than that. They were robbing banks and trains to fund a group they belonged to."

He looked around again, as if thinking about how to proceed.

"You ever hear about a group called the Knights of the Golden Circle?"

"Not really, Bud. Are they part of something like the Knights Templar?" I tried to sound like I knew what he was talking about, but the fact was I knew very little about that group. I knew the Templar Knights were on the quest for the Ark of the Covenant, the Holy Grail and other religious relics. I had made numerous studies with my associate Dan of how they arranged the various cathedrals throughout Europe to make certain geometric patterns. For what purpose, at the time, I wasn't quite sure.

"In a way, yes," Bud continued, "only something more like how a second cousin is related to you. I've been studying the KGC for the past ten years and have gotten pretty good at learning how to decipher their codes. For instance, those turkey tracks are part of an elaborate coding system they used to mark where they buried their treasures and stolen money."

So that was it. Buried treasure. I guess I hadn't really thought about Jesse belonging to some secret organization like KGC. In fact, I wasn't even sure that Jesse and his gang had made the coded markings.

"So what are these Knights all about?" I asked.

He smiled, as if a fish had just made a first nibble at a big fat worm dangling from his line.

"Whoa there," he replied. "A little tit-for-tat here. I've shown you part of my hand, how about a little reciprocal trust being shown by you?"

"What do you want to know?"

"Well, where are these caves, for one?"

He didn't know. That was in my favor. And as much as a poker player as he must have fancied himself, it was written all over his body that he wanted to know—badly.

"Well, it's a little premature to talk about location at this point," I stated, as I internally began strategizing my position. "But I'll tell you what. How about I send you a couple of photographs of the codes, and if you can decipher what they mean, we'll go from there."

He wanted to close the deal right there, I could feel it. But then some thought seemed to cross his mind and his whole body relaxed. "Ron," he said, slapping me on my back and smiling, "I think that's a fair deal. You send me a couple of pictures of the place, and I'll show you I can read the code. Then we'll make a deal about how to get to these caves and see if what I've read about the treasures they buried applies to the site."

Although the exhumation itself was a disappointment, the trip itself was *not* a huge waste of my time. In fact, it was an invaluable experience for many reasons. I met former Texas Attorney General Waggoner Carr and spent many hours picking his brain. He was convinced that Dalton was "the" Jesse James and held many historical documents to prove it. He sat there with Dalton's hat in his lap all day. Little did I know back in May of 2000 that he had all the DNA needed right there in the sweatband of that hat.

I was also able to spend some quality time with Dr. Glassman discussing the physical anthropology and DNA recovery from historic remains. I had been trying to figure out how I was going to come up with the DNA to prove my case. Eventually, we were going to have to exhume the grave in southeast Kansas to harvest Jesse's DNA. I tried not to let the overwhelming thought of how to accomplish that awesome task occupy my mind.

I just knew I was going to make it happen, somehow.

Knights of the Golden Circle

I sat in front of my computer, hoping that more hits would come back, but that was it. I had searched for the Knights of the Golden Circle in several different ways, including fully spelled out, then with the initials KGC, then again with initials and periods, all to no avail. Assuming there was a secretive group active during and after the Civil War, there was very little literature written about them.

So it came down to this. If the Knights of the Golden Circle even existed, it was apparent that finding out about the clandestine group was not in the cards. I'd have to resort to good old-fashioned manual research.

The main blurb I did get out of my Internet searches was that this group was a secret order of Southern sympathizers in the Northern states and known as Copperheads (like the snake) and that the Knights were especially active in Texas. My critical analysis buzzer went off when I read that, Texas being a Southern state.

Was this a mere misdirection or part of some overall plan to continue keeping the group a secret? I admit I must have been watching too many episodes of "X-Files" at the time.

Another web site stated that the KGC was largely composed of peace Democrats who opposed the Civil War and whose sole purpose was to expand slavery. Again, contradictions abounded.

The word "secret" was more of an issue for me. If Jesse was part of some secret organization, then what was his role and why was he part of it in the first place? What about his brother and the rest of the gang? Were they also part of it? Who knows, maybe this Bud guy is just a brick or two short of a full load and he made the whole thing up in order to get me to reveal something. I needed to bounce this off someone who was more objective. I turned to General Skelton since he'd been so helpful in the past.

I got Larry on the phone and filled him in on where the research was heading. I gave him an overview of what I had found in and around the caves, and then the subject turned to the conversations that I had in Texas. That's when I broached it.

"Larry, I met the sponsor of the Grandbury exhumation, who mentioned that Jesse was part of a group known as The Knights of the Golden Circle. Do you know anything about them?"

There was a noticeable pause on the other end of the phone.

The main thing General Skelton told me during the next few minutes was that it was a secret spy ring that operated for the South during the Civil War. This group went by various other names including the Confederate Secret Service, for one.

"But I've got to warn you here," he continued. "Don't go too far into this. And especially, don't go onto the Internet and start typing in key words regarding this group."

"Why not?"

"It's still on the NSA's list of active white terrorist organizations. You don't want your name coming up on any of the governments databases."

"Why is that?" I was shocked at what he was saying.

"That's all I can tell you."

After I hung up, I sheepishly thought about why I hadn't told him I'd already been on the Internet for the past two weeks looking for information. I admit it. I felt like an idiot and I didn't want General Skelton to agree. On the brighter side, it confirmed the track I had continually found myself relying upon: start from an academic point of view and do the research. It was the key that helped steer me in the right direction in the first place by tracking down the original documents on Jesse.

Over the next few days, I sent out inquiries to the usual destinations—libraries, research centers, University archives—requesting papers on the Civil War era KGC. Finally, I received a positive response from the San Bernardino library, specifically relating to KGC operations in California before and during the Civil War.

After I received and read the paper, I became aware of just how important California was to this group. It was the cornerstone of a much larger plan.

The paper stated that KGC's primary purpose was to secede from the Union and take with them the thirteen Southern states along with New Mexico, the Nevada/Arizona territory and California. The next phase would be the conquest of Mexico and Central America, culminating in taking Northern South America, continuing through the Caribbean Islands and finally into Cuba. This would form what they called the Golden Circle, which would add at least one hundred new congressional votes to the power base of the Southern states. The political doctrines would be a blend of commercial capitalism and socialism where the working class served the hierarchical ruling class.

So, from the surface of it, this secret organization formed in the 1840s was the result of the classic perceived problem of the Southern states being overpowered by the Northern industrial states, what one of my history professors used to say was the battle between the Jefferson populists verses the Hamilton federalists.

I reasoned that if this was simply a case of political or philosophical differences, admittedly massive, how did all of this intrigue tie into Jesse and his disappearance? And why was it that the James clan seemed to be at the middle of many of the key events of the era? The Coles, Zerelda's family, ran the Black Horse Saloon, frequented by many prominent politicians. Captain George James (J. Frank Dalton's father) allegedly fired the first cannons on Fort Sumter. I didn't think it was a coincidence that years before the James, Cole and Younger families had suffered terrible attacks on their Midwest farms by John Brown followers and federal dragoons.

Suddenly something didn't sit right with the circumstances of Jesse's father's death. I wondered: who was it that he went to California with?

And then I got a break.

I found another article relaying that near the end of the war, the South started getting low on money to pay the troops. When this happened, they would go to prearranged locations and dig up gold that had been previously buried for that specific purpose.

This was interesting, because if Jesse and his gang were members of these Knights, it could make sense why they were robbing locations specifically for gold. They could then bury it using secret codes to mask the locations. More importantly, it helped to explain why he needed to appear dead rather than simply missing. Authorities had been spying on the KGC for years. They had to know Jesse was a member. If so, it meant the law not only wanted Jesse, they also wanted his codebook and the locations of where he had buried the vast gold spoils. If he were dead, the trail would be cold.

Another parallel story started to emerge. Jesse's father, the Reverend Robert Sallee James, had inexplicably decided to go to California in 1850, well before the start of the Civil War. Supposedly, Robert went to get in on the gold rush. That didn't make sense to me, because the James family, although not exceedingly wealthy, had a successful farming operation. It also meant he would be away from his family for an extended time. Jesse had an uncle in San Francisco, Drury Woodson James, and a thought started to percolate in my consciousness. What if it wasn't for the gold? What if he, or they, were also part of this Golden Circle group?

A picture began to emerge as to how a group of powerful, well connected individuals could have easily staged the disappearance of one man, Jesse's father. He supposedly died of food poisoning and pneumonia in the California gold fields. Robert James was allegedly buried in an unmarked grave near Sutter's Mill. His body was never recovered. Yet another unlikely story for a preacher.

Later, while inspecting some additional pictures from the James collection, I found a picture of the Reverend Robert Sallee James, as an old man—a good twenty years after his death—a man supposedly killed in 1850 at the age of forty-five. And there was the rumored story that he returned to Clay County, Missouri and married Sara Mulkey. Could all of that be true?

Now it had come full circle to the same question that had taunted me: "Why would a prominent minister, founder of William Jewell College and a seminary, suddenly feel compelled to pursue personal wealth in the gold fields out West?"

Some answers came from the book *Uncommon Men.* The book revealed Rev. Robert James' traveling companions on the journey to California: Lorenzo Merriman Little, his brother Olmstead, Andrew Mome Diggs, William Tucker and Dan Schowalter, veteran miners from North Carolina. I'm assuming at this point they merely formed a mining firm as a front for their political activities. I didn't see the Reverend toiling in the gold fields of Sutter's Mill.

I also uncovered some interesting accounts of gold shipment robberies from the railroads around San Luis Obispo amounting to millions of dollars during that same time.

No way. That's just too coincidental!

- - - - - - -

In the summer of 2003, I tracked down another man from Kansas who claimed that he too was a grandson of Jesse James. When I went to meet Charles Johnson, he told me his family history and presented original photos and documents as proof.

Charles said that the Reverend Robert Salle James successfully left his unfaithful wife by faking his death in California. He returned to Clay County, Missouri to claim a new bride. Robert also advised his sons Frank and Jesse that he was alright. He took the name Robert Johnson and married Sara Mulkey who was thirty years younger then he was. They had a daughter named Susan Johnson. Robert later died during the Civil War. Jesse visited the young widow years later, and she bore them an illegitimate son after Jesse's alleged death in 1882. Charles Johnson claims that his grandfather was Jesse James and showed me a family photograph from the 1890s. The man in the photo is a match to the photo of Jesse at the Nashville barrel factory. These barrels would also come up again later in my research.

After looking at the historical photos and recording his story, I went to the archives to test the information. It was solid enough for me to have a detective from the sheriff's department come down and collect a DNA sample from Charles Johnson.

It was an intriguing story and it matched J. Frank Dalton's version of history. That's when I decided to do a photographic study of Jesse.

The Three Jesses

To begin with, I gathered up all of the photos of Jesse that I could find and analyzed them to see if there were common facial characteristics. It didn't take long before I had three distinctly different groups of photos. They were:

Group One

Jeremiah "Jesse" *Woodson* James, also known as Jere Miah James: He had an almond shaped head, ears with a pronounced notch inward on the outer rim, a fine pointed chin, an enlarged right nostril and parted his hair on the right. He is the one commonly pictured as Jesse James the outlaw.

Group Two

Jeremiah "Jesse" *Robert* James, also known as J. Frank Dalton. He had an oval head with large round ears, a square chin and parted his hair on the left.

Group Three

Jeremiah "Jesse" *Mason* James, also known as Tom Howard. He had an almond shaped head, with round ears, with a congenital birth defect notch in the upper rim of the ear. He also had a long square chin and parted his hair on the left.

Group One

Jesse Woodson James

Jeremiah Woodson James 1864

J.W. James 1872

J.W. James 1877

Jeremiah M James 1906

Group Two

Jesse Robert James (J. Frank Dalton)

Nashville 1865

Nashville 1866

Tom Johnson 1890

J. Frank 1950

Group Three

Jesse Mason James

Jeremiah M James 1860s

J.M. James 1870s

J.M. James 1870s

Jesse James Death 1882

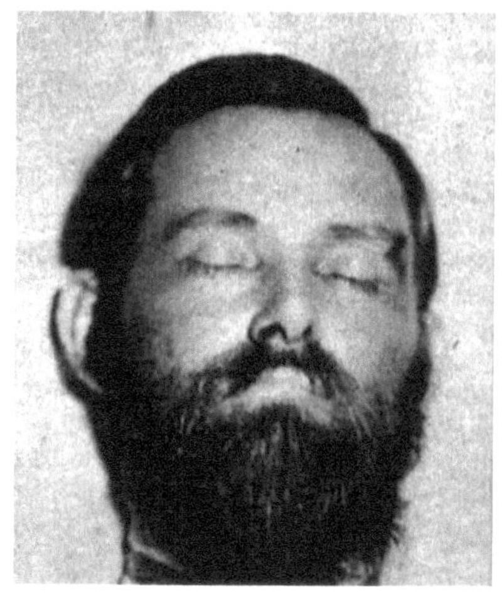

Just seeing the visual differences helped tremendously. I had them grouped and separated into three different body types in a chronological progression. This way made it easy to see that group one was the Missouri outlaw Jesse Woodson James and he had nothing in common with the two other men. I was able to match up group two with J. Frank Dalton. And group three was the cousin who would figure prominently in a discovery I made later.

All three of these Jesses had the same grandfather, meaning their fathers were all brothers that grew up in nearby Scott, Logan and Carter counties in Kentucky. It took many long hours of genealogical research, but I finally found the records.

I used large poster boards to map out all of the data and draw line diagrams to show the connections and relationships. It was very confusing for a while, but it finally came in to focus. I had empirically analyzed the theory into reality.

Now I could refer to them by their key (middle) names to keep them straight.

Their End Game

During the next couple of months, a troubling pattern started to emerge in my dealings with Bud. I had sent a non-disclosure agreement (NDA) to him the same day I arrived back home from Texas. I kept calling him, but somehow managed to miss him. Finally, I called late one evening and he answered.

"Bud? Hi, this is Ron. We met at the exhumation and I was telling you—"

"Ronnie, how are you my boy," Bud said. "I'm sorry to have not gotten back to you sooner, but I'm working on this deal here and it's been busting my balls. You know what I mean?"

"I do. Say, did you get that NDA I sent you?" I quizzed him.

"Sure did. Been meaning to get a look at it and sign it. But hey, I've got an idea. Why don't I just meet you at the site? I'll bring in a couple of horses, and we'll go have a look at the caves together. I'll start to decode the markings for you right on the spot. How about that, Ronnie?"

How about that? I thought. "That" is bullshit. That's what I wanted to say, yet at the same time he was my only lead to what those marks meant, and I didn't want to alienate him. I hated those types of dilemmas.

"Bud, as I've already mentioned to you, I need to have the NDA signed before we do anything." I purposely drew out the word "signed" to make my point. "If you can sign those and return them, we'll talk more about the site. Can you do that Bud? Sign them, I mean?"

"Well of course, Ronnie," he assured me. "I've been meaning to all along. I was just trying to save us some time. You know, get that trust issue moving along. Heck, I got them right here in my hand.

I'll sign and send them right out. Then you can send me some of those photographs you spoke about and we can get right into it. Is that okay with you, Ronnie?"

"Absolutely, Bud. That's all I wanted. Just a show of good faith."

"That's right, my boy. And I've got plenty of that to go around. I'll look forward to receiving those pictures."

Next time, I told myself, I'm definitely going to speak to him about his little "nickname" for me. In the meantime, I'll just wait and see if he mails out the NDA. True to his word, I received it a couple of days later. I promptly sent back a couple of the rock carving photographs to him and waited to see what he would come back with.

And wait I did. First one week, then two and finally it was almost a month, and still nothing. I called him up, and it was almost as if we'd never had a conversation before. Nothing had been done. Of course he's working on the deciphering, he told me. It's hard work. And he reiterated his "generous offer" to meet me at the site and bring those horses so we could get down to deciphering the symbols right then and there.

Once again, I politely declined his offer, after brushing the straw from my hair that he seemed to think resided there, and suggested that trust would be built upon his deciphering the photos I'd already sent him.

"No problem, Ronnie. I'll send them right out as soon as I'm done," he finally said.

As of this writing, they must still be on their way. It appears I'll never be able to tell him about how much I detested his use of the name "Ronnie" either.

However, soon after our last conversation, another stroke of luck occurred. At least I thought so at the time. After scouring the Internet, I finally found a web site that had a book and videotape for sale about the Knights of the Golden Circle, in which it promised to contain the information to decode the symbols I had found. The price? Only fifty dollars. Not being in a position to throw another fifty dollars down a never-ending sinkhole of research, I decided to call the author and ask if he thought I might be on the trail of a possible cache site. The man on the other end of the phone, Michael G., was located in Midway, Oklahoma. He thought there was a good chance I may have stumbled onto, and possibly found, what is known as the "guerilla cache" site. I told him it would be a couple of weeks before I ordered the book and left it at that.

The next week, I received an email from Michael stating there was a man in Kansas who was fairly skilled in the art of code-breaking. He was a private detective, so I could trust him. He gave me Ron W's email address and I quickly sent him a note.

He immediately got back to me and agreed to sign my non-circumvention, non-disclosure agreement. After I received it, we talked at length and ended by his agreeing to meet our team near the site where we would guide him in.

- - - - - - -

It was a sweltering day. We met face to face after he exited the mini-van he arrived in. He was tall, sported a military-type crew cut and had a noticeable gap in his smile. After the perfunctory greetings, we spoke for a while, and it appeared he was a pleasant enough guy. We gave him a tour while he commented about the symbols being very important—this one was probably for this, that one for that, always pointing and animated. Excitement hung in the air at his revelations.

Finally, we had someone on the team who could help us in a meaningful way. Someone who could unlock the mysterious codes that lay waiting to be revealed.

When I mentioned "team" I was referring to four trusted men working to map the site and all of the rock drawings.

We met with Ron W. numerous times over the next couple of weeks, and as we progressed, something began to feel amiss. Every time we'd meet, I'd ask him for the previous weeks' decipherments, and he had always either forgotten them or he gave a number of other "lost high school homework" type excuses. I also noticed that whenever I'd ask him a question, he would conveniently change the subject and end up side stepping it completely. Very frustrating.

I'd also observed that he was ever so slightly creating a little friction within the team—subtle yet snide comments about my ability to actually lead the expedition. I let most of them pass because I wanted everyone to get along. My main focus was to break the codes and keep the team moving in a harmonious direction. In hindsight, however, that was a big mistake.

One afternoon, the team and I arrived at the site a couple of hours earlier than when we'd told Ron W. to meet us. To our surprise, we saw our "trusted" private detective showing the site to another man. I was doing my best to control my anger. I had been very careful to protect the location of the site, and now a stranger was there.

I approached Ron W. and asked him what he was doing. He said that this was his friend and partner Michael, also a private detective. He explained they had just gotten off a case and were driving by when he decided to show him the site.

The team pulled me aside and expressed their concerns about his bringing this guy here, mirroring my own thoughts. Why would he do it? What was he thinking? And what was I going to do about it?

"You got my back?" I asked to my team. They all nodded an ascent. I approached the two again.

"Do you realize you're covered by an NDA," I said in a serious tone to Ron W.

"Don't get huffy here," he shot back. "He's a partner of mine. He's covered by it too."

"The hell he is! I need him to sign one right now, and as far as we're concerned, we need to have a discussion on how we'll proceed from here." I turned to his partner.

"So, are you going to sign it?" I asked.

"I'd have to have my attorney look at it before I sign anything," he responded.

Why didn't that surprise me?

"Then you'll both have to leave, now!"

Well, you could have heard a gnat fart at that moment. I quickly assessed the situation. Ron W. was in front of me wearing his flack jacket with a .45 holstered on his chest. His partner Michael was on his flank.

My team members were to my sides, all three of us armed as well. Ron W's face was flushed and looked as if he were deciding if he would take a shot at me. At that point, I didn't care. This was a trust broken, and I had zero tolerance for betrayal.

It was a long few seconds of what you might call a Mexican standoff. Fortunately, calmer judgments prevailed. Not to mention, the odds were in my favor. I could tell he felt they could not win this one, and they decided to get on their merry way home.

He cracked a wide gap-toothed grin. "I'll be in touch," were his parting words as we escorted them off the site.

I thanked my team for covering my ass, and one of them replied, "Hey, we thought you were pretty easy on him. Who knows what *we* would have done. We would probably be digging a big hole about now."

Of course, it could all have been an innocent gesture on Ron W's part, I reasoned; a simple mistake of judgment that wasn't thought through. After I cooled down, I was open to giving him the benefit of the doubt. But what he did next was shear madness.

Over the next few weeks, he started to contact the individual members of my group to impress upon them the folly of having someone like me as their leader.

That was it for me! I'd had enough and immediately terminated his contract. I even considered contacting the Attorney General and having his P.I. license pulled. However, that might have exposed my project to open discussion, so I decided to leave it as a lesson learned.

Ron W. then contacted and convinced Jesse V that it would be a good idea to take him to meet his dad Chuck at the farm. Later, when I found this out, I explained to the Jameses that Ron W. was no longer part of our team (Ron W. conveniently neglected to mention this to Chuck) and that he was now considered untrustworthy. This was also another violation of his NDA.

When he discovered I had contacted the Jameses and exposed him, he went ballistic and immediately sent a three-page diatribe to each of the team members outlining my shortcomings as the project leader. Of course, I received a copy of it.

And then I saw it.

Buried in this vitriolic rambling was a phrase that caused my heart to sink lower than I knew possible.

"...just who do you think Bud's code breaker is, anyway?"

Betrayal. He knew Bud H., and now I knew I had been taken in by all of them. I never saw it coming and was unprepared for the consequences that would certainly ensue.

I later confirmed that Ron W. was associated with Michael G., the man who ran the KGC web site I had contacted. It may have even been the same Michael he brought to the site for all I knew. And they were both in cahoots with Bud H.

It had taken them a full year to infiltrate my group and get the information they wanted. I had lost a year of my life in the ruse and I seemed no closer to breaking the codes than when I started, a position that was no doubt planned by this group from the beginning. Then, I remembered one good thing to come of it. I did end up with a copy of the Knights of the Golden Circle codebook and an original copy of the secret wolf map—a prize that would prove invaluable very soon.

My attorney offered no hope either. The expense of trying to enforce a contract with no monetary end game was hardly worth the effort. He reminded me that the rocket ship had already taken off. Though not a major site, they knew the location.

The site.

That's when it hit me. If I put my limited resources into controlling the site, then that might stave off an end run by these less than forthright individuals. I instructed my attorney to draft an agreement with the landowner to give me the exclusive rights to explore and research the site.

I then decided to investigate the malefactors themselves. Very interesting stuff. From the various people I spoke with and the papers I was able to find about them, it appears their whole idea of research involved infiltrating and enticing folks like me to give up our hard earned research and then use it for their personal advantage.

That was their whole agenda.

I wondered. Were they part of the modern day Knights? If so, they would no doubt justify their ruse as being for a higher cause. And if they were not part of the Knights, then they were just as they made themselves out to be, greedy little men who wanted to steal someone else's hard work and efforts. Either way, I hoped they would fail miserably.

The money for the attorney was well spent. Agreements for the sites were executed by the landowners and under exclusive contract with my company, NGS. That meant anyone caught on the sites would be arrested for trespassing. We also had the technology to remotely monitor the sites with video surveillance equipment.

But the sting of being suckered like that is still with me to this day.

Plan B

The James family, at least as far as Chuck's side of it was concerned, were extremely disillusioned with most of the people they had dealt with throughout the years they had safe-guarded the collection of artifacts. There were many more Tim's (the fellow I had originally met at Cave Springs) that had approached them with tales of great wealth and fame. Each time they were left with the bitter taste of either outright deception or extreme disappointment with the final outcomes. I was counting on this when I started to develop a plan.

It was simple enough, really. Because of all the research I had completed and the story that was emerging about what really happened, my enthusiasm had grown exponentially. Some of the pieces were still missing, but on the whole, I thought that I could paint a very compelling "case" for Jesse Woodson James faking his death and how he might have pulled it off. The reason he did it was still not completely answered (I was still doing research on the KGC connection), but that was not the issue. History had been duped and I wanted to reveal how it had happened—and set the historical record straight. The public had a right to know the truth!

When I approached the family about my plan, they were at first hesitant. However, when I followed up with a written outline describing it in detail, they became ardent enthusiasts. As I had suspected, they were tired of dealing with the "pinheads" as they called the traditionalists who were not even interested in seeing what evidence they had.

This was a great day, and I could finally make more sense as to the convoluted way the universe seemed to guide me these past couple of years. First, I had to understand the story, then I could tell it. But in order to understand the story, I needed to research it and then basically let it seep deep into my bones before I truly got it. But now I did.

Now I was ready to lay it out to the world.

I'd heard about a retired doctor who was quite well known in this area as an avid collector of archeological treasures. When he retired, he opened a museum to house his collection. He divided the collection into three different halls: the first held American treasures, the second European and the last one old world and ancient artifacts.

I decided to propose the idea to Doctor Jon of using a small area of his American treasures hall to house some of the James artifacts and pictures that were now in my care and control. He was an extremely amicable, distinguished-looking and accessible man, which no doubt played a great part in his success as a physician. I decided to take a rather unique tack with him. I realized he had a great location with many spectacular and rare pieces that were quite wonderful. But there was very little tourist traffic that visited his museum. That gave me an idea.

"How about I create a little buzz with the local newspapers and get some stories printed about your place?" I suggested to him. By that time, I had already made a number of connections with the local and state media. The doctor was more than open to it and seemed appreciative of the fact that someone was willing to help him.

I called a local reporter and spoke with her extensively about the museum. Unfortunately, since it had already been open for nearly a year, as far as she was concerned it was old news.

"What if the museum was displaying the lost collection of Jesse James artifacts and treasures that I uncovered?" I asked her. "Would you be interested in doing a story on that?"

She perked up immediately. I could feel her visualizing the headline: *Local boy discovers outlaw treasure story*. Controversial. Mysterious. All the elements that newspapers look for to get their rags off the news racks and into their readers' hands.

"Of course, that would be a different story," she told me. "We'd love to follow up on that."

Great, I thought. Now I actually needed to pull this off with the doctor. I told him the gist of the conversation with the reporter and laid out what I had discovered about the James story. I told him of the artifacts and then asked if we could open a small exhibit for ninety days—just enough time to do the story and bring him some publicity. He liked it. In fact, he seemed genuinely excited.

"Of course, we can make room for you. Let's sign a ninety-day exhibit contract and see how it goes," he enthusiastically responded.

"Wow!" I was just as enthused.

All the work I'd done over the past few years. It was finally going to be in a museum. Okay, it was not the Smithsonian and it was only for ninety days, but it was a foot in the door and critical for the next part of my plan.

A plan that contained the boldest step I'd ever taken.

Contact

I'd known of Bill Kurtis' work for a number of years through his documentaries on television. Because of the less than enthusiastic response from my earlier contact with the History Channel, I'd pretty much discounted contacting them again. Bill Kurtis seemed different, though. I'd always harbored the belief in the back of my mind that there had to be at least one objective journalist out there who would ultimately see the value of my efforts to present a fair and accurate version of the whole Jesse James story.

Coincidently, Kurtis was scheduled to give a talk in Caney, Kansas, which was only a two-hour drive for me. I called his office to let them know that I wanted to speak with him about some exciting new evidence regarding Jesse James and his death. I mentioned I had amassed and housed the proof in a museum in Wichita. I figured that was warning enough for my approach to him.

On the appointed day, I arrived at the event and waited until Kurtis finished his speech. After the usual accolades that the local officials liked to lavish upon someone famous, I approached him.

"Hello, Mr. Kurtis," I said, holding out my hand. "I'm Ron Pastore. I left a message at your office about the Jesse James artifacts. My museum exhibit sheds new light on what really happened. Do you have a couple of minutes so I can share a little bit of the story with you?"

He smiled and graciously agreed to five minutes. I quickly laid out the general scenario including a brief overview of the artifacts. He asked questions about the 1995 documentary, which I answered and countered with a list of the discrepancies I had uncovered. I invited him to come to the museum exhibit and listen to the whole story before making a decision. He listened intently and said he'd be happy to meet me there.

There are certain moments in life when, for whatever reason, it seems like your body, mind and soul align in a way that you know you're on the right path—an overall feeling of oneness with the world. The conversation with Kurtis brought that feeling to me, in a way that made all of the work seem worthwhile. Finally, someone might actually get it.

That feeling stayed with me the entire drive home and lasted all of another thirty minutes after I'd settled down inside. That's when I got the return phone call I'd been waiting for from the reporter of the local paper. She had given one excuse after another for why she was unable to get out to view and critique the exhibit. Fortunately, I had been able to sign a second contract with the doctor to extend the exhibit for another ninety days. Doc was quite supportive, especially since people really started to take an interest in the artifacts when they came into the museum. We were beginning to draw larger crowds, and they ate it up.

However, every time I had contacted the newspaper, the reporter had something else a little more pressing. I was getting nowhere with her and realized that I had to go up the ladder to get any media coverage. Finally, out of pure frustration, I called the editor about the exhibit ending soon. I asked when she could send a reporter over, and she lit off like a cat running from a firecracker. She snapped back with a surprising attitude more appropriate for the *New York Times* than the *Wichita Eagle*.

"You know, you're not the only story in this area, and if you don't like it we'll just forget about covering it at all!"

Wow, what the hell was that about? I started to get mad, not only for this totally inappropriate attitude, but also for bringing me down from the high I had been on only a few moments earlier. However, I gracefully signed off with the ungrounded hope that the paper might visit the exhibit in a month or two.

In the meantime, the next Monday, Kurtis came to Wichita and I gave him the grand tour, just as I had been giving it the previous three months. He was very inquisitive and nothing got by him. At the end of the tour, he invited me to lunch and we spoke for almost two hours.

He was extremely complimentary about my research, the realistic way in which I presented the information and how I tied in the artifacts to the overall story. He agreed that it played like a television special from end to end.

"I'd like to do a show on your story," he said. "I can pay for the exhumation and DNA study, get a documentary made and put it on the air. The great part of the whole deal is that you've already done all the research, Ron. You can be the historical consultant. Are you interested in doing that?"

After I nearly fell off my chair, I said, "You bet I am. When do we start?"

"Give me a couple of weeks and I'll contact you," he said, smiling back at me, obviously amused by my puppy dog enthusiasm over his support of the project.

I decided then and there that I would take the next step of my vision for the story and start to look for a location to open my own Jesse James museum. I reasoned that the documentary would give it national exposure, and I could tap into the controversy the show would surely create. It would be the pinnacle of all of my efforts. Finally, the public would get to know the truth. All the efforts, disappointments and joys would pay off, and history itself would be rewritten. I felt great!

Funny how those feelings never seem to last that long.

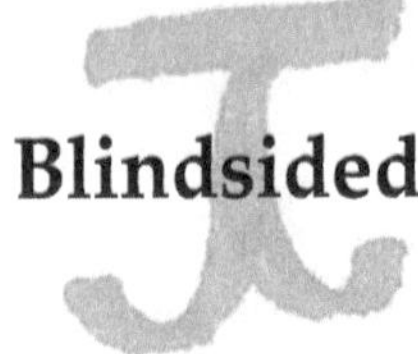

Blindsided

My first inkling that something was amiss came when the good doctor's checks for the Jesse James exhibit started arriving late. At first, it was only a few days, which soon started stretching into a week and then longer. This was very perplexing, since I believed money was obviously not the issue with him.

However, I had noticed that spending those greenbacks was always challenging for Dr. Jon. On more than one occasion, I had set up advertising contracts with local newspapers or magazines, which he authorized, only to find out later that he had tried to cancel the deal after the fact. It seemed to be more of a control issue, if I had to put a tag on it. But perplexing, nonetheless.

The Jesse James exhibit at his museum was an unqualified success. Due to my marketing efforts, more people were coming into the museum, and everything was going well. So well, in fact, that the doctor had offered me the position of marketing director for the museum. I presented a formal marketing plan on how to bring in additional foot and tour bus traffic. He accepted it, and I became quite involved in promoting the museum as a whole and at the same time continuing to push the Jesse James project ahead. Everything proceeded nicely over the next few months.

Or so I thought.

That ended abruptly when I called the museum about picking up the check for the exhibition, and I was informed by his assistant that they, meaning Doctor Jon, had resigned the agreement for the exhibit directly with the Jameses. His assistant said they did it on the advice of the James family attorney. I remember hearing it, at least the words, but not being able to process it. As if it were a bad dream, and all I had to do was wake up and it would be over. I had a difficult time even forming words. The pounding of my heartbeat overshadowed all background noises, leaving me with overwhelming waves of shock, isolation and outrage.

I finally managed to spit out something.

"Thanks, I'll give them a call," I sheepishly responded.

They couldn't do that, I told myself. The Jameses and I had a deal. The museum also had a renewal deal according to our contract. Now, they both where breaking their contracts and had resigned without me. It was time to lawyer up.

I sat down on my couch and ran what just happened through my mind, searching for something I hadn't heard that would make the full impact less hurtful. I'm not sure of the time frame—an hour, maybe two, I really don't remember. I was grasping at ghostly straws that would somehow make these feelings subside.

But it didn't work.

I reasoned that it wasn't the money, at least as far as I was concerned—most of that had gone to Chuck anyway. Money was never the issue with me. It was always about getting the truth out, letting the world know what had really happened. Kick a little traditional academic ass.

Two other emotions from this revelation swelled within me: anger at the outright betrayal by the James family, as well as the loss of control. I couldn't decide at the time which upset me more. Truth of the matter was I never saw such treachery coming. I was completely blindsided. That was a wakeup call. It's not like I couldn't have at least thought about this possibility. Almost from the beginning, right after the contracts were given to Chuck for signing, little things started to happen. Most often they were phone calls from him ranting about one thing or another. I took it as peculiar at first, deciding that it wasn't difficult to just listen with patience and then either suggest some logical solutions or put to rest his groundless concerns.

But those rants grew in intensity as the months pushed on. I was beginning to suspect that the calls might be related more to personal problems he was experiencing, including bouts of manic depression. I didn't know for sure, and I had no reason to believe that it would lead to anything other than calls that at worst were a bit unpleasant, and at best somewhat amusing in their twisted logic.

Within days of the phone call to the museum, things quickly changed from irrational phone calls to threatening legal action from Chuck. At one point I received a cease and desist order from his attorney barring me from ever using the name of Jesse James. An outrageous claim even for Chuck, since my job was to prove they were related to Jesse in the first place. I had already copyrighted the story, photos and artifacts so I wasn't concerned. But I felt this letter was totally unwarranted.

It was time for me to take back control.

I searched for and found the perfect building and signed a lease for what would be the Jesse James Museum in the historic Delano District of Wichita. I was committed and on the hook for it. My attorney knew it too, which was why he was so concerned about my alienating Chuck and his lawyer. But at that point, I didn't care.

One of the business precautions I had taken near the beginning of this whole adventure was to professionally photograph all of the artifacts and scan the documents. First, I did it for archival purposes, in case something was accidentally lost or destroyed. Additionally, I wanted to be prepared as there had been rumblings that the other side of the James clan were out to close us down. Those were the ones who derived revenues from the James venues in Missouri and from the myth that he was killed in 1882. I remember the bumper sticker from the "X-Files" era that said:

Just because I'm paranoid, doesn't mean I'm wrong.

Turns out I wasn't wrong.

My back-up plan was to open the Jesse James Museum with only the photographs, if necessary. I didn't need the Jameses to make that happen.

I was moving ahead and feeling better about how I handled the whole situation.

However, the loss of income from the doctor's museum started to take its toll. I was scrambling to make ends meet and, added to this, my family had an ongoing disagreement with me regarding the direction of my life over the past few years. The final blow to my income came when my family accepted a financially attractive offer on a real estate trust that I was paid to manage. They sold it, and I was out of a job. They must have thought I had lost my mind with this Jesse fixation and wanted no part of it. The next week, another crisis arose.

"I can't file any legal actions without a retainer," my attorney called to inform me. "And quite frankly, we need to settle up with the legal work I've already done these past few months."

I totally understood. This wasn't his battle, although he was very supportive and cut me a lot of slack to continue on with the quest.

I began to feel like a clock was counting down toward zero, and I was running out of time for this whole Jesse adventure. I was afraid it would be yanked from me with someone else grabbing the credit for uncovering this amazing story. And it wouldn't be the first time someone high jacked one of my creative projects.

Fear of loss can be a tremendous motivator, and that's the juice I was running on. I got into high gear.

I had sent copies of the original DNA report to a number of people and now I was committed to follow up on it. I also knew that Kurtis was determined to make a documentary, but there was still no deal. I couldn't let him learn that things were falling apart. I had to find a way to get everything back on track.

Even though outwardly I was going through the motions, inwardly I was not very hopeful of the outcome. Why couldn't Chuck and the rest of the people I was dealing with have just kept their agreements? *Was their personal greed the only virtue those people possessed?*

My attorney finally arranged a conference call between the Jameses and their lawyer on one end and us on the other. After much discussion, most of it contentious, Chuck's attorney finally asked what I planned to do if we didn't work things out.

I jumped up, bent over the speakerphone and shouted, "Damn the torpedoes, full speed ahead!"

That was the first time my lawyer told me to shut up, and I did.

By the end of the call, I was slightly optimistic. The Jameses agreed to support the terms I had originally laid out. Yet, historical dealings with them were not in the positive column of my radar, and I knew our new understanding could change instantly. All I could do was continue moving ahead any way possible.

My hope was that all was resolved.

Hope does spring eternal.

Section V

Yin and Yang

Turnabout

November, 2003

It was almost sundown. Hues of amber rays painted the rolling hills forming a picture of serene tranquility. My own feelings of tranquility had eluded me for the past couple of weeks, I mused as I sped down highway 54 toward Delano to the soon-to-be open Jesse James Museum. With only a handful of pictures and artifacts to grace the walls, I was worried it might not be enough. My mind raced over recent events. Despite my declarations that nothing would stop me from moving forward, I hadn't counted on the magnitude of the "nothings" that started to rise up within me. I struggled to fight off feelings of discouragement, hurt and rage as well as questions that challenged my inner convictions to the core.

"Why go on? What's the point? So what if you let people know the truth? Then what? And why are you busting your balls to do this, when no one else wants to help?"

Great questions. In fact, too good. I wasn't coming up with equally great answers. My self-motivation was becoming more and more difficult to sustain.

I pulled up to the nearly deserted street in front of the museum and quickly made my way up the stairs to the one bedroom apartment. I had created a humble abode above the museum to provide security for the priceless collection of Jesse's heirlooms. I was so immersed in my thoughts that I almost didn't see the blinking red light on the answering machine. I tossed my notebook onto the desk and hit play.

"Ron, I just wanted to let you know I forwarded the DNA report and the other materials to our news station in Missouri and they were floored. Tomorrow they're dispatching a worldwide news release saying they have the exclusive evidence to show the conclusions and content used for the 1995 documentary on Jesse James were false. They're going to do a four or five part series on it. They think it will make international news. Congratulations, dude. All your work is finally paying off."

It was Jim R., a news reporter with a network affiliate in Missouri. No way, I thought. They'll never air it in Missouri.

The dial tone sounded only a few more seconds until the machine beeped me out of the numbness. I hit play again and re- listened to make sure I had heard it right. Unbelievable. In fact, it was more than that.

It was vindication. Of a kind I never expected to experience based on the previous few weeks' events.

The next message was from my attorney, asking me to give him a call as soon as possible. But I wasn't listening. I quickly put in a call to Bill Kurtis' production company to let them know, but it was already past eight o'clock in Chicago and no one answered. I left a message, popped open a brewski and jumped down the stairs to the museum. It looked awfully empty. I started imagining what it would be like with people coursing through, soaking in the evidence and how they would finally understand the truth about Jesse James. I even imagined news cameras pulling up outside with reporters grappling for a scoop on the ten o'clock news.

The next day, I awoke to the ringing of my phone at the un- godly hour of eight a.m. It was Jeff, my attorney.

"Didn't you get my message yesterday, Ron?" he asked.

"Yeah, I did. I took a drive out East and didn't get back until late. Thought I should wait 'til morning to call. What's up?"

"What's up? Didn't you hear about—"

"Yeah," I interrupted, "I got a message from the people in Missouri telling me about the news story. Pretty great, huh?"

"How did they learn about it in Missouri?" he asked.

"I sent them a copy of the original DNA report and some papers outlining how they actually lied on the documentary."

"Ron, what are you talking about?"

"I got a call about a five part news series on how they manipulated the evidence about Jesse's DNA report. It's going to be an international story."

"That's really great. I didn't know anything about it," Jeff said.

Wait a second, I thought. I was sure he had heard about the news story and wanted to be the first to let me know.

"Then why did you call?" I inquired. "What was your news?"

"Chuck's attorney called. As you had predicted, Doctor Jon tried screwing them with the contract, so they have a new offer for you to display the artifacts at your museum."

"You're kidding?"

"No, I'm not. They've agreed to stick with the terms of our original agreement—all remains as is. By the way, that's really good news about the TV story, Ron."

"And your news, too," I said. "Now I'll have something to actually put in the museum. Thanks Jeff."

As I rose out of my bed, I started to realize the full impact these two events were sure to have on my life. The museum was a cornerstone. I needed it to branch out into television, movies and books. Now I had that. And the news story in Missouri. That would provide some legitimacy to what I had discovered. I didn't care if I got the credit, which surprised me. What I did care about was that a journalist had seen the results of my labors and made an independent judgment as to its validity.

Fully awake, I made my way into the living room and tossed the phone onto the couch. I'm not sure if I've ever jumped that high yelling "yes" before in my life.

I took possession of the future Jesse James Museum location in June and was busy working away, utilizing every spare minute of my time building display cases, printing exhibition tags and signs— the works. The time flew by so quickly that I found myself in November, still without the artifacts.

Where was Chuck with the collection? I wondered.

Finally, a few days later, Chuck arrived at the museum door. He brought back the collection and returned all the money the family had taken from the museum exhibit I had set up with Dr. Jon. Together, we inventoried the various items as he brought them into the museum.

The next few days were a whirlwind of activity. Chuck and I, although not technically kissing and making up, got as close to that as two men living in the Midwest could. It didn't matter. The artifacts were now at the museum, being put in their proper places on display in the public domain, just as I had envisioned it.

The opening day was a truly wonderful event. I'd sent out press releases and people were waiting at the door when I opened. The exhibit was set up in a chronology to tell the story and reveal the truth about Jesse's life as visitors walked through. It was so compelling that not a single skeptic left unconvinced.

A week later, I received a call from Kurtis telling me they were going to proceed with the new show on the History Channel about Jesse based on my research. I could expect paperwork within the next few days. We discussed what my role would be and how the show would play out. I realized I had subconsciously been running the show over and over in my mind. When Kurtis asked about it, I was easily able to convey the way I thought it should run editorially. He was fantastic to speak with, and I felt totally at ease that he was the right person for this project.

I was busy day and night at the museum, giving tours and fine tuning the exhibit, preparing for Kurtis' eventual arrival to shoot the documentary. The days and weeks seemed to fly by at break-neck speed, providing me with little time to worry about what could go wrong or even that anything would.

It wouldn't be long, however, before Chuck would show up again and renew my faith in the old saying that a leopard can't change their spots.

The New Documentary

"You did what?" I shouted at Chuck.

"I'm sorry about that. I thought it would be important to have with us," he sheepishly replied.

I couldn't believe it. Six months of preparatory work were now at risk because of Chuck's pulling another of what I had begun to call "Chuck-ups" without even consulting me.

Once Kurtis got the go ahead from the History Channel for the television show, I became totally involved. I was asked to do various jobs, including scouting for locations, deciding who they should interview, scheduling shooting times, as well as addressing a great number of other issues. At the same time, I was writing notes about the overall theme of the show, with theories about how the documentary could address them.

In short, all of my work and the whole thrust of the show were contained in my production notebook. I had been zealously guarding this document. If the conclusions of the show got out, there would be big problems for the History Channel and Kurtis Productions. The whole idea was to be the first ever to reveal what actually happened—a world scoop.

Additional research was needed, so I decided to take a trip to St. Joe, Missouri before the exhumation and reluctantly took Chuck along. My reasoning was that we could double our efforts covering the various materials, and it would allow me some time with him during the drive to go over the project in detail. One of the stops along the way was to visit Dan W., who had a rather controversial and conflicting theory about Jesse James. I wanted to see what research he had. I never knew if someone might have found another photograph or document that would be helpful in some way to my research, so I made it a point to follow up on every lead. Dan was amicable, well-researched and the visit was pleasant. Yet, it didn't yield anything new.

About a hundred miles south of Kansas City, a good three hours into our return trip home, I asked Chuck to hand me the production notebook from the back seat. I always kept it with me in case I had any ideas I wanted to write down, especially while driving.

"I think I may have left it in Dan's house," he said.

"You did what?"

"I left it in his house."

I pulled the car over to the side of highway I-35, unable to focus on the road while the blood rose into my temples, creating a throbbing that boomed throughout my head.

"Why in the world would you even touch my notebook?"

"I thought we might need it there."

"You had no business touching it, Chuck," I said angrily. "And there was no way in hell we would have needed it. If we had, I would have taken my book into the meeting myself."

It was like speaking to a doe in headlights. His blank stare underscored his complete inability to grasp the gravity of what he had done.

"Did you notice Dan had a copier on his desk? If he copies this and lets out what the show is about, we're screwed. That notebook details every aspect of the production plan."

"Well, I didn't think it was a big deal."

That was it, his biggest Chuck-up, yet. I raced to the nearest phone and called Dan's house. No answer. I reasoned there was nothing I could do at this point and I needed to get home and follow up from there. A number of phone calls went unanswered, and I was getting very nervous. How did it come down to this? Three years of my life wrapped up in a folder left at a relative stranger's house. And if that information got out, I was pretty much thinking the production would stop, I'd be sued and who knew what else.

Finally, around ten at night, I got Dan on the phone.

"Dan, it seems Chuck left my notebook at your place. Did you see it?"

"Yeah, Ron. I found it on my couch after you left."

"You didn't, you know, look at it did you?"

"Of course not," he said. "It's your notebook. I'd never do anything like that."

Okay, I thought. Human nature being what it is, I think I would have had a problem not looking at it. But at this point there's nothing I can do about it.

"Well thanks for being so honorable, Dan. Can you ship it back to me FedEx overnight?"

"Be happy to," he replied.

Thirty-six hours and dollars later I had the notebook back in my hands and everything seemed to still be there. I had no way of knowing if anything was copied. However, I still believed in chasing windmills and I chose to believe Dan's a good guy and trust he kept his word.

- - - - - - -

The actual production process of making the new show was a joy, made even more so by the calmness of Bill Kurtis as the producer. He and his people were professional and really appreciative of the help I was providing.

I thought I had found the perfect job for Chuck in this whole process. Because we were exhuming his great grandfather, I had asked him to contact all of the James family members and let them know about the production and what we were planning to do. More importantly, his task was to explain to them why we needed to keep this project in complete secrecy. We didn't want the public spectacle that surrounded the last two exhumations and accompanying circus of reporters. He jumped at the opportunity and constantly updated me on his progress. So far, he relayed, no one had any objections to the exhumation.

The day before the exhumation, we were shooting B-role or secondary video and bank robbery reenactments at the Old Cowtown Museum. I received a call from my attorney informing me he was getting swamped with calls from various James family members who were livid they had been kept in the dark about what we were doing. What, I thought? How could that be?

And then those intuitive hairs started to rise up the back of my neck as a frightening thought started to form. What if Chuck hadn't been contacting anyone? Another Chuck-up!

I cornered him by the saloon and bluntly asked what the hell was going on?

The beet red flush of his face told it all. He mumbled on about wanting to keep the project secret and he felt it would leak out if he told his family about it.

"This was the only thing I asked you to do, Chuck. The only thing. And you screwed it up. Now I look like an idiot, and more critically, the production crew is going to be down at the cemetery in the morning. We can't afford to have anything stop the exhumation and your family is threatening to file an injunction today. Don't you get it?"

He didn't. But I did.

I immediately got on the phone and started talking to the family members, some of whom were extremely upset. "Why weren't we told?" "How could you do this without letting us know?" At great length, I explained we were trying to not have this turn into a media circus to avoid desecration of the cemetery and gravesite. *We* "thought" Chuck had already contacted them. There were rumblings about blocking the exhumation, and I replied that we would have to file a counter suit. That would bring wide-scale media attention to the exhumation, creating serious security problems. Additionally, that type of publicity would no doubt bring hundreds of people to watch what was going on. I suggested that it was best to allow us to proceed with the security and secrecy policies I already had in place. In the end, they were kind enough to agree.

Everything I had been working toward for the past three years boiled down to this pivotal event—the exhumation.

My academic studies and my contacts with the anthropology department at WSU over the past seven years now were put to the test. Together we set up the recovery protocol and methodology for collection of the physical remains. Once the remains were recovered, we would study the anatomic and skeletal morphology to identify past injuries and the possible age of the body. I started discussions with the Sedgwick County Regional Forensic Science Center several years prior, knowing this day would come. The staff guided me in a general study of genetics and interpretation of the mtDNA evidence.

Further, my discussions with General Skelton at the Geological Survey assisted my studies of soil composition and stratification. My association with local law enforcement afforded me the opportunity to attend security and firearms training. A meeting with the homicide detectives at the Sedgwick County Sheriff's Department instructed me on evidence handling. The funeral home director covered transportation of human remains protocol. I had discussions with the County Coroner and the DA's office regarding the documentation needed to conduct an exhumation.

I had gained valuable experience in Texas during the 2000 J. Frank Dalton exhumation in Granbury, especially on what *not* to do. Uncountable hours were spent in archival research and data collection. I assembled a team for excavation of the burial plot. Even the car I had purchased for the museum, an unmarked Highway Patrol cruiser, would provide a security presence during the three days at the cemetery. Now everything was in place.

A three-zone security perimeter surrounding the cemetery was set up. A secondary zone secured the burial plot from any possibility of DNA contamination of the remains from current James family members. The area around the grave site was tightly restricted to forensic and production staff only.

The next day, the excavation site was set up for filming and you could feel the excitement in the air. We would finally be able to provide the hard evidence that would be examined on a scientific level.

I noticed Chuck milling around in the background, nervously looking around. What now, I thought? I'd seen that look many times before, and it usually preceded something he had screwed up. It wasn't long before I found out what.

The sheriff had given me permission to block the county road to the cemetery. I posted guards at both ends of the road, giving a half mile buffer zone to intercept intruders. Suddenly, the radios started crackling with chatter.

CODE RED - SECURITY BREACH AT THE MAIN GATE!

A plume of dust fronted by a pickup truck blasting its way toward us was the first hint of trouble. It skidded to a stop, and out stepped a man who was obviously mad as hell. My security team was moving to stop him when I realized it was Chuck's father, Charles, and advised them to stand down.

"What are you all doing here?" he shouted.

So that was it. Chuck didn't even tell his own father we were exhuming his grandfather. No wonder he was so fuming mad. Quickly glancing over at Chuck, I could see he was getting ready to flee the scene like an arsonist from the inferno he'd just lit. I quickly ran over and grabbed him.

Fortunately, Bill Kurtis saved the day. His warm, endearing style finally won over Chuck's dad and he relented to allow the exhumation. I brought Chuck over, who again tried to get away. Kurtis put his finger through Charles' belt loop to keep him there, while an astute cameraman turned the camera on and caught the scene. Kurtis ended up with a wonderful first hand interview with Chuck's father, who admitted publicly that he thought his grandfather was the notorious Jesse James.

The digging part of the exhumation took almost three full days. After many interesting events, we finally were down to the human remains.

The only thing really out of the ordinary was the fact the glass viewing window of the casket, which is normally placed over the upper portion of the body, seemed to be over the lower portion of the body instead. I didn't know what to make of this, whether it was some kind of metaphor or had been done in order to keep anyone from seeing the face of the person who was in the coffin. I had been told in the past that when the KGC buried someone whose identity did not match the headstone, they would bury the body upside down like the one that had been exhumed in Kearney, Missouri in 1995. However, this was a different situation because the body was buried right side up in the proper position. It was only the glass that had been reversed. Most curious indeed.

By the end of the third day, we had completed the exhumation and all of the remains were then placed in a transportation container to be taken to the lab in the anthropology department at Wichita State University. Several specimens were bagged separately and sealed with evidence tape provided by the sheriff's department. After the remaining soil had been sifted for possible fragments of bones, nails and remnants of the coffin, the dirt was placed back into the hole. The anthropology crew returned to Wichita, and I left for St. Joe, where the following day I was to film my interview segment in the Jesse James Home Museum, the scene where most people believe the killing took place.

Scene of the Crime

I drove by way of Oskaloosa to see how far it was from St. Joseph, Missouri. To my surprise, Martha Jane Presgrove's home in Oskaloosa was only about twenty miles from St. Joe. (She was Jesse James' wife) I wanted to follow up on whatever I could find out about her, since I believe she may have played an integral part in the cover up. At about eight p.m., I arrived at the hotel where the production crew was staying and checked into a very nice suite provided by Kurtis Productions. Before checking in, I asked the hotel to have their security staff keep an eye on my car.

For the first time in three days, I got a good night's sleep and was fresh and relaxed for breakfast the next morning. I met with Bill Kurtis and went over the day's activities. I noticed the author of the documentary, Ted Yateman, who was recruited for a segment of the show, was sitting by himself, talking to nobody. I had yogurt and a bagel and got ready to leave

When I went out to my cruiser, I found the doors were unlocked and the contents had been rifled through, although nothing obvious was missing. So much for hotel security. Since this was a situation over which I had no control, I decided there was nothing to do but head out to the Jesse James Home Museum and set up for the interviews and re-enactments.

As I was entering the museum, which was Jesse's home and where he supposedly was killed, I was confronted by the curator, Gary C., who objected to allowing me into the museum to shoot my segment of the interview. In fact, his exact words were, "I'm not letting that son of a bitch in here to shoot his interview! If you insist on having him here, then the whole thing is off and you can't do your production here at all!"

I was completely shocked as I had spoken with the man several times and he was always civil—at least he seemed so. I decided not to circumvent what Kurtis had planned for the production and left.

I was more than a bit upset about it since I had gone to the trouble to include their point of view (that he was killed by Ford in the house), and yet they were not going to allow me to express my opinion. I got on the phone and called the Secretary of State's office to find out who was the chairman of the Board of Directors of the corporation that owned the museum. I received the information I needed and attempted to contact the director in order to see if I could overrule the curator. But, I was unable to reach the individual.

Much to my surprise, I received a phone call from a newspaper reporter with the St. Joe Gazette. He said news traveled fast in a small town and he had already heard I was having a little difficulty at the museum. The point I made was that it seemed awfully undemocratic not being allowed to express my opinion when I was the one who arranged for them to have their say.

Later that day, the film crew and I went out to the James Farm Museum outside of Kearney, Missouri where I was allowed to film my interview. All of the people at this museum were friendly and cordial and made me feel quite welcomed. In fact, John C., of the KC Crime Lab, actually provided me with a copy of the report from 1978, which covered the remains found during the excavation of the 1882 burial site. Very helpful.

The production wrapped and the crew packed up and shipped off the tapes for final editing.

Part of the production agreement was that the results of the DNA tests would not be released to anyone before the show aired. That included me. I honestly had no idea what the results would show.

Now I had to hurry up and wait.

I thought I would use the time to focus on one of the mysteries that had been continually nagging at me: the markings at the caves and what they might mean. I was pretty convinced that Jesse and his gang were affiliated with the Knights of the Golden Circle. I also believed the robberies were somehow tied to it. Unfortunately, the last two attempts to unravel those cave symbols ended up in treachery and disappointment.

That changed when I received an unexpected call from the author of a new book that helped answer some of the underlying reasons for this whole charade that had been perplexing me from the start.

Code Keys

"Hello Ron. My name is Warren G. I wanted to introduce myself and discuss your exhumation project. I co-wrote a book called *The Sentinels* with Bob B. about the Knights of the Golden Circle and their role throughout history. Have you heard of it?"

As a matter of fact, I hadn't heard of his book. But he had my attention just mentioning the Knights. He also activated my now automatic distrust radar whenever I received calls like this.

"The reason I'm calling is because I read an article about your museum and the exhumation, which totally surprised me. I wanted to at least meet you on the phone and see what you're following up on?"

I asked him about his theory regarding Jesse, and he said he came to the conclusion that Jesse changed his name to J. Frank Dalton. That was a theory I had dismissed years ago. Warren gave his reasons, which sounded good, except I realized right away he had made a few wrong turns regarding Jesse's identity.

We made arrangements to talk again after I ordered and read his new book. A week later, it arrived in the mail and I quickly read it. What surprised me was the depth of research he had done regarding the purpose of the Knights of the Golden Circle, not to mention all the people supposedly involved.

There were numerous pictures and references to people Jesse had known and befriended, from Billy the Kid to Wyatt Earp. It hadn't previously occurred to me that they were anything more than friends or acquaintances. When I finished *skimming* through the book, I called Warren back. After a few minutes speaking with him, it became apparent that in my myopic quest for the truth about Jesse, I may have overlooked a much bigger picture of what he was involved in.

After some small talk about the little nuances of why I thought J. Frank Dalton wasn't Jesse, he went on to mention, in his pronounced East coast accent, he had also found some translation keys to the codes the Knights were using. My heart started racing at this point.

"Really?" I asked. "What do you mean?"

"We found these code translations that are very similar to the codes the Masons were using. My writing partner is more familiar with them than I am, but we did include a few in the book."

I quickly flipped through his book until I found pictures of the codes and markings he had mentioned. Chills rushed up my spine.

The problem was, the code keys were rather blurry—apparently a copy of an original document. That didn't matter. Here I had confirmation of my discoveries regarding Jesse and the caves. I was thrilled.

Warren was very friendly and especially so after I mentioned I had found some caves with those same markings and JJ's initials. He suggested we share some information and that he'd like to bring his writing partner Bob into the conversation. Great, I thought, since Bob is the technical source of the codes. And, he knows the meanings, not to mention the locations of some of the sites. He's the one I really need to talk with.

I spoke with Warren several more times before he gave me Bob's number. I figured I should take the time to thoroughly read the entire book before speaking with him.

And then I found it.

Bob mentioned that "he and his good friend Bud H…" The very Bud, I assumed, who had befriended and later betrayed me was working together with Bob and Warren exploring the different sites mentioned in the book. Man, I thought, this *is* a small world.

I started to wonder: are these guys trying an end run to accomplish the balance of what Bud and Ron W. were not able to find out? I had shown Bud only one of the sites before the proverbial crap hit the fan. Maybe this was another ruse they were using to find out about the rest of my site locations.

Bob was a lot less "polished" on the phone than Warren, but amiable and friendly. Yes, he had found the original codes and understood their meanings. Yes, he could send me a clearer copy of the code keys. Yes, he'd like to see photos of the markings I had found. And of course he would help me in any way he could. We talked briefly about the different locations.

"Bob, you mentioned Bud H. as a good friend of yours in the book."

"Yes, we've been working together on this project for quite a while."

"I just wanted to let you know I consider him a fantastic actor," I said.

"What are you talking about?" Bob asked.

"I just thought you'd want to know. He had me fooled through and through as to his intentions."

I relayed the story and all its intricacies, including the letter from Ron W. that mentioned Bud in it. And then something interesting happened. At the end of my story, there was a long pause. Bob finally stated that, as a matter of fact, after he had taken Bud to the various sites, he heard from him less and less often. You could almost feel the light bulb of revelation starting to glow. I knew how he felt, if indeed that wasn't an act.

He said he would get those copies to me, and I should contact him in a few weeks. That turned out to be most difficult. I never received the codes, and when I tried calling there were no return calls. I called Warren and explained what was going on. He stated Bob was busy with a construction project and not to take it personally. He also suggested we start to share whatever information we had regarding Jesse and the codes, so we could learn more about the overall connections.

I didn't feel comfortable doing that, especially knowing Bud was involved in any way. But I did mention that maybe we could NDA each other and start sharing some of the basic information. I was right in the middle of preparing for this book, and I told him I didn't want any of my material ending up in a new book written by either him or Bob. He agreed to my request for confidentiality agreements.

When I finally reached Bob, his mood was markedly different. Curt, distant, far less friendly and completely unhelpful. I suppose it could have been a number of reasons unrelated to me, but the conversation basically went nowhere, and after a few minutes, I got the impression he wasn't open to helping at all. Okay, fine. I felt at the very least, I had dodged another bullet by keeping what I knew from being taken again.

The important part of this story and the coincidence of meeting those guys on the phone was that they confirmed there were codes out there that may shed light on what the markings I found in the caves may say—perhaps a last message left to us from Jesse and his Knights of the Golden Circle.

Whether they will ultimately lead to vast treasure troves or simply information about their organization, I was not to discover for many years. One thing was certain, though. Until the messages the codes contained were finally unlocked, there was no way of knowing.

All's Right in the World

The production of the documentary took a lot more energy than I thought it would, although it's the kind of energy I didn't mind expending for a project I was so passionate about. It's the same as getting absorbed in a good book or working on your favorite car in the garage until four in the morning. I was running on all eight cylinders, waking early every morning and staying up quite late working on the next day's details.

Once Bill Kurtis' crew packed up and left town, it was a different story. I literally collapsed from the fatigue and exhaustion of little or no sleep during the previous weeks. I decided to take a couple of days off from the museum and the everyday grind I had to deal with and try to recharge. A few days later, I started to feel like my old self again, at least enough to start conducting tours at the museum. This always brought me a certain satisfaction, especially when the visitors had that ah hah! moment. It was that magical conscious "click" when they got the whole picture and realized what all the evidence really meant.

My next move was to call back a writer I had been in contact with throughout the past four years of my journey. I was keeping him informed of my adventures from the time I first found the artifacts. One day he had phoned me with a totally unexpected suggestion.

"Ron," he said. "I have an interesting proposition for you. What do you think of the idea of my co-writing a book about all you've been through regarding this Jesse James adventure?"

"You know," I replied, "there are hundreds of books out there now about old Jesse. I don't see what the big deal would be."

"I'm more interested in how you got involved, how you discovered all this information," he responded, "and I think others would be too. That's the focus of the book. Although the information is truly amazing, I think your journey down the path of discovery is equally as intriguing."

My journey? I thought. I guess I never looked at it quite that way before. It had always been Jesse's journey I was trying to bring to light. Although not completely sold, I decided to at least see where it would lead.

"Okay," I finally told him. "Let's do it."

We quickly worked out the details and had it "papered up" within a couple of weeks. The critical part was coordinating the release of the book with the airing of the History Channel show.

For the next few weeks, he conducted daily telephone interviews, and it was actually pretty exciting reliving all of the details about how I got to this point.

One night during these interviews, although still almost one-hundred degrees, I decided to take a walk along the river to think things through—sort out the events that had brought me to that point. So much had snowballed within the past couple of months that I wanted to get a real perspective of where my journey had taken me. Not where I would like to be, but an honest assessment of my objective progress to date. Plus, there were still financial pressures, and I hoped this walk would lighten up my mood a bit.

The first realization I had was I needed to focus on all the events that had transpired and were positive. So much negativity had been seeping into my adventure. But the fact was a lot of good had resulted from my efforts: the History Channel show, the new book and the museum that was open and running. I was also in discussions with another writer for creating a screenplay about what really happened to Jesse.

Okay, that's all good stuff, I told myself. Yet why was I still feeling this nagging "something" deep in my craw? An intense feeling of foreboding. Was it because I didn't think I would succeed? No, that wasn't the problem—I'd always had success in ventures I'd been involved with. But I admit, this feeling was different. It was as if I were waiting for the other shoe to drop, as it had consistently done at every turn of the journey so far. I'd never in my life met so many less than honest people. It was a real surprise to this Kansas boy. I was taught to trust people and those characters sensed it. But objectively speaking, at that moment in time things couldn't be going better.

Dripping wet from the near one hundred percent humidity, I decided to head toward the comfort of the air-conditioned museum. On my way back, I remembered the glass half full, half empty analogy and made a decision. It wasn't a lightning bolt moment, but rather a sort of inward resolve.

Why not focus on what's right and at least enjoy it—even if it turns out to be short lived? I thought. These are the kind of moments that don't show up very often. Carpe diem! If this silk purse does turn into a "sow's ear," then at least I'll have had some positive experiences to balance it against.

"That's it!" I shouted out loud. Whatever those apprehensions are, I'm going to override them and focus on the glass being half full. Slowly, a wave of calm blanketed my body. That's it, I again told myself. That's what I wanted to feel. It'd all been worth it, at least to me.

I hurried through the door to the more frigid eighty-degree air inside the museum and looked around, taking stock of it all. A smile crept over my face, turning into a full grin. I breathed in the ghost-riddled artifacts of Jesse James filling every corner of the place, seeming to cry out to tell his story.

"Jesse," I said quietly to myself. "The world will finally know the truth of your life story. It's been a long journey, my friend. But all worth it."

My mind and body knew it.

Now, my soul knew it too.

Carpe diem.

Close, but No Cigar

The City of Wichita had notoriously bad timing when it came to civic improvements. After I moved into the building and opened the Jesse James Museum, I was informed by the city they were planning to make that historic section of Delano a tourist destination. That would entail some "slight" improvements to the streets and sidewalks in the process. Three months into these improvements, the streets and sidewalks were completely torn out in front of the museum, leaving no way to get to the door, even if anyone could find it among the construction work. This was playing hell with the limited cash flow I was generating. When I called the city to complain, they seemed to have a playbook everyone within the office read for these types of calls.

"It will be over real soon, Mr. Pastore, not to worry about it."

"I'm not worried about it. I think I'm actually pissed off about it."

Oh well, ya can't fight city hall, I told myself.

I was pleasantly surprised when FedEx delivered the manila envelope that contained both a transcript marked "working copy" on the cover and a rough cut VHS tape of the Kurtis documentary. The cover letter asked me to give it a look and make any notes on what I thought needed attention as to accuracy.

Part of my agreement with Kurtis included this very item of final review, and I was glad to see he was keeping his word.

I decided to watch the video first, then, if I had any questions, compare it to the transcripts afterward. I'm glad I did it that way.

In hindsight, I think my expectations were way too high. I kept thinking of the three years of my life that led up to that pivotal moment, and my excitement at finally being vindicated was taking front seat to my normally objective nature.

A big mistake.

I saw it coming almost from the time the opening titles of the show appeared. It was subtle at first, but I detected a hint of an agenda just from the wording that was used. By the time the video was over, nausea had swept through my body. I just sat there on the couch, remote in hand, unable to even comprehend what I had just seen.

It's hard to explain the next few hours. I experienced a combination of feelings of betrayal, anger, feeling stupid and just plain disbelief. Dazed and confused as Led Zeppelin had said. I called John, my book's co-author and tried to relay what I'd just seen. He suggested I re-watch the show and take notes on the major flaws.

I had to go to work that evening (another part time job to help support the museum), so in the midst of customers making their normal demands, the minutes dragged into hours as I went over in my minds' eye what I had watched earlier. Finally, it was time to go home, and I rushed back, grabbed a notepad and watched it again.

After the third time, I hit the stop button at the end and just shook my head. I had ten pages of notes for a forty-seven minute show, and I was sure I had still missed a lot. But I did get down enough to realize the name of this game.

The ending statement by Bill Kurtis summed up the whole piece: "Does the DNA of this body match the results of the 1995 study? Close… but no cigar."

"Close but no cigar?" What the hell does that mean? What kind of scientific investigation even uses a phrase like that, especially with no explanation as to what it means?

Unbelievable.

My mind was racing a hundred miles a minute. Close to what? What was he even talking about? Then it started to become clear.

He was saying the new DNA results were "close" to the DNA samples taken in the 1995 study. The same 1995 samples this new program was trying to demonstrate were a fraud. But how could that be? I mean, was he trying to say there were flaws in the earlier studies or not? When we met and made our deal, Kurtis and I agreed the point of the show was that the results from the 1995 study were *not* the remains of Jesse James. The actual DNA report I was finally able to locate—and which I gave Kurtis a copy of—stated that the DNA samples from the 1995 study were not those of Jesse Woodson James.

And now, in this show, Kurtis was saying that *since the results of this new DNA do not match the "flawed" results of the 1995 show, this body wasn't Jesse James either.*

What a piece of crap journalism!

Worse than that. It was idiotic.

If you started with the premise that the 1995 study was true, there would be no point to this show. The reason? No matter whose DNA or grave you test, it will never match the DNA in the 1995 gravesite, because you were already saying the DNA in the 1995 study *was* Jesse James. Furthermore, there cannot be two of the same person. Kurtis had presented a flawed argument.

There can't be two copies of the same man. Duh!

And since it doesn't match, well, close but no cigar.

How could it, when you set it up like that?

And that was only the beginning. There were many other problems, all based on interpretations of what was presented.

It was painfully obvious they really were not investigating history. Because an investigation would look at and objectively weigh everything connected to it before an opinion was rendered. What he did was start with an opinion and then slant the evidence to support it by not covering all the facts.

Maybe slant is the wrong word, I told myself. It could be that they just didn't get it. I mean, I gave them everything they needed—access to all the artifacts, letters, newspapers and interviews. I thought we were on the same page. Here was a chance to show that there could be another scenario for why all the evidence contradicted what the first documentary showed. It's possible they just got off the track.

Maybe.

I had one shot left. Kurtis and his team wanted me to send a letter covering any discrepancies I noticed, so I was readying a six- page letter detailing all the points I had found.

In it I included some of the areas I felt gave a conflicting scenario and needed explaining. However, the main issue was the whole DNA premise. Kurtis was trying to compare the DNA to random teeth found in the James farmyard in 1978. Starr had *not* recovered any DNA from the 1995 exhumation. If they didn't get the scientific premise correct, everything else was a joke anyway and didn't matter. (see Appendix K)

But it did matter to me. What would this faulty conclusion mean regarding all the work, research, blood, sweat and tears I'd put into the project? Had it all been a great exercise in futility, with no historical value in the end? Basically, a complete waste of my time?

A surprise phone call gave me hope.

Let's Face It

"Who is this again?" I asked.

"Bob S., we spoke a couple of weeks ago about running the facial recognition test."

It took me a couple of moments to orient my thinking. I had completely forgotten about calling him. A documentary I watched on the History Channel a couple of months earlier had gone into some detail about a new technology a division of General Electric had for facial recognition. The thrust of its development had been for Homeland Security, but it had dawned on me this could possibly be used for matching people from their youth to old age. Of course, I had an ulterior motive in wondering if it would work.

Family Portrait found in Trunk

The documentary had wrapped about a week before I started my search to track down the man in charge of that division. After a few dead ends, I ended up getting a call from Bob Schmitt, who stated he would try to answer my questions.

I gave him a brief background on what I was involved with, including the documentary, especially focusing on the photographs of the young Jesse in Rebel uniform at age sixteen and the older "supposed" Jesse at the age of eighty-three that was one of the pictures Chuck had discovered in the two trunks. Part of the evidence on which I based my theory that Jesse had faked his death centered on this photograph. It was a picture of an older Jesse, or so I believed. Obviously, if it was Jesse, then he could not have died in 1882. I asked Bob if it would be possible to use the two photographs—the younger one and the older one—to determine with any degree of accuracy if they were indeed the same person.

"We've never done that before," Bob said, "but that doesn't mean it can't be done. The main problem, since I haven't seen the pictures, is that I'm unable to tell whether the plot points match up as far as angles go. If they don't, I need to determine if there's enough leeway to mechanically line them up. And that's not to mention the huge differences in age."

Jesse James alias Jere Miah James

He dissuaded me from thinking I could compare generational pictures to prove a linkage—the technology may not be advanced enough to do that. I still felt it was worth a try, and at last he relented. "Why not send them and let me see what I can do?"

He went on to tell me about what else they were working on, which at the time sounded pretty exciting. I made notes to myself to remember as much of it as I could, in case I needed more confirmation in some future project. It seemed the technology could be a boon for archaeological and genealogical work someday. I sent him the pictures for comparison that same day.

I also made a note to myself about the irony of what I was asking him to do. Part of the reason the technology was being deployed was to combat terrorism. And that's exactly what law enforcement back then thought Jesse and his gang actually were— historical terrorists.

"Hi there, Bob," I finally answered. "Sorry about not placing you at first, but you wouldn't believe how my week has gone."

"I totally understand, Ron. Listen, I was able to put those images you sent me through the system. It was a little tricky and to tell the truth, as I told you when we first talked, we've never put the system through a test like this before."

"I understand," I said, preparing myself for another negative outcome.

"But it worked," he said.

"What?"

"It was a match."

After a moment of "thinking" I'd heard what he said, I asked again. "You mean the two subjects matched?"

"What I mean is, according to the parameters we set up for facial recognition, I would say these two pictures are the same person. No doubt about it!"

"You're kidding?" I could hardly contain myself.

"I was surprised too," he continued. "But when you get down to the actual facial, head and ear characteristics between the two, they were a match—even allowing for the sixty-plus years between images. I've put together a PowerPoint presentation that shows how we did it, including the conclusions, and I'll send it off to you tomorrow."

"Thanks a lot, Bob. You have no idea how much this may help."

"No problem. We always love a challenge here."

I started to hang up when I heard, "Congratulations, Ron. Seems like your theory is spot on."

The process above is to normalize the two photographs. This is done by making the distance between the eyes equal in both photographs. The distance between people's eyes does not change over time.

What's interesting about these photos is that the space from the hairline on the right and left side of the face is identical in both photographs. If it's the same person it does not look like he lost much hair, and therefore this is a telling similarity.

Sample of Facial Recognition Slide

I hung up the phone thinking about the facial recognition results for a couple of minutes. Finally, empirical evidence that Jesse lived until at least 1935. That's good, but how does that square with the results from the DNA tests contained in the documentary?

Maybe it didn't matter, I thought, especially if they were using the old samples of the earlier study. But if not, then why is the DNA different from the remains in the grave we just exhumed?

It was a question I would have to ponder later. All I could do right then was wait until I received the facial analysis presentation from Schmidt.

I did call Kurtis' office to inform him of this critical breakthrough. I was cryptic, but with an urgency in my voice. "I don't know if we have time, but this facial recognition match sure seemed like pertinent information that would really go well with the piece," I said to the recording that greeted me.

The email with the PowerPoint from Bob arrived as promised the next day and it was fantastic. There, laid out with explanations and measurements, was the case for both images being of the same person.

"Yes!" I shouted out loud.

I called the production offices, got a hold of the associate producer, told her about what I'd come up with and then sent the presentation off to them. She warned me they were already close to a locked print and may not be able to get it in, but my persistence must have worn her down to the point of at least looking at it.

I finished my notes on the video and transcript, adding this new bit of evidence to the list of why they needed to balance the show a bit more and sent it by overnight courier.

Feeling pretty good at this point, I decided to sit back, call in a no show to work, select a bottle of wine and pop the cork. I still had a lot of problems to deal with, not the least of which was the documentary. The producers needed to get their facts right. As to being balanced? Well, I'd have to meditate a while about how to deal with that. And then there was Chuck with his mood swings and the museum overhead, which were both quickly draining my reserves and my nerves.

But all that seemed almost like a dream. Aware, yet the full significance of its reality floating in the background. Yeah, I'd have to deal with it, alright. However, at that moment, I had finally found someone who, through a thoroughly scientific approach, with no agenda to color the results, confirmed what I had been saying all along.

I had found Jesse Woodson James. Alive at age eighty-three. That meant it wasn't Jesse Woodson James in that 1882 grave. Period.

Because of my research into body types, I also had a good idea who really was murdered, having already decided to release that information later, more than likely in the book.

The merlot was sliding down my throat quite smoothly, and I was looking forward to the inevitable buzz that followed to gently bring me to a lumbering sleep that night.

It would not last long.

Not Again

One of the many incongruities throughout this convoluted adventure was a bit of information told to me by the James family in my earlier interviews with them. It was about the night Jesse James, under his new name Jere Miah James, died in Neodesha. The story they relayed was that Jesse's wife died on December 27, 1934. He was so distraught over the loss of his wife that he went to bed and refused to eat. Jesse ultimately died of a broken heart on February 9, 1935.

Their story went on to say that one of his five sons ventured out into the night and returned the next morning carrying ten thousand dollars in dirt smudged cash. The amount represented a considerable fortune in 1935 dollars. What also intrigued me was that the funeral itself only cost $134.75 according to the bill. So, the money wasn't just to cover the burial costs. I remember thinking it was all pretty strange. Maybe they dug up some of his treasure stash after he died.

Now, I needed to rethink this bit of trivia, mainly because of a theory that was starting to develop within my subconscious, a potential outcome which would lead me on yet another adventure.

But, first things first. A little logical "mentiation" was in order.

As far as I could discern, I was left with three possible scenarios to the work I had done so far. Unfortunately, I wasn't particularly happy with any one of them.

The first possibility: I'm completely wrong and Jesse actually was killed that fateful day in 1882. Everything else which contradicts that outcome is not relevant; the coincidences and leaps of logic are just that and nothing more. Of course, this conclusion is the one I liked least of the three.

The second possibility was he *did* fake his death. However, I'm wrong about the identity he took after his "death". In other words, he lived out his life elsewhere under a different name. This, by the way, was the contention of two other groups—one in Missouri and one in Texas. I suppose it was possible. But how do you explain the family resemblance of Jesse V, the descendant's possession of the artifacts or the facial recognition data I had just received? Especially since there was no other collection of Jesse's artifacts like this held by any other James family.

The last possibility, and one that was starting to percolate to the top, was that he faked his death and was the person I thought, yet perhaps he wasn't buried in the Neodesha grave. I hadn't really entertained this outcome before, since there was no reason to suspect the body in the grave wasn't that of Jesse James. But now, with clouds of doubt rising with this new documentary, right or wrong, it's a scenario I felt needed a harder look.

That's where a phone call from Texas came in. It was from the former Attorney General of Texas, a man who definitely was well respected and one I had no reason to doubt. Although, after hearing his story, that's exactly how I reacted.

"Ron, I've been following what you're doing through the newspaper here," he told me. "I don't know how this fits in with what you're working on, but I have in my possession an affidavit from a Joseph A. Hines, in which he swears he is in fact the original Jesse James. It's signed and dated 1936 and was sworn out in front of witnesses in Florida. Now, I don't know what to make of it, but I have it if you're interested."

I had forgotten about the call, which had come in months ago, until the videotape raised the possibility that it wasn't Jesse in the grave. The 1936 date is about a year after he supposedly died, and the name on the affidavit sounded familiar to me, so I decided to do a little research.

It didn't take me long to find out where I'd heard it before—it was mentioned as an alias of his in one of my research books.

That's it, I inwardly shouted.

He'd done it again.

My mind started comparing this revelation against all the anomalies I had been running into.

Why would his son need to get ten thousand dollars for the funeral? He didn't get it for the funeral. He got it for his dad, Jesse. Why was the viewing glass on the coffin at the feet instead of the head? Simple. It wasn't Jesse in there—again. And, it was a trick consistently used by the Knights of the Golden Circle, a ritual for burying someone other than one of their members, to throw people off their trail.

How was it that a man in Florida, over a year later, claimed to be Jesse? And further, why would J. Frank Dalton go to the trouble to have his attorney get Jesse to sign an affidavit acknowledging them both? Dalton was going to great lengths to prove his own identity, and he wouldn't have risked using an imposter.

Some additional questions arose. Why was Jesse in Florida? Why would he make that affidavit? Who was in the Neodesha grave? How could that corpse have the same injuries as Jesse?

The choice of the Florida location was a little easier to surmise. It was a known gathering spot of the Knights of the Golden Circle. This was mentioned in a number of books and articles about their "hope" for the South to rise again. Certain Knights, as part of their commitment to the cause, had to work as guardians to protect the assets of the KGC. If this were true, Jesse apparently took on one more assignment in his older years.

The reason for signing the affidavit and letting the world know about his ruse?

That one I wasn't sure about. In the affidavit he mentioned that J. Frank Dalton was also masquerading as Jesse James the outlaw.

He really was full of secrets.

The question still begged in my mind: Who the heck was in that coffin in Neodesha that Kurtis and company dug up?

That took a bit more research, but a plausible answer was swift in appearing. One of his sons, while digging a grave for Jesse's wife, fell asleep against a tree and was covered with snow when he woke up. That was in the winter and one of the coldest months of the year. He caught pneumonia and died.

Yet, the death certificate stated he died a year earlier than Jesse!

Here's the strange part. A family photograph showed Jesse and his brothers next to the grave of his son, *and there are green trees in the background!* That would have been impossible in winter. And it proved Jesse outlived his son.

It would have been quite possible to put his son's body in the coffin. With the viewing window at his feet, his face wasn't seen and no one would be the wiser.

Then he was free to move to Florida.

I had to start laughing to myself.

That old son-of-a-gun; he fooled us all again, I thought. Only this time, he came clean about it at the end with the signed affidavit.

A reasonable doubt emerged. And another lead to the seemingly endless litany of those I had to follow up.

- - - - - - -

However, I not only felt trapped and unable to get my story out, but it didn't seem like the media was interested in listening to it even if I did. Yet, that attitude contrasted starkly with everyone who came through the museum and were totally enthralled with the story.

I called my co-author and laid out the whole scenario to him and he got it immediately. We needed to focus more on *why* he faked his death, he suggested. Discover the root cause of everything. He reminded me of one more thing that had been absent from my thoughts for the past six months.

Once he brought it up, it made all the sense in the world.

The Yin and Yang of Chuck

In spite of all the grief and stress I got from dealing with Chuck, there were moments when he could be just as nice and welcoming as a cool summer breeze on a warm September night. I never knew from day to day which Chuck I'd get, the one who was angry and antagonistic or the good 'ole boy Chuck that just can't do enough to help you with whatever you're doing.

When the phone rang and I heard his voice, that familiar electric shock of stress that can run straight to my stomach, quickly reared itself. I gripped the phone a little tighter in anticipation of whatever was to come next.

"Hey there Ron, I found some things you might be interested in for your museum and thought I'd bring them over. That okay?"

"Well sure, Chuck. What do you have?"

"I'd rather show ya."

Okay, so he had me intrigued. I was hoping it would be a couple of photographs he'd shown me in an earlier visit that he was unable or maybe at that point unwilling to find again. But who knew? It could be a utility bill he though would interest me, Lord knows why. I could never tell.

I'd already spoken to Kurtis' production company about the changes I thought the documentary needed. The staff was polite and said they would look into the corrections. After I asked them if I could see the corrected version of the new script, I had a suspicion they were waffling. "There wasn't enough time." "We're still working on it." Most disappointing of all, they had no interest in using the facial recognition data, which I thought could be the most compelling piece of evidence of the whole show—a real world exclusive.

"Maybe we could use it in a follow-up piece sometime in the future," Kurtis said. It was their final way of wearing me out. Yeah, and maybe a pig will fly past my window in the future, I thought.

Chuck was prompt and arrived at exactly eleven o'clock that morning with a paper bag.

"I found these with the rest of the stuff, but didn't think they were too important at the time," he started off. "I took a quick look through 'em and thought they could be used here at the museum."

"What are they?" I asked as he opened the bag.

"I believe they're Jesse's diaries."

Might not be important? I thought. You forgot about them? I'd been busting my chops for the past three years trying to find out as much as I could about him and you have some diaries? Are you kidding me?'

"So what do you think?" Chuck chimed in, interrupting my thoughts as he handed them to me.

There were four small notebooks in various sizes, the largest about three inches by six inches. Well worn and stained with sweat. I quickly opened one and thumbed through it. It was beautiful. All hand written in script. I was almost speechless.

"Well?" Chucked asked again.

"They're very important Chuck. I need to look through and read what they say, but I think they will help the museum."

"Good. Okay, gotta go. How y'all doing here anyway?"

"Well, you can see from the street the town's still torn up," I answered, "so we hope to get a little busier once the construction ends. They promised it would be fixed up by the end of the month. But you know how that goes."

"Hell yes," Chuck said. "Government's always fixing something, ain't it?"

He started to walk to the door and stopped as if remembering something.

"How we doing on those payments for the artifacts you've got?"

"What?" I answered automatically.

"You know, our agreement?"

Well there was a zinger if I ever heard one. That'd been a bone of contention between us for the past year. Chuck was the representative for the James family ever since they moved the artifacts out of The Museum of Ancient Treasures. Our deal called for a non-profit museum to expose the story. The museum and all the expenses were in the hole, big time! I'd been funding most of it out of my own pocket by working a second job at night.

"You know Chuck, there is no money yet. The exhibit payments were coming from the deal with Dr. Jon, but you messed that up when you tried to cut me out of the picture, remember?"

"Oh yeah, I guess I did," he replied sheepishly.

"We agreed to put this out in the public domain as a non-profit, free to the public. This museum is strictly a promotional project. I'd have to go over the books to see how much we're in the red. In the meantime, I'll have my attorney send you an accounting."

"Appreciate that, Ron," he said. And then he left.

That whole exchange didn't feel right. If he was trying to mimic Detective Columbo, he needed a lot more work. However, the diaries would take precedence over my ominous feelings. I sat down and started to look through them.

What emerged was truly amazing.

It seems the James brothers had quite a few business enterprises, not the least of which was a sizable number of livery stables. The interesting part of this is how many employees they had—dozens of them. I wondered why they needed that many men on the job.

What also interested me about the diaries were Jesse's poems. Hand written poetry. And it was pretty raw. One was even an ode to Budweiser! (See Appendix M)

There were entries for payroll, personal notes in the margins and a mix of information that would typically be found in a running day-to-day diary.

I designed a way they could be displayed at the museum and started to work on the exhibit. This was an exciting find on many different levels and I wanted to get it out in the public domain with the rest of the exhibit as quickly as possible.

Over the next couple of weeks, I made multiple copies, studied the diaries and took notes, while I worked evenings to make enough money to pay for the ever-increasing museum expenses.

In addition, I now found myself following up on the ever escalating and unreasonable rants of Chuck and his attorney, demanding to see an accounting of my venture and all its expenses. I sent their requests off through my attorney and hoped for the best. The problem was that the expenses were deeply in the hole, and it would take a lot of effort to get it into the black. I was counting on book sales and the rights for a potential movie to accomplish this. Otherwise, I was basically out of dough, and Chuck wouldn't receive any more money.

- - - - - - -

Out of the blue, as the saying goes, I received a call late one afternoon from a friend named Dan. He had produced an excellent documentary on my discoveries about Native American burial mounds which I had researched years earlier. What I discovered back then was that the mounds were not randomly arranged, as had been thought, but actually formed geometric patterns. That was very important to the Indians both symbolically and literally, as it led to sacred sites they wanted hidden from unworthy presences. It was a fascinating project I'd spent years with as a full time "hobby" until this JJ project took hold. We spoke at length, and then he said something quite interesting:

"You know Ron," he said, "it wasn't just the Indians who did this. I've been studying the work of writers and archaeologists who've been researching sacred sites in Europe. They're finding all kinds of correlations with what we were looking at. In fact, it turns out the Knights Templar built their chapels in Europe to form various sacred geometric designs. They're just now starting to realize these patterns and map them out.

What caught my inner listening was the mention of the Knights Templar. They were the precursors to the Knights of the Golden Circle, which were part of the Masonic order. What if? I wondered.

I told Dan of my hastily devised theory of the possible background of the burial sites, and he gave me a few tips as to what he learned regarding shapes and where they point, wishing me good luck on the project.

"Great," I thought, "another potential lead."

I promised myself to follow up on that right away. However, I hadn't counted on Chuck.

The call from my attorney later that night seemed urgent. He didn't usually call after business hours, but when I got home from work, there was the message.

"Please call as soon as possible Ron. You won't believe what I received from the James family."

Since it was past midnight, I had to wait until the next morning, and a fitful, sleepless night ensued. I couldn't imagine what it would be, but then again, it could be just about anything and was probably centered on bad news.

At eight o'clock the next morning I called Jeff, and his tone was hair raising.

"Ron, you're not going to believe what's happened. Chuck's attorney called and asked us to produce the signed agreement you two have, and further, he said he was faxing a list of items that they want to address right away. I received the fax this morning and it's an extensive list. Plus, they want it all answered within ten days. Before we get to that, though, you do have the agreement, don't you?"

That question caused a few moments of awkward silence.

"Jeff, I've checked our files here, and we have the agreement, but the copy signed by Chuck seems mysteriously missing from my file."

"Well… that could be a problem," he replied. "I've got to be frank here, Ron. It sounded like they know something we don't," he stated.

They did.

It was a reality I was hoping never to face. A few years earlier, Chuck and I had signed the agreement. Shortly after that, we had gotten into a disagreement over Chuck's not honoring my exclusivity to the story by speaking with other writers, researchers and production companies. At the same time, Jesse V, his son, was living at my house. I told Chuck the agreement was binding, and I had no intention of dissolving it. We got into a bit of a shouting match, and Jesse V chimed in on behalf of the family. I hit the roof, since I had literally been supporting him for the past year, and truth be told came down on him pretty hard.

The upshot of the situation was we resolved it and moved on. At least I thought we had. However, when Chuck did an end run around me at the Museum of Ancient Treasures a year after this incident, I had tried to find the agreement in my home office. It was gone. Not to brag too much, but I keep meticulous records. So the idea of its not being in the file was untenable. However, not thinking nefarious deeds were involved, I brushed it off as a misfiling I would correct later.

Besides, I knew Chuck had a copy, and he darn sure knew what the terms entailed. When we finally worked out the details of the new Jesse James Museum, we verbally agreed we were operating on the original contract, and Chuck stated he would re-sign the agreement as a good faith gesture. I had sent it to him several times over the next year. Each time he agreed to do it but never sent it back signed. Again, no red flags went off for me. I simply thought it was his usual way of not following up regarding business matters.

Now, they were asking *me* for a signed copy and Chuck was claiming he "never got no signed contract". I had to face the fact that maybe more than fate removed that contract from my files. An unpleasant thought for sure, because thinking of people in those kinds of terms was something I was not accustomed to in business, although it was slowly changing.

In fact, it seems I've only had to watch my behind since I started dealing with the Jameses, and it was surely getting a bit tiring.

"What's the bottom line, Jeff? What can they do?"

"Well," he continued, "if there is no signed contract, they can claim you have no right to display the artifacts and you'll have to remove the exhibit."

"And if I can find the agreement?"

"Then they're bound by its terms and you have possession of them until it expires. But you've got to act quickly. The attorney said there's no leeway past the ten days for answering these questions and coming up with the contract."

Like I've said before, you never knew who you were dealing with whenever Chuck was involved.

The Last Clue

When I turned on the light in my storage area, I realized the extent of the task before me. There, amongst the dressers, tables and other "stuff" accumulated over the past twenty years stood over forty boxes of notes and office folders I'd packed up when I moved from the last office. It was daunting and I didn't really want to do it.

I searched through the two boxes I thought the agreement was most likely to be in first, but to no avail.

I loaded up twenty boxes and took them back to the museum so my secretary Tiffany could search the files. This is *not* going to be easy, I reasoned. And true to course, it took substantially longer than I thought it would. In the midst of this search, Tiffany died in a tragic car accident. I buried my sorrow at her loss by digging deeper into my research and work, while at the same time I mentally reviewed what I'd recently learned by reading and studying the diaries of Jesse James.

I was still plagued by the fact that the livery stables owned by the James brothers and mentioned in the diaries were so well staffed. There were way too many people employed for any legitimate livery needs. Especially, in light of the small communities in which they were located. I noticed they were also located close to each other, relatively speaking. But what started to intrigue me more was what else a livery stable might have done back then.

And why the welders, carpenters and boilermakers?

The significance of this question eluded me at that moment; it only became clear a little later on. But the fact remained that they had over a hundred employees supposedly shoeing horses. Either they were a terribly mismanaged business, or there was some other reason, a different scenario that called for the employment of such a large workforce.

Earlier that week, I received a topographical map of the area I had ordered a few days after discussing my theory with Dan on the telephone. It was a "far out" idea as we used to say in the sixties, but a lot of ideas in this quest had started as far out and ended up in fact. I was hoping this would be a repeat.

The theory was shaping up as follows: Jesse and company were part of the Knights of the Golden Circle, an offshoot of the Masons, which was founded based on the Knights Templar theology. That being the case, there might be more to these livery stables and, more particularly, the *locations* of these livery stables than previously thought. I say previously thought, because as far as I could tell, no one knew about them or their true ownership until I had read the diaries. So, no one else had a clue to even look for them. I had read a mention in my earlier research by J. Frank Dalton in his obscure memoir *claiming* he was a secret partner to his cousin Jesse James in a chain of livery stables. These diaries seemed to confirm that assertion.

In order to confirm my theories, I quickly learned I needed to get a more detailed topographical map of the area in order to pinpoint and plot the actual locations of these stables and then see what showed up.

Easier said than done.

A lot of the locations were sketchy, and their names had changed since the diaries were written, which according to Jesse's hand, was from 1914 to 1928. But after considerable research and double checking names of towns and other data, I was able to plot their locations.

Now the fun part. Did the plotting of the locations or, more accurately, these "points" on the map, mean anything? I started to connect the dots to see if a pattern revealed itself. Nothing. Okay. Let's look at it from another perspective. Maybe they pointed toward something, like an arrow. But again, they were such a mishmash that there didn't seem any rhyme or reason to the locations. No matter how I connected them, the designs didn't fit a pattern.

And then it happened.

While studying the map a little more closely, the name of a canyon jumped out at me, one I was intimately familiar with. One, in fact, that sent shivers up my spine. When I located its position on the map, I connected the dots in a particular way, and there it was.

They formed a crescent moon, the Royal Arch. The kind you see in children's books with a cat sitting inside.

It was also the symbol of the Knights of the Golden Circle.

The tip of this crescent pointed directly to that canyon. The same canyon where I had found the turkey scratches and the JJ initials a year and a half earlier. The spot where Jesse and Coronado had both rested, supposedly burying loot and arms.

The other end of the moon pointed to a location with which I was also familiar. It's currently under investigation as an archeological dig site and a potential treasure site for the James gang.

Maybe, I conjectured, they needed all those men at the various livery stables to bury large caches of arms and other things, like precious metals. And all that loot was to finance the uprising they were committed to see happen—the eventual Phoenix-like rise of the South. Hence, the many blacksmithing facilities and massive pool of manpower.

Could it really be true?

And yet, in spite of those revelations and the potentials their answers may have held, there I was, searching through dozens of boxes trying to find a contract Chuck says he never signed, so I could hold onto the artifacts and keep the museum open.

It didn't seem like a good use of my resources. I had to ask myself, What am I really interested in doing? Running a museum or going out into the field doing research? As it was looking, a new choice would be available very soon, and I didn't want to be left without either of those two options.

Moira, the goddess of fate, was a master of many a humorous moment in my life. This was no exception. Just when I thought things were figured out, she stepped in to throw a curve ball, just to see if I was still on my game.

In this case, she threw what we called in softball a "lobber," something really easy to hit. I didn't realize the gift it was at first, but this indirect event helped make up my mind on which way to go.

Turning Point

I was a little nervous about speaking before such a large group, as I suspect most people are. It wasn't as if I didn't like doing it—speaking, that is. I truly did. In fact, presenting my work is what made all the research and perseverance to overcome obstacles worthwhile. I've been speaking in front of various groups for the past twenty years.

And it wasn't an inner fear of getting in front of people that I was feeling. It was the group itself. They had contacted me months before and invited me to speak at a breakfast meeting of their members. The man who contacted me, a longtime family friend, had been to the museum and was fascinated with the concept that a local boy had pulled off such a *coup d'etat* and thought his "temple" would like to hear about it too.

The Masonic Temple.

The local shrine in Wichita was modern and stylized, surprisingly devoid of any distinguishing architectural features, save the traditional sign over the door with the familiar crescent and star.

I had agreed to speak because at the time, I had an ulterior motive—I wanted to go through my theories in a very linear and concise way before a group of people. Particularly, a group with no previous exposure, to see what their reactions, questions and doubts might be. People walking into the museum were one thing. They were expecting something. However, this was a group of people who would hopefully have few preconceived ideas and listen objectively.

By gauging their reaction to the research, I would get some feedback from them.

A practice run for what was to come.

Section VI

A New Direction

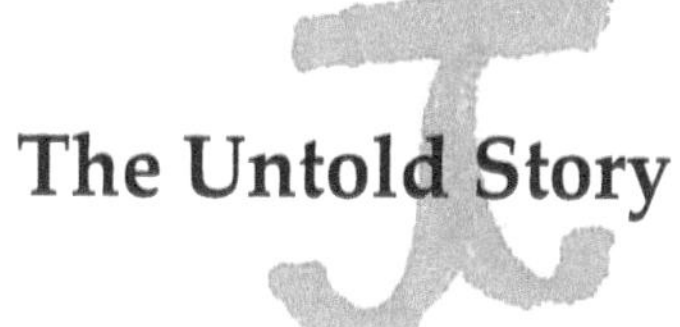

The Untold Story

My Speech at the Masonic Shrine Temple

I made one very important promise to myself. I would not bring up anything to do with the Knights of the Golden Circle directly, only by indirect reference. I thought it might cloud their objective listening. More importantly, I wanted to see if the scenario stood on its own without the clandestine secret society connection. So instead, I would simply mention the "Secret Service of the South", which sounded less sinister but was, in point of fact, the same group. I was just going to roll out the facts according to what the evidence and original records showed.

I arrived about ten minutes early, and set up my pictures and Colt Navy 1851 replica pistols to show the group. The excitement was building within me as it came time to speak; adrenaline was pumping its way through my body. After I was introduced, the apprehension completely vanished and I was relaxed, cool and in control.

An overview of that speech is contained in Appendix E.

What's important to note was the paramount question that invariably popped up at the end of my talks from this new information about Jesse…

"Where is all the money Jesse and the gang stole—especially if the secret of it didn't die with him in 1882?"

This was a major point in light of recent data that showed how much Jesse and his gang may have actually absconded with.

According to a book J. Frank Dalton wrote before his death at one hundred and seven years old, the gang *collectively* stole over four hundred million dollars worth of gold and silver. That included the proceeds of a huge Civil War era robbery of the Federal Reserve in St. Louis. Dalton methodically listed the various treasure caches and amounts. A king's ransom even by today's standards. But remember, that was in late 1800s dollars. The horde could be worth fifty times that today—a staggering billion-dollar treasure.

The question then became more than a passing curiosity.

I continued speaking and reminded the group that the James boys were part of a movement that was anti-North, or more correctly, pro-South. It was spearheaded by a close-knit group of people working through the Southern Secret Service. Part of the strategy of the Southern forces and their provisional government during the war was to bury money in caches to pay for troops, ammunition and expenses for the armed forces. After the war, some of these groups were still active and planning for the South to rise again. In that vein, they were amassing money, ammunition and political influence to help move that goal forward.

From my explorations of the various sites and from clues left in the artifacts and books written by contemporaries of Jesse, I came to the conclusion that the majority of these caches had as yet, *not* been found. I based this on a number of reasons, the most prevalent being that until 1978, no one even knew of the existence of the artifacts and diaries except Jesse and Daisy (Jesse's Daughter) who had kept them hidden.

The next clue that the treasures had not been touched was the way the Jameses lived. Never in luxury and never spending much more than they had. Yet always having what they needed.

I believe Jesse buried the loot and left cryptic maps and clues as to where it was laid to rest. Clues only others of their group would know how to understand and decipher. Theirs was a higher goal— the resurrection of the South. They would no sooner have spent that money than betray their cause. It was their honor at stake, and a death sentence if attempted.

This theory also shed some light as to why he needed to "kill" himself off in 1882. The federal authorities were aware of all those robberies, especially of the Federal Reserve funds. They wanted the gold back. And the rewards were starting to reach astronomical figures for those days. Jesse and his group realized the Feds end game was to find the caches of gold, which they could not allow to happen. If he were proven dead, then the government was at a dead end. With no one to pursue, the money would remain safe until needed by the South. That also explained why the U.S. government sent the governor of Missouri himself to confirm Jesse was indeed dead. The government wanted to confirm the gold was lost forever.

I also mentioned in my talk that I believed Governor Crittenden was in on the plot. I had found evidence that he was also a part of the Southern Secret Service group and had met with Jesse, his brother Frank and J. Frank Dalton several times to plan the ruse. The chain of evidence was there to see and left no doubt that Jesse James faked his death in 1882.

I then concluded my half hour talk to the Masons. That's not all I had wanted to tell them, but it was enough.

Be Careful What You Wish For

The Masons were exceptionally supportive by the end of my talk, and to put it modestly, I was a hit. There were all kinds of offers for help. I was grateful for their rapt attention to my speech. Their comments were unequivocal accolades. And they didn't seem to want to ask anything about the Knights of the Golden Circle, which I was especially glad about.

That last part of the talk however, the part about continuing my research and learning the final answers to this quest, was completely spontaneous. I had actually considered in the days before this speech giving up the whole venture and getting back into the financial consulting business. However, my co-author had suggested something to me a few months earlier that must have planted itself in a deep subconscious layer, only to resurface at that moment.

"You alone hold all the pieces to the puzzle, Ron." John stated. "The cave locations, the codes and glyphs, the placement of the livery stables, the amounts of the caches and the knowledge of what they may hold. Most importantly, you hold the key to why; why they would go to such extremes to accomplish all of this. I think you should go out and find the damn caches. That's what you love to do. This other stuff, the museum, dealing with the Jameses, the financial pressures—you don't need all of that. Follow your passion."

My passion.

That sounded good. I remembered the exhilaration I felt when I first found out about the cave that had JJ's initials, when I first met the Jameses and got to view and touch the pictures and artifacts. Those were great moments, and I missed them.

I had pushed myself to the point where I was spending ten to twelve hours a day in the museum. Expending that kind of energy was at cross purposes with what I was trying to do. In effect, I think it was sabotaging the real research I felt was important. What I needed to do was push away from what I was doing and return to my passion.

And that passion was the search. The thrill of the hunt and discovering things that have been forgotten or lost. That's where my best talents lay.

It wasn't a week later, the eleventh day after receiving the Jameses' demand letter, if I'm calculating correctly, that Chuck showed up unannounced at the museum door with his son, Jesse V. He demanded the return of the artifacts right then. And I got it. I needed to do that. Let them go. No resistance. I returned them all, had him sign off the inventory listing to that effect and watched him drive east on Douglas Ave.

I walked around the museum, looking at the empty cases that had contained the artifacts which started me on this journey, surveying the walls pictures had once graced, taking stock of all the events that led up to this moment. The newspapers I had blown up from 1882 were still hanging on the walls, so I stood and reread their historical accounts.

"You were one hell of a man, Jesse," I whispered, continuing my walk around the newly echoing space.

I knew I wouldn't wallow in it. In fact, I couldn't. There had been a shift in me that was almost complete. A subtle change that grew and forced me to be thankful I was no longer tied down to the museum, that lifestyle and the 24/7 obligation of guarding the collection.

I was free to pursue my passion.

The landlord understood about my not renewing the lease. I moved my office upstairs into the apartment I'd been living in over the museum.

Funny enough, when I drove to work that evening taking my usual route through town, I noticed Chuck's car parked in front of the Museum of World Treasures. That was a bit ironic. The ghosts of the past seemed to have come full circle now. The collection was back at the place where I had first set up the exhibit. Maybe that was the best place for this unique treasure.

- - - - - - -

The next couple of weeks were a whirlwind of activity. I set about getting new topographical maps with more elevation and geological details and writing up documents with the landowners to get permission to research their land

I also came up with another plan. In order to continue with my vision, I knew I would need some funding. I was hoping the museum, the book, maybe even a movie or documentary would provide the needed funds. But that didn't seem to be working out at that moment. So, I decided to create a company and look for investors. Many times when I was sharing about my discoveries, especially about the possible hidden caches of treasure, people had asked if they could put in some money. This seemed like the perfect time to see if they were sincere. So, I set about creating working documents for those investors who I hoped would fund my studies.

It seemed I had always anticipated that someday Chuck would figure out a way to screw things up. I was constantly scrambling to make sure that wouldn't happen. Now that he had, there was nothing to fear. The feeling I was experiencing was a Zen-like sense of knowing.

It had all happened just the way it was meant to.

It was a great day.

Tinkerbelle

I decided to sit down and pour myself a shot from a scotch I'd been saving for a special occasion. I figured this qualified. There's nothing else in the world as smooth or warming as a single malt scotch swooshing around a thin-walled glass.

It had been a month since I closed the museum when John, my co-author, called asking me how I was doing. We had already finished the bulk of the book and I just needed to write the introduction and do another proof.

"I'm feeling terrific, John. I'm actually feeling free for the first time in ages."

"That's great, Ron. I'm returning your call about one of the investors who wanted to speak with me."

"Right," I said with anticipation. "They want to talk with you about the book and they keep asking me about the locations before they'll sign an NDA. They seem like nice guys, and they have the money to put into the project."

"They won't sign the NDA?" John asked.

"That's what they say."

"Let me ask you a question, Ron. What is it exactly they have that you need?"

"Money. You know how much it will take to pull this off," I explained. "I need a rather expensive ground penetrating radar unit, about six months worth of research capital to make it happen, not to mention the—"

"Okay," he interrupted. "Now, what do you have that they need?"

"Well, I have the charts, the location, I know exactly how to locate the caches—"

"Hold it right there," John interrupted. "Let me tell you what you have. You have the magic pixie dust. You have everything. You're holding all the cards. If they don't want to put in the money, believe me, someone else will. Because there is plenty of money around, but only you have the magic pixie dust. Without you and what you know, they're sunk. Do you get it?"

I got it.

I like that, I thought. I have the magic pixie dust.

I remember going to the movies as a kid and seeing that little guy flying around the city, fighting pirates and being chased by alligators. In spite of all of those obstacles, he kept his childlike enthusiasm and wonderment about the world and he never gave up.

Peter Pan always was a hero of mine.

Problem With the Book

Six months had come and gone and still no one was putting money into the company. Even though there were many people telling me they were going to do it, no checks appeared. I found it rather amusing, after the initial disillusionments. I lost count of the times I was told someone was just waiting for this or that to happen and then the money would be there the next day. Apparently, a lot of stars did not align up for many of these investors. However, they all had one thing in common. They wanted to know where I was going to search.

John called and said he had a couple of strong leads on getting our book published. Great, I thought. That's one way to get some capital. However, he brought up a point that had never occurred to me. Not from lack of critical judgment; rather, a naiveté as to how people think.

"Is it possible," he asked, "for someone to read the book and figure out where the caches might be located?"

Wow. I had always focused on the academic and historical part of the equation. It was important to me to get the new information out and clear up a one hundred-year-old mystery. However, the other side of the equation did contain the revelations of Jesse being part of the KGC, his motives for hiding the treasure and his methods for doing so. In effect, I was laying out a blueprint for others to follow and try and discover where he buried the caches.

So what to do?

"Ron, where are we on the funding for the company?" John asked.

"I haven't been able to close anyone to this point," I admitted.

He was quiet for a few moments.

"Here's what I think," he said. "Let's put the book on hold for now, and focus on raising the funds. Once we do that, you can conduct the field studies and searches. We'll wait until you're through, and publish the book then."

"What if we don't get funded? Then all of my work will be lost and not get out to the public"

"If we put it out now," John pointed out, "you'll win the battle but lose the war. As to the funding, I'll see if I can find some people to put in the money. Worst case, I'll fund it. The important point is to not lose control of the knowledge you've discovered—that Jesse James not only faked his death, but he buried the gold and you think it's still there."

"Okay then," I said, feeling somewhat relieved. "I'll start searching for the equipment we'll need."

"Good. In the meantime, we'll continue writing about all you're doing and include whatever you find as the final chapter. Deal?"

"Deal."

Jesse's story to the world would have to wait a little while longer.

However, a select group would get to hear about it first.

Vindication II

I had one more avenue I was pursuing during the fund raising time period. I had learned from speaking with the editors of the local newspapers that they felt their readers lacked the intelligence and the attention span to grasp the story. I also found that many historians found it untenable to revise the popular legend regarding Jesse James. It seemed no one wanted to know the truth. Then it struck me. I needed to focus on the one area that made the difference in my unmasking the inconsistencies in the 1995 study.

Academia!

It wasn't just a thought out of the blue. Dr. Peer Moore-Jansen had encouraged me to apply to the American Academy of Forensic Sciences ever since we started the exhumation project. My plan was to correct the misinformation presented at the 1996 AAFS meeting by Professor Starrs and his associates. I wanted to get the *facts* of the case on the record once and for all.

The problem was the application process required submitting an abstract prior to the conclusion of my study. I would have to write it based on what I had found so far and what was as yet forthcoming. Lacking the credentials as a forensic scientist, why would they even consider approving my request to speak? Not to mention the fact that Professor Starrs was co-chair of the 2004 forum. His pull alone would surely keep me out.

Undaunted, I logged onto the American Academy of Forensic Sciences web site and found that the next annual meeting was just a few months away. I entertained visions of nailing Professor Starrs on the finer points of this case. So, I plunged in and submitted an abstract to speak at the next conference.

The detailed overview of a forty-five minute presentation covering the forensic evidence received a quick reply: an email requesting that my abstract be reduced to one-half page in length. The final paper was submitted a week prior to the deadline with little hope of approval. I dismissed the effort as futile and was satisfied I had at least met the criteria for consideration by such an august body as the AAFS.

To my surprise, I got an email stating my abstract was accepted and I was scheduled to present my findings. Wow, I can't believe it's true, I thought. They really want to hear the facts. Amazing! How on earth did this get past Starrs?'

Without answering that question, I started laying out a PowerPoint presentation and it quickly took shape. I had only fifteen minutes to present the finer points on the true forensic nature of this case. It finally boiled down to a one hundred and twenty–year-old cold case murder file. If what I was presenting was true, then someone had been successfully murdered in Jesse James' place. The same questions I'd been asking myself all these years required a reasonable and logical analysis of the case. Motive, means and opportunity, backed by historical record and illustrated by period photographs. I had designed a ten-point criteria of evidence, met that test and showed the logical outcome with my new evidence—most of which was the actual historical documentation.

I finished building the slide show a few days before the trip, showing a review of the source material from the empirical view of the audience. I was speaking to a group that made their living doing what I had only taken on as a personal passion to solve. I couldn't make a mistake.

The drive to Dallas was surprisingly relaxing. I left Wichita a full day ahead of schedule to ensure my timely arrival. It was surprisingly warm and sunny for late February. I had plenty of time and no need to speed, so I enjoyed the sights along the way. The Arbuckle Mountains of Oklahoma brought back many tales of James Gang treasures buried in them there hills.

After reviewing the research data, I got a good night's sleep and awoke early. When I arrived at the venue, I found the hall and moderator for the program. A review of the program guide showed that I was last to speak. I wondered if anyone was even going to hear my talk. The hall seated four hundred people easily, and it was nearly empty at nine a.m. when the first speaker went on. By ten a.m. it started filling up a bit. And by ten thirty, it was nearly half full. The next thing I knew they were talking about me!

"At this time we'd like to present what we think is the best, which we saved for last. We've read Ron Pastore's abstract and find it a compelling body of research. We think you'll be impressed with his work on the book, Jesse James' Secret."

Suddenly it struck me. I was the final *featured* speaker. It was real. I would either fall on my face or dazzle them with my research.

Relax, I told myself. You've done your homework. You've walked the land and held his bones. You know it's him, now tell them about it.

I took the stage and thanked the moderator, a Special Agent from the Office of Naval Intelligence. I first made it clear that I was not a forensic scientist, merely a student of history with a de facto Ph.D. in Jesse James. My B.A. in sociology led to an interest in ancient cultural linguistics and petroglyphs. In the course of my research, I encountered numerous cave sites that held post Civil War era glyphs of historical figures, including the initials JJ. That led to various descendants with claims to direct lineage. But it could only be true if history was wrong and Jesse had lived on to father more children.

I started with square one, the day of the killing. "In order to objectively analyze the case, there must be a criteria of evidence," I said. I then laid out the ten basic points that constituted proof under scientific scrutiny. I presented the evidence and how it measured up to the criteria. The audience was very vocal in their appreciation of my findings. It was all so obvious when you put it in logical black and white, cutting through all the rhetoric and bull. Simply stated, it was all a big ruse and they got away with it. Now, who is the dead guy if it's not Jesse James?

I proceeded to show them slides of the various Jesses and their body types, separating them into three groups. Three subjects, under one alias, Jesse James. And then I proclaimed who the real victim was. A cousin and train robber, who had gone astray from the group and finally became a sacrificial lamb for the common good.

When I presented the facial recognition software analysis segment that matched my older subject to the younger Jesse James, the audience was ooohing and ahhing out loud. Fortunately, one of the speakers before me had covered biometrics and Bertillian facial recognition techniques, so they really got this bit of evidence.

I showed the handwriting comparisons and covered the medical records, the victim's autopsy and the death photo. By the time I got to the DNA evidence, two things were clear. There wasn't enough evidence available yet to determine this case with DNA. And when viewed in reverse order, my new DNA evidence was in fact, a very near match. But my study got the opposite results than the 1995 study. Go figure.

Either way, I stated the DNA evidence was still not conclusive enough to say yes or no. It would entail an entire DNA catalogue of all three DNA types: X, Y and Nuclear, from all the families in question before DNA can solve this case. I wrapped up my talk by summarizing my ten points of evidence and stressing that a preponderance of facts met the burden of proof.

My closing remarks were met with loud applause and accolades, bringing the audience to their feet. As soon as the room quieted down, a man in the back row raised his hand. It was Dr. Peer Moore-Jansen, the physical anthropologist from WSU.

A thought flashed as I acknowledged him to speak. What the heck is he doing here? Dr. Moore-Jansen stood up and said something to the effect that since the DNA didn't match, doesn't it prove he wasn't Jesse James?

Holy crap! He was trying to discredit me right in front of the audience. Yet, he was the one who encouraged me to speak at that meeting. Those thoughts and more raced through my mind, and I was pissed.

"With all due respect, Dr. Moore-Jansen, I've already addressed the DNA issues. But if he had matched the 1995 DNA, it would have made my subject a brother. We did our study based on the contention that the 1995 data was flawed, so it's not valid to test against, period! Frankly Peer, you failed to complete your report on the physical remains we exhumed, which showed three injuries consistent with Jesse James. The only opinion you should have is based on the evidence you failed to provide. So until you do, kindly sit down and shut up."

I could see him turn beet red as he left the room in a huff. The audience applauded me loudly, and more hands went up to ask questions. The rest of the inquiries were very supportive, intelligent questions and comments. The moderator had to cut the crowd off. She invited them to come up and speak with me personally as she ended the symposium.

Many of the attendees came forward to congratulate me as I came off stage. Those scientists, anthropologists and investigators were openly acknowledging their agreement with the unadulterated evidence. It showed I had solved a one hundred and twenty-year-old murder case.

I went home to my ranch in Kansas high on the feeling I had finally found a venue for the truth. Funny enough, nothing really changed after that. But it gave me the drive to retool the book and present more of the personal experiences along the way.

And start to plan how I would finally find the last of Jesse's secrets.

End of Act II

It'd been over a year since Bill Kurtis' fine piece of journalism aired. Fortunately, the program only received about eighteen hours of advance promo. So, among those who did catch the show, the comments were generally the same: lots of fluff...long on background reenactments...short on substance...often stopping short of actually making an important point...it was in essence, a complete disappointment. They had missed the mark in spite of my long letter to Kurtis explaining the critical errors.

I came to the realization that the only way to get the truth on record was to both publish this book and produce my own video. It was the only way I could envision all of my evidence being presented without someone else's agenda or interpretation. It would allow the opportunity to receive objective peer review of my many discoveries.

However, as I mentioned earlier, the book would have to wait until I finished my field studies and research. And I hadn't the funds to make my own documentary.

So, I returned to the field to study the rock carvings in their remote hideaways until something changed.

While working on this book, an old wagon master, John Hogoboom, told me a story about Jesse James and company robbing the Butterfield Overland Stagecoach. I decided to check out the area of the holdup at a remote Pony Express depot. It was an unusual spot with massive round lava boulders atop sandstone pedestals over ten feet tall. They were so covered in graffiti that it would have taken hours to search for any remnant of older petroglyphs. I expanded my search to the surrounding valleys where Jesse may have sought cover. I followed a stream wherein a bluff came into view. The face was completely devoid of a single mark.

The newest field team member, Michael, noted that the cliff face had recently collapsed, which was why it had no glyphs. The rocks were face down with the glyphs lying beneath the large boulders that choked the natural spring. Then, we noticed thick chunks of ice had refrozen vertically and the mud splatters were still crystallized. Since it had rained two nights before, this cliff had fallen only the night before. But those clues were now gone forever.

The geological clock was quickly running out on those sandstone bluffs. Within a few years, all of the clues left by Jesse would be gone. I had recorded everything I found in my field journal, taken photos and marked the GPS coordinates of the glyphs so far. But there was so much more to cover before it was too late. With my newfound freedom, I was able to focus on that task and collect all of the data I could find as quickly as possible. It was up to me to get the job done if anyone was ever going to solve the mystery.

We had to press on to see what else the valley might reveal. It was an extremely productive survey where we found many unusual glyphs and signs. Among them was an inscription in the rocks high on a cliff, some fifty feet above the valley that read:

"WILLIAM BRADY AND VERNON SMITH FAWT INDIANS HERE 1847".

That passionate feeling of discovery reeled up within me again. I was where I needed to be.

Section VII

The Truth Revealed

Four Years Later – 2008

While my co-author John was working on other projects, I was busy preparing for what I hoped would be a full-scale expedition to uncover the last of Jesse Woodson James' secrets. That involved creating a company, team and protocols for the undertaking. It also involved researching what it would entail to accomplish this feat.

First and foremost, I needed to identify the sites with the most potential, and then secure the rights to explore and excavate if necessary from the landowners. The former was not difficult. I had already found many sites with the glyphs and JJ's initials. More importantly, I had identified Hanson's cave and the moon shape that pointed to it.

I found the owners' names through county records, and finally was able to reach them on the telephone. My company, National Geometric Surveys, Inc. or NGS, was already known in academia as a registered archeological survey company. After meeting with the owners and explaining the scope and goals of the project, they agreed. (Actually, it was a bit more involved... including getting together a few siblings that were geographically quite distant). The point being, I had an agreement in place to start exploring the cave and surrounding area. I also located and started to obtain additional land agreements with surrounding owners in the area.

About a year earlier, I had realized the only way to effectively find anything buried to any great depth would be a ground penetrating radar, or GPR. Keeping in mind the earlier unanswered questions of why Jesse James would need so many people to run his livery stables, I surmised the reason might be to bury the caches so no one would find them outside of their fellow knights who knew how to read the codes.

After extensive research, I located a GPR unit in Greece. That unit was important, because it had a specialized antenna that would penetrate over sixty feet down into the ground. These units were now illegal to sell in the United States. However, this one was manufactured before the ban and was grandfathered in. A price was reached with the broker, and then the hunt was afoot. How was I going to pay for it?

I called John and told him the great news about locating the radar. Realizing that if we didn't act immediately it would be lost (it was highly sought after because of its depth range), he agreed to purchase it. I attended classes, along with JD, one of my key team members. Without going into too much detail, let's just say it's an amazing machine. It provides 3-D rendering of the different layers of soil and artifacts in the ground. In color!

A client of mine owned a brand new Kubota RTV, and after some negotiation I purchased it. This would be used to pull the GPR across the ground. Finally, I found a trailer to house everything. In a word, NGS was getting ready to launch a full scale, professional operation.

Then, a surprise phone call came with an offer that was hard to refuse.

The Chance for Truth

"Hi Ron, it's John. Do you have a few minutes?"

"Sure do. What's up?"

"I have an interesting story for you. I was having lunch with a friend, Matt, and just before we were leaving, I told him about our book and the idea of our going out and searching for the caches Jesse may have left behind. He got really excited, and then when I returned home, he called and asked for more information. I sent him what he wanted, and now he thinks he would like to present this to a couple of networks and see if they want to do a special on it."

"You're kidding," I said, disbelieving.

"Nope. And here's the cool part. He was really interested in the fact that Jesse faked his death and how he did it. So let's collaborate on a proposal for him so he can take it to the networks."

It didn't take any coaxing for me to agree. We wrote up the general outline of the story, and then went back and forth with Matt's company until we created a proposal we were all happy with. John suggested we secure additional sites and that I take the GPR unit out and get some more experience with it.

A few weeks later we had the verdict. And how ironic it was. The History Channel had agreed to go ahead with a two-hour special. The gist of it was to follow me on the search for the buried caches, while at the same time revealing the story of how Jesse James faked his death.

When I heard the news, I felt both elated and scared. My last experience with Bill Kurtis and the History Channel was horrible. However, *this* would be different. It would be based on the book. And, John would be one of the Executive Producers on the project.

It took a while, but it finally dawned on me that this was the perfect circle to the overall journey. There was now a chance for the truth to get out on the same network that broadcast the initial untruths. A karmic vindication of sorts.

Those thoughts were quickly superseded by another realization. It was real now. All the work, theories, conjectures and hopes were soon to be put to the test. We really were going on a hunt, where the quarry was over one hundred-year-old buried treasure. There was no wiggle room. I, and the world, were soon to find out if my theories had any validity.

As for the actual theory of Jesse Woodson James having faked his death and the evidence backing up that claim, I was steadfast and certain. It had passed numerous vetting and always stood the tests. But the buried caches were another matter.

However, I was committed, and so were the production company and cable network. I had work to do.

Passionate work.

The Payoff

Whatever misconceptions I was harboring about the creation and production of the documentary were soon dispelled by the collaborative nature of this show. As I mentioned, it was based on my theories and the manuscript of this as yet unpublished book. The writer and producer, Mike K., wanted to do it right. We spent weeks in preproduction, coordinating the overall script and securing locations for the shoot.

The locations were the biggest challenge. Although I had contacted the owners of these particular locations, they were hesitant on a number of issues—not the least of which was privacy. They didn't want the location of their land advertised on the network for fear (arguably correct) treasure hunters would start descending on it after the show. We finally worked those details out, and days before shooting received the final signed releases.

My team was trained and prepared. The equipment was in place and ready to be used. The locations were set. It was now time to get out in the field and start the process.

As adventurous as treasure hunting sounds, it's a lot like watching water getting ready to boil most of the time. That's not to say it was boring. More akin to tedious. Though, the excitement of the team and film crew was infectious. But still, it took long hours of following specific protocols to search the areas we had designated. In between the scans, we conducted interviews and location shots.

We filmed for over five weeks, total.

The reenactments were filmed in Oregon. I wasn't able to be there, but was very excited to learn they were going to do many of the scenes my co-author and I created in this book.

Again, a chance for vindication. And for truth.

The show aired as 'Jesse James Hidden Treasure', and was watched by millions of people worldwide. The world now knows what we found and whether or not my theories hold up to scrutiny.

They do.

Jesse James' "secret" has now been revealed for al;; to see. He faked his death, and in so doing created a myth that survived for over one hundred and fifty years.

A chance meeting in 1996 on a small piece of land called Cave Springs was the beginning of my journey to unravel that myth. Along the way, I discovered larger mysteries surrounding the enigmatic outlaw: secret societies, hidden agendas and a story that needed to be told. It took over ten years of relentless and dogged determination to wrench those secrets from his grave.

Yet, those secrets led to further mysteries still crying out for discovery. He was a very resourceful and fascinating man.

And I'm still on that passionate search today.

Final Note

It is understood by the author that this book is not consistent with traditional history. I have brought to light a whole new view based on facts and evidence uncovered from over a decade of research. This is by no means the final word on the life of Jesse James. It is the beginning to understanding the life he led and what became of him after the 1882 ruse. These and other issues will be addressed in an upcoming follow-up book, which will include an expanded version of the detailed analysis of the forensic evidence, along with a closer look at the subsequent years of his long prosperous life, until his death in 1935.

Postscript

During my years of research, I came across an even greater secret hidden for centuries. I see now that Jesse's loot was just the practice round for the *find* of the millennia. I learned what was at the heart of all this secret society agenda of subterfuge.

In one of my mapping studies, I unlocked a geometric puzzle that led to this discovery: that in fact, the *true* Templar legacy, from which the Knights of the Golden Circle descend, has been hidden here, *somewhere* in America!

Conspiracy Fulfilled

The "Murder" of
Jeremiah "Jesse" Woodson James

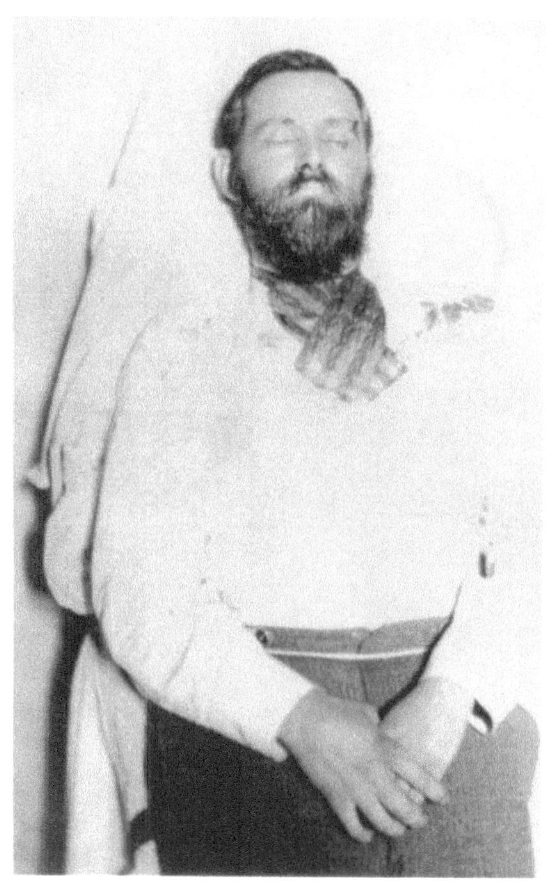

Wednesday, March 22, 1882

The biting cold pierced through his clothes as Jesse Woodson James rode up toward his childhood home. Memories flooded his mind as he passed the old tree where the Yankees had hung his stepfather nearly twenty years earlier. As his horse ambled up to the house, he could see his cousin J. Frank Dalton standing on the porch, talking with the Ford brothers. A group of familiar men huddled together around a fire near the barn nodded toward Jesse as he dismounted his tired horse.

Although sporting a new beard and darker hair, Jesse was immediately recognized by Dalton and the Ford brothers.

It was a long hard ride for Jesse, and he'd had plenty of time for uninterrupted thought and introspection. He knew it was only a matter of time before someone would try to turn him in for the reward money. The price on his head had grown to the point that even his most trusted men were starting to get nervous. In order to stop the pursuit of the Pinkertons and federal authorities once and for all, they had met months earlier in Denver to devise the plan. It was daring—every conceivable detail and contingency having been discussed. If perfectly executed, it would finally allow him the safety and freedom he desired. The Knights would be assured that the gold they had been hiding for the past seventeen years would remain secure until it was needed by the secretive KGC.

Although most people and the authorities believed otherwise, Jesse did not much enjoy killing. This flew directly in the face of his exploits with Quantrill, where it was not uncommon for them to kill hundreds of men in a single day. That was war, he reasoned, and it was justified given the circumstances. He could live with that.

After the war ended, the gang continued robbing trains and banks to fund their efforts at secession. They always tried to make sure no one was hurt unnecessarily. But he was prepared if anyone resisted, and they suffered the merciless consequences. Jesse had learned his lesson only too well in the case of the Northfield bank robbery where his gang was decimated and innocent people were wounded and killed. It was still a kind of war in his mind, given that the proceeds would be used later for the greater cause he believed in. It was serious business and casualties were inevitable.

However, what they were planning then was different. The reason for this killing was the need for a body double, or it would not work. They also faced the issue of his cousin Jeremiah disobeying strict orders and placing the group in jeopardy. The days passed on the ride to the farm gave Jesse a chance to view the situation from all sides and justify it in his mind. And he could live with that as well.

"You look dead dog tired, cousin," offered Dalton as Jesse walked up the porch steps.

"Long ride from Neodeffee, cousin," he replied.

"Yeah, cold as hell too," Dalton added.

Jesse nodded as he walked through the door, grabbed a cup and poured some coffee from the warm stove.

Dalton and the Ford brothers followed him in.

"Where's Frank?" Jesse asked.

"In town with some of the boys," Dalton said.

Jesse absorbed the answer along with another swig of hot coffee.

"Where are we on the plan?" he asked.

"Everything is worked out," said Dalton. "We've had men in St. Joe watching Jeremiah for the past couple of weeks, and we got his habits down pretty well. We've called up the rest of the men and have a total of fifty-two of them who are all fellow Knights sworn to the cause. About half of the boys are already in town with Timberlake. We're ready."

The door opened and in walked Dick Liddel and Jim Reed, two of the group's most trusted men. Jesse nodded toward them.

"Nice beard there, Jesse," smirked Dick. "Almost didn't recognize ya."

"That would be the point," Jesse shot back, half smiling. "So what exactly is the plan, boys?"

"I think the best place to get Jeremiah is in the stable behind his house," Dalton started, "just as we planned back in Denver. We need him out of the house, especially since his wife and kids are there. Once he goes out to the stables, we confront him. We'll take him down and then wait until the morning when Bob here will go into town and tell Timberlake that he shot you… I mean Jeremiah."

"You okay with that?" Jesse asked Bob Ford.

"Sure am Jesse. But I ain't having no part in killin' 'em," Bob insisted.

"Me neither," his brother Charlie piped in.

"Relax boys," Dalton told them, "we're taking care of that." They both looked relieved.

"Besides Bob, you'll be the one who gets the reward money," Dick added as he winked. "That should help ease your conscience a bit."

The group laughed at the quip.

"What about his wife and the kids?" Jesse asked.

"A couple of the boys will keep them quiet in the house," Dalton replied. "After things calm down, we'll set them up somewhere new."

"Why are we shootin' him so early?" Jesse asked. "Won't the coroner know he was killed the night before?"

"If we leave him in the barn, he'll stay cool until the morning," Jim replied. "Rigor shouldn't have set in much. The problem is we gotta set the scene up to make it look like you live there, Jesse. We'll need some of your personal effects, rings, jewelry and such to lay about the house. And we have to secure the wife and kids to make sure they don't witness any part of it. It'll be easier if we do it the night before while the town's asleep."

"Seems reasonable," Jesse said as he poured himself some more coffee, thinking. "When are ya planning to do it?" he finally asked.

"We have to get it done before the election," Jim continued. "Crittenden is running a tight race and he could lose. If so, we'll have no backing from the governor's office. So, we'll set it up for the evening of April 2nd, like we planned."

"Cutting it pretty close, wouldn't you say?"

"With all the commotion of the election and such, Jesse, I think it will be the ideal time," Dalton responded.

"Okay then, we'll meet at the World Hotel the afternoon of the 2nd and get started," Jesse said. "I'll stay here until then. J. Frank, why don't you go into town April 1st and make sure Timberlake swears in our men as deputies. Get it all legal."

Dalton nodded an "okay" to Jesse. "All our men will be wearing the Lone Star badge or their Copperhead pins."

"Well men," Jesse said, "this is gonna be an interesting time in our lives—a tragic end and a brand new beginning, free from the feds forever."

He raised his coffee cup in a salute.

"To the successful death of the famous outlaw, Jesse James."

Sunday, April 2, 1882
1319 Lafayette, St. Joseph, MO. – Early evening

Jeremiah "Jesse" Mason James, Jesse's cousin, had finished supper and was waiting for his children to go to bed before feeding the horses. Lighting a kerosene lamp, he kissed his wife and stepped out into the bitter cold. He walked along the south side of the "L" shaped house toward the stables where he opened the door and entered.

Once inside, he headed for the feed stall when he saw a match struck and then rise toward a face. He froze and reached for his gun. The match created a glow around the face of his cousin, J. Frank Dalton, and he relaxed. Dalton shook out the match while Jeremiah walked closer with the lamp, illuminating not only J. Frank, but Jesse, Dick Liddel and Jim Reed.

"You fellas scared the bejeezus outta me," Jeremiah exclaimed. "What are ya' all doin' here at this time of night? Why didn't you just come up to the house?"

"We need to talk with you privately," Jesse responded.

"What about?"

Jesse stood silently looking at Jeremiah, following his movements as a snake does its intended prey.

"You've been robbing trains and such these past few years against orders," Dalton told him.

"That's *my* business, cousin. I need to support my family here."

"Problem is, *cousin*," Jesse interjected, "you've been sayin' you're Jesse James, and the law thinks it's *me* doin' the robbin'. That's bringin' all kinds of pressure down on me and our brother Knights. It ain't just you in this. There's a greater cause at stake here. That makes it my business."

"Like I said," Jeremiah responded, "I've gotta make a living, Cause or no Cause and I'll do what I choose, no matter how you or the KGC tells me different."

He stood up defiantly to Jesse. Dick and Jim slowly moved around, flanking Jeremiah on both sides.

Silence gripped them as Jeremiah observed their motions. "Well,

Jeremiah," Jesse finally spoke, "therein lies the problem.
We can't let it continue. I guess you always wanted to be me, pretending and all. So, it looks like you're going to keep on foolin' people into all eternity."

"What the hell you talking about?" he snarled back.

Jesse nodded slightly toward the others while his right hand quickly pulled a pistol from the reverse holster on his right side. He swung the butt of the weapon toward Jeremiah and slammed the hammer into Jeremiah's left temple. To Jesse's surprise, the blow merely stunned the stout man rather than knocking him down, as planned.

Dick and Jim got behind him and grabbed his arms. Jeremiah was dazed but yanked his right arm away from their hold, drew his gun out of the holster and started to take aim at Jesse.

Dalton instinctively pulled out his bowie knife, grabbed the barrel of the Jeremiah's gun with his other hand and quickly slid the blade along the top of the barrel, slicing off Jeremiah's thumb before he could cock the hammer to fire. It was a trick he had used during the war that always took the victim by surprise.

Jeremiah screamed out in agony as the gun was twisted from his grip. He grabbed his bleeding hand and fell to the ground on his left shoulder, writhing in pain. Jesse took aim and fired a death shot straight down into the right side of his head. His body went limp in an instant.

Jesse looked over at the others and motioned his head authoritatively toward the body. They un-holstered their guns and each took a single shot into Jeremiah's chest.

Four other men had entered the house right after Jeremiah had walked out to the barn and gathered up his wife and two children.

They were forcefully removed to a wagon and quickly whisked away until morning.

A man walked into the barn, carrying a lamp.

"Everything okay in there?" asked Dalton.

"The house is secure," the man answered.

"Good." He turned toward the others and said, "Leave the body where it is. We'll bring it into the house before sun up. In the meantime, you check with Timberlake and make sure the deputies will be ready in the morning."

"Yes sir, Colonel," said the man as they left.

"I guess it's done, cousin," Dalton said to Jesse.

"The ruse has just begun, cousin. We've still got a lot to do."

Monday, April 3, 1882
1319 Lafayette – Morning

It was an exceptionally cold April morning. Frost had taken hold of the town and the ground was frozen. Clouds of steam shot from the snouts of their horses as the Ford brothers rode up to the house just before dawn. They quickly dismounted and walked up to the back door. Jesse, J. Frank Dalton, Dick and Jim were sitting inside next to the fireplace as they entered.

Everyone present was silent. A few moments passed before Bob spoke.

"Everything okay?" he asked.

"Exactly as planned," Dalton responded.

Silence reigned again as the fire crackled in the fireplace.

Finally, Jesse rose from his chair. "Time to set this thing up," he said. "Jim, Dick, bring in the body. Bob, we need to get your story straight here. I've been thinking about how this whole thing plays out. You tell the sheriff I took off my gun belt to dust off a picture up about right here," Jesse said as he pointed to the wall. "And then, when I turned my back to you, you shot me in the head. That means I would be standing on a chair to reach up that high."

Jesse grabbed a chair from the dinner table set and moved it into position. He stepped up onto it.

"Shot you in the back, Jesse?" Bob asked.

"No one would believe you took him in a fair fight, Bob," Dalton stated matter-of-factly. "So you shot him in the back of the *head*."

Jesse looked perturbed by the interruption.

"If you're standing over there, Bob," he impatiently continued, pointing, "then your bullet should hit somewhere around here."

Jesse pointed to an area on the wall with his index finger, and jumped down from the chair.

"Go ahead and take aim on that spot and pump a bullet into it."

Bob pulled out his .44 caliber Smith and Wesson, carefully took aim at the spot on the wall and fired off a round. The back door swung open, and in came the boys with Jeremiah's body.

"What should we do with him?" Dick asked.

"Put it over here next to the chair," Dalton told them. "Then we'll push the chair over to where he woulda fell."

"Good thinking, cousin," Jesse noted.

"What about blood?' Jim asked.

"I've got an idea," Dick responded. "I'll be right back"

"So you've got the story straight, Bob?" Jesse wanted to know.

"Yeah, yeah, Jesse. We came over to visit him, I mean you," pointing to Jeremiah on the floor. "You was dusting off a picture, standing on that chair. While your back was turned, I pulled my gun and shot you in the head. The bullet went through and hit the wall. It seems simple enough to me."

"It is. But it must always be consistent. If it doesn't hold up, then we've all wasted our time here and nothing will change."

"It'll be consistent," said Bob. "I'll make sure of it."

Dick walked in with a bowl.

"I've got some chicken blood here, Jesse. Put your hand in it, and then make like you tried to balance yourself on the wall after you were shot. I'll pour some on the floor next to his head."

Jesse dipped his hand in the bowl, stepped back up onto the chair and pressed it onto the wall near the bullet hole.

"Looks all official like now, don't it?" he laughed.

"Dead is dead," added Dalton as he looked down at Jeremiah's body. "And you sure look dead enough to me, Jesse."

"You and Charlie better get off to Sheriff Timberlake and tell him the 'tragic' news of my demise, Bob."

The Ford brothers exited the house, jumped on their horses and galloped off to summon the sheriff.

Monday, April 3, 1882
1319 Lafayette, St. Joe., Missouri – 9:00 am

Bob Ford turned himself in to Sheriff Timberlake, telling him and a couple of deputies the story of how he killed Jesse James. The sheriff wired the marshal in Kearny to notify Jesse's mother and have her come to St. Joe immediately. Once the telegraph office knew of the death, it wasn't long before the news was wired all across the country.

Sheriff Timberlake swore in extra deputies, all to a man were members of the James Gang. He sent them to secure the crime scene and act as crowd control for the multitudes that were sure to show up. Townspeople were already being awakened by their neighbors with the news that the famous outlaw Jesse James had been murdered over on Lafayette Street. The sheriff also sent a couple of men to fetch the assistant coroner, Heddens, to accompany him to the crime scene and take charge of the body.

When the sheriff, coroner and Bob and Charlie Ford arrived, there was a crowd gathering around the house. The deputies were making them keep their distance. The foursome made their way past the crowd and into the house. They found the body lying on the floor with a pool of blood by his head and a chair turned over beside it.

"Is this how you left the place?" asked the sheriff.

"Yes sir," Bob replied.

The coroner knelt down and started to examine the body.

"So your story is that you and Charlie were here to visit Jesse, and he took off his guns and got up on that chair over there to straighten out that picture?" Coroner Heddens questioned while pointing."

"Yes sir."

"And that once he turned his back, you shot him through the head?" Sheriff Timberlake added.

"That's how it happened, Sheriff."

"And then what?"

"Well sir," said Bob. "He grabbed the back of his head, fell toward the wall… I think he reached out to brace himself against it, and then fell off the chair onto the floor."

"Anyone else in the room with you here?"

"Just me and my brother Charlie was in here," he said, nodding in Charlie's direction. "His wife and kids was in the kitchen fixin' breakfast."

"That how it happened, Charlie?"

"God's truth, sheriff."

The coroner looked up at Bob. "Is that the gun you used, son?"

"It is."

"May I?" he asked holding out his hand and giving an expectant nod. Bob unholstered and handed the gun to the coroner. He examined it carefully, opening up the cylinder and checking to see that only one chamber was fired. After he sniffed the end of the barrel, he handed it to Sheriff Timberlake.

"You better hold on to this as evidence, Sheriff." He returned his attention to Bob.

"And you say this whole event happened only about two hours ago?"

"Yes sir."

"Interesting," he stated softly to no one in particular. He became markedly quiet and introspective for a few moments, his eyes seemingly searching for an answer to some puzzle.

"Sheriff," the coroner finally continued, "I'll need you to send a couple of men to the funeral parlor and fetch a wagon. We'll take the body there where I can finish my examination and conduct the autopsy. We'll also need a next of kin to positively identify the body."

"I sent for his mother, Zerelda. She should be here later this afternoon. We're holding his wife and kids in protective custody at the World Hotel."

"I'm sure that will do." He stood up, surveyed the room and fixed his gaze at the wall where the bullet hole and bloody handprint was visible.

"Very interesting."

Monday, April 3, 1882
Funeral Parlor – Afternoon

The coroner examined the body and what he found was troubling. He discovered two more bullet holes in the victim's chest when he removed the shirt. There was no blood from the wounds, which could only mean they happened *after* the victim was dead, simply for the fact that his heart had stopped beating or blood would be present. He observed that the holes had entered the right chest below the breast.

He found that the victim's thumb was amputated, and recently. Yet, no thumb was found at the crime scene. He also noticed a deep gash in the victim's left temple, the indentation closely resembling the hammer of a gun. Then, there was the problem of rigor mortis. He estimated the body had been dead for at least twelve hours before he found it.

Perhaps the greatest surprise to him was when he removed the brain from the skull. Inside he found a small .36 caliber round ball type bullet, similar in style to the kind of weapons used during the Civil War. They used a round ball and not a lead bullet. He also found no exit wound through the front of the skull. He remembered the gun Bob Ford had showed him, a .44 caliber.

So how, he wondered, did Bob Ford shoot the victim through the back of the skull with a .44 caliber gun and have it enter the wall with no exit wound in the skull? And how was it there was a .36 caliber round ball still stuck in the skull?

Furthermore, how did he get those two holes in his chest—*after* he died? Nothing added up to him.

He returned the brain to the skull and noted these anomalies in his report. Then he released the body to the undertaker and left.

Later that day, a photographer arrived to take photographs of the body. It appeared someone during that time had dyed the victim's hair with boot polish, evidenced by the staining on the pillow in the coffin. A picture was taken with his shirt off, which showed the two bullet holes in the chest. Later, they took more photos of the body in the coffin with his shirt on, and still more when he was surrounded by people in the funeral home.

The coroner stopped by the sheriff's office and relayed his concerns regarding the round bullet he found in the skull. The coroner laid the flattened lead ball in Timberlake's hand and tersely stated, "There's no exit wound out the front of the skull Sheriff. What do you make of that?"

"Can't explain it," the Sheriff said, "but we'll bring it up at the inquest. I'm sure it will all sort itself out."

"This is a mighty troubling case, Sheriff. I don't think I can sign off on this autopsy."

"Doc, the important thing is that Jesse James is dead. And it's imperative he stay that way, you catch my drift?"

"Loud and clear, Sheriff."

Zerelda James-Samuel arrived in town and went straight to the funeral parlor without checking in with the sheriff. When she arrived, the coroner was there along with a reporter and some of the deputies who were recently enlisted to protect the body. She viewed the victim and stated emphatically, "No gentleman, that is not my son."

The reporter wrote down what she said and ran out of the room. One of the deputies hurried out and fetched J. Frank Dalton, who rushed into the parlor and pulled Zerelda aside. He looked around to make sure they were alone.

"Zerelda, of course it's not Jesse. We've set this whole thing up. We tried to catch you before you got here. You've got to play along, Aunt Zee."

"Who is that in the coffin?" Zerelda inquired. "He sure looks familiar."

"That doesn't matter right now. Point is, we've got to pull this off or they'll be chasing your Jesse for the rest of his life."

"What's in it for me?"

"Ah ha, now the Zerelda I know and love has shown up."

He looked around again and continued. "We'll drop off some gold after the burial. A thousand dollars worth. That should help you to remember how sad it is to see your favorite son lying dead in that casket, right?"

"Two thousand would make it much less painful, J. Frank."

"All right then, two thousand it is."

"Where is my Jesse?" she finally asked.

J. Frank pointed across the street to a man leaning against the corner of a building. Jesse tipped his hat and smiled at them.

"Now go back over there and set them boys straight. And buy your 'son' a nice fancy funeral while you're here. Nothing but the best for Jesse James, ya hear," J. Frank said as he winked at his aunt.

"I understand completely, nephew. You can count on me."

"I knew we could, Auntie Zee."

During that time, Sheriff Timberlake had collected signed affidavits of over twenty men swearing that the man in the coffin was indeed the famous outlaw Jesse Woodson James.

However, two detectives arrived on the scene from Kansas City. After looking at the body, they were convinced it couldn't possibly be Jesse James.

A messenger arrived with a telegram for Sheriff Timberlake from Marshal Craig in Kansas City. It stated he was coming in on the afternoon train to take charge of the body. They were to escort the body to Kansas City for positive identification. Sheriff Timberlake showed the telegraph to J. Frank.

"We've got to get that body back to the farm and bury it quick," the sheriff remarked. "If it goes to KC, they'll figure out from the injuries it ain't Jesse"

"Agreed," said J. Frank. "But the next train isn't leaving for a couple of hours."

"Let's move him to the ice house until we can load up the train," Timberlake suggested. "That way, we can say we missed them and the telegram. Governor Crittenden will back us if push comes to shove."

"We don't want to play that card if we don't have to, Sheriff. Once we get my cousin's body into the ground at the farm, they won't be able to do anything about it. Sacrilegious and all," Dalton said with a smirk.

"I'll get the men to move the body and we'll all meet at the train," the sheriff told J. Frank.

Monday, April 3, 1992
Train Station – Late afternoon

The train arrived from Kansas City with Police Marshal Craig eyeing the scene at the station. There was a coffin, Sheriff Timberlake and twenty plus deputies standing guard. He quickly stepped off the train and walked up to Timberlake.

"I'm here to take charge of the body," Craig commanded.

"I have not been authorized to turn it over to you."

"Did you not receive my telegram? I'm here from the highest authority."

"No, I didn't get no telegram," Timberlake responded. "And I don't give a damn whose authority you are here on. This county is my jurisdiction under constitutional authority of Posse Commitatus. And these men are my sworn posse.

"I have determined that all the evidence we need has been discovered and that this body is released to the next of kin for burial," said the sheriff.

"This is outrageous," replied Craig. "We have no evidence that Jesse James is in there. We need proof before we can release the reward money."

"I have affidavits from twenty men who say otherwise. The body has been positively identified as that of Jesse Woodson James. All is legal here and you will release the money."

"We'll see about that, Sheriff."

The deputies loaded the casket on the train and stood ready to escort the body to Kearny, Missouri. Craig motioned to two detectives who took their places on each side of him while opening their coats and displaying their guns.

The sheriff's "deputies" spread out and pulled back their coats, clearing their weapons to draw. Several men had rifles raised in

Craig's direction. Timberlake silently watched the scene unfold as he looked Craig in the eye, not flinching one iota.

"What's it gonna be Craig? You're in my yard and I have twenty officers here who intend to back my authority."

Craig held his gaze on Timberlake. "I have my orders."

"Your orders don't look like there gonna serve you and your two detective friends too well here, do they?"

Suddenly a conductor, watching from the doorway, ran up between the two groups. "Gentlemen, for heaven's sake don't draw your pops here!" he pleaded.

Craig and Timberlake looked over at the station operator, mildly humored by the man. In that moment, they acknowledged the seriousness of what was about to take place. A stand off that could only end badly for the marshal.

Finally Craig relented.

"Looks like you won this one, Sheriff. But you can be sure the governor will hear about this and take appropriate action against you."

"I'll deal with that," said the sheriff. "Now, if you gentleman will move aside, we can be on with our business of getting Jesse James' body back to his home."

Tuesday, April 4, 1882
James Farm – Kearny, Missouri

The deputies hauled the coffin to the James farm and set it next to the small family burial plot. Four men had been digging for several hours through the frozen ground, and at last the grave was ready. Six men unceremoniously grabbed the coffin, shoved ropes underneath and slowly lowered it into the ground.

Zerelda motioned for Dalton to meet her alongside the rear of the barn. To her surprise, another man joined them.

"Jesse, my lord, I had such a fright."

He tipped his hat respectfully as she turned her attention to Dalton and continued. "I will need more money, J. Frank. The pressure is really on me to say that it's not Jesse." She looked over at Jesse, "I mean it's not you, son, in that coffin. It'll be really hard keepin' it secret."

"How much more do you want, Auntie Zee?" asked Dalton.

"Double."

"You know Ma, that's a lot of money," Jesse said. "I'd think you would be glad just to see it wasn't me in that there grave."

"I am son, I am. But business is business. I'm gonna need more."

Jesse looked at Dalton who shrugged his shoulders in a "what the hell can you do" way.

"Okay Auntie, I'll take care of it," Dalton said. "But you've got to swear at the inquest that it is Jesse in that coffin."

"Oh, you can be sure they'll believe me once I get through," she assured him.

"Likely they will," Jesse responded. "Well, I guess we better get," he said to Dalton as he turned back toward Zerelda. "Been a pleasure as always, Ma." He bowed his head again in a respectful manner.

"You take care, son."

"I'll come see you in a couple weeks, after the inquest," Dalton told Jesse as he departed.

"Look forward to it, cousin."

Jesse mounted his horse and tipped his hat as he rode away.

At the inquest, it was ruled that Jesse Woodson James was in fact killed by Bob Ford—in spite of the coroner's report that contradicted the entire story and numerous eyewitness accounts that stated it was not the famous outlaw.

A copy of this Coroner's report is available on the website

www.JesseJamesSecret.com

The Final Proof

The exhumation of "Jere Miah James" of Neodesha, Kansas in May of 2003 and the application of modern day CSI investigative methods conclude without a doubt that Jesse Woodson James went on to live a long and happy life.

As a final note of proof, I leave you with the only known wedding photos of Jesse Woodson James. He is seen with his one and only lifelong wife, Martha Jane Presgrove, both in 1872 and again in 1902.

New wedding photo 1872

Jere Miah & family 1902

Martha Jane had eight children with Jesse James and died December 27th, 1934. Jesse was so distraught over the loss of his beloved Martha that he went to bed and refused to eat.

Jeremiah "Jesse" Woodson James died of a broken heart on February 9, 1935.

Dedication

I dedicate this book to the most important people in my life, my family and dear friends. It is solely due to their patience and understanding that I was able to invest myself in the project. I want to thank my parents, Don and Valerie Pastore for equipping me with the tools I would need to overcome all of the obstacles and drama thrown in my path.

Special thanks goes to my daughters, Abigail and Veronica for all of the great questions their inquisitive minds came up with. Seeking out the answers for them led to many discoveries and insights. They have been real troopers on our excursions, exploring many wondrous places. They have marched through wilderness, climbed mountains and crawled through caves with me. Amazingly, they never complained no matter what the challenge.

I also want to thank the girls' mother, Lynda for her extreme patience and understanding throughout our lives, both together and apart. I am indebted to her in many ways, but most of all for the way she raised our children. She is an amazing woman and I am very fortunate to have had her in my life.

I must also thank my team of fellow explorers and researchers. We have gone on many a rigorous march through rugged remote areas. They have bravely faced dangers I had no right to ask anyone to endure. Yet, they took it all in stride and relished the adventures—traveling through severe weather, rockslides, freezing wet caves and encounters with a myriad of wild and human beasts. Yet, we have remained a team, tolerating my relentless drive without complaint. They are the best allies a man could hope for and have helped make it happen.

Finally, I have to express my deep gratitude to my co-author, John O'Melveny Woods. He has followed this project for many years and encouraged me along. His advice and ultimately coming on board helped bring this book to fruition. John's insight and intuition allowed him to bring out the moment of the experience as it happened. His suggestion to write this book in its' present format has made it a richer experience, and reads much better than my previous attempts at simply regurgitating dry empirical facts on the subject matter. The intent is to educate with the facts and entertain with a look at my personal path of discovery as well.

I hope my story will inspire others to take the risk to follow their dreams.

RJP

Appendix

A – *KGC Aliases*

B – *List of Robberies*

C – *James Gang Members*

D – *Pall bearers at Funeral*

E – *Masonic Temple Speech*

F – *Mysterious Joe Vaughn Manuscript*

G – *Robert Sallee James*

H – *Jesse Frank Dalton*

I – *Inquest search*

J – *Northfield Bank Robbery*

K – *DNA Explanation*

L – *Notes to Kurtis Productions*

M – *Parody by Jesse James*

N – *A deck of cards*

O – *For Sale*

About the Authors

APPENDIX - A

Names of groups known to be associated with the Knights of the Golden Circle (KGC)

Knights of the Outer Circle
Copperheads
Knights of the White Camilla
Keetoowah Society
Knights of Pythias
Albert Pike Lodge
Ku Klux Klan (Closed Club Clan)
Scottish Rite Masonry
Night Riders
Old Populist Party
Patteroos
The Lone Star
Red Shirts
The Legion
Regulators
The Home Council
Modern Woodman
The Order
Odd Fellows
Knights Templar
Order of Sons of Liberty
The Blue Lodge
International Anti-Horse Thief Association
Order of American Knights

APPENDIX - B

LIST OF KNOWN ROBBERIES
(Amount may vary depending on the source)

- February 13, 1866, Clay Co. S&L, Liberty, Missouri. **$105,000** (Cash, gold, silver & bonds)
- October 30, 1866, Mitchell & Co. Bank, Lexington, Missouri. **$2,000**
- 1866 Adams Express, New York, New Haven, & Hartford R.R. **$700,000**
- May 22, 1867, Hughes & Wasson Bank, Richmond, Missouri. **$4,000**
- March 20, 1868, Southern Deposit Bank, Russellville, Kentucky. **$15,000** ($5,000 cash, the rest in gold coins.)
- February 13, 1869, Richmond Bank, Richmond, Missouri.
- December 7, 1869, Daviess County Savings Assoc., Gallatin, Missouri. **$700**
- June 3, 1871, Ocobock Brother's Bank, Croydon, Iowa. **$6,000**
- April 29, 1872, Columbia Bank, Columbia, Kentucky. **$6,000**

- September 26, 1872, Kansas City Fair, Kansas City, Missouri. **$10,000**
- May 27, 1873, Savings Association, Genevieve, Missouri. **$4,100**
- July 21, 1873, Chicago & Rock Island R.R., Adair Iowa. **$26,000**
- January 15, 1874, Stagecoach holdup near Hot Springs, Arkansas. **$8,000**
- January 31, 1874, St. Louis & Southern R.R., Gads Hill, Missouri. **$22,000**
- April, 1874, Austin Stage Line, Austin, Texas. **$3,000**
- August 30, 1874, Waverly Stagecoach, (amount unknown)
- August 30, 1874, Lexington Stagecoach, (amount unknown)
- December 7, 1874, Tishomingo Bank, Corinth, Mississippi. **$10,000**
- December 8, 1874, Kansas Pacific R.R., Muncie, Kansas **$55,000**
- September 5, 1875, Huntington Bank, Huntington, West Virginia. **$20,000**
- July 7, 1876, Missouri-Pacific R.R., Rocky Cut, Missouri. **$17,000**
- September 7, 1876, First National Bank, Northfield, Minnesota. **$100,000**

- October 8, 1879, Chicago-Alton & St. Louis R.R., Glendale, Missouri. **$50,000**

- September 3, 1880, Express Stagecoach, Mammouth Cave, Kentucky. **$1,800**

- March 11, 1881, Gov't. Paymaster, Muscle Shoals, Alabama. **$5,200**

- July 15, 1881, Chicago, Rock Island R.R., Winston, Missouri. **$15,000**

- September 7, 1881, Chicago & Alton R.R., Blue Cut, Missouri. **$15,000**

- Sub-total of robberies = **$1,202,800** *in 1865 dollars.*

In today's dollars…?

APPENDIX - C

James Gang Members

Note: 44 of the 82 gang members were Quantrill's Rebel (Aliases noted in parenthesis)

Jesse W. James* (Tom "JD" Howard, Wm Campbell, Charles Lawson, Tom Johnson… 22 known aliases)
Alexander Franklin James* (JB Woodson, Buck Woods)
James Anderson*
Daniel Tucker "Ike" Bassham*
Sam Bass
James "Ike" Berry* (Boze Kazy)
John "Jack" Bishop*
William "Bill" Blackmore*
Felix Bradley
Richard "Dick" Burns*
Bill Chadwell (Bill Stiles, Jack Ladd, Jack Ward, Cherokee Bill Brown)
John Chatman*
William "Bill" Chiles*
Mike & Tom Clearey
Archibald "Archie" Clement*
Bradley Collins
James "Jim" Collins
Ben Cooper
James Robert "Windy Jim" Cummings*
Benjamin H. "Jack" Davis*
Edwin Daniels
Jim Devers*
Andrew Moorman "Mone" Diggs

J. F. Edmondson
Isaac "Si" Flannery*
Will Freeman*
Charley Wilson Ford
Robert Newton Ford
Frank Gregg*
James "Bill" Hickman*
John James Hinds* (Hines)
Clarence Bowler Hite
Robert Woodson "Wood" Hite*
William Hulse*
John Jarrette*
Payne Jones*
Sam Kaufman
Jack Keene* (George, Preston, Thomas Webb)
William Keoughman
Hobbs Kerry
John Land
Jack Latche
Andrew James "Dick" Liddel* (Joe Smith, Dick Little)
Lorenzo Merrimon Little
Arthur McCoy*
William "Bud" McDaniel
Thompson "Tom" McDaniel
Andrew "Andy" McGuire*
William Miles
Edward "Ed" Miller
McClelland "Clell" Miller*
Red Monkus
Allan H. Palmer* (Allen Parmer)
Bud Pence*
Donnie Pence*
Joab Perry*
Samuel Pipes
Charlie Pitts (Sam Wells)

Dave Poole*
John James Poole*
Robert Pop
Ed Reed*
James "Jim" Reed*
William "Whiskey Head" Ryan (Bill Ryan, Tom Hall)
Bud Singleton
Allan Shepherd
George W. Shepherd* (G. W. Smith, One Eyed George)
Oliver "Ol" Shepherd* (Robert Boggs)
William "Bill" Stiles (Alvin Steven, Bill Chadwell)
Joe Vaughan*
Samuel Wells (Charlie Pitts)
Richard "Kinch" West* (Little Dick West)
George White
James White
Joseph White
William "Bill" Wilkerson*
James "Jim" Wilkerson*
Jack Wymore
James Henry "Jim" Younger*
Robert Ewing "Bob" Younger
Thomas Coleman "Cole" Younger* (Thomas "Bud" Coleman, J.C. King, Tom Coburn, Charles Coburn)

*** Quantrill men**

APPENDIX – D

Pall bearers at "Jesse James" 1882 Funeral

Sheriff James R. Timberlake*
Deputy James Reed* (James Gang member)
Ben Flanders
James Joseph Vaughn* (James Gang member)
Charlie Scott
JB Henderson
JD Ford (Older brother of Bob & Charlie Ford)

***Member of Quantrill Raiders**

APPENDIX - E

Ron's Speech at the Masonic Temple

I started out explaining a bit about Jesse's early years, recalling some of his childhood incidents with his brother. How he got involved with the South's fight, including the time the North tried to assassinate his stepfather, Dr. Rueben Samuel, by hanging him.

I then shared a little bit about my adventure of becoming aware of the artifacts' existence and then went into the incredible untold story.

I mentioned Jesse was a prolific train and bank robber. The problem was being too prolific, that is, of committing more robberies than physically possible. So how could that be true?

I mentioned this point because it led into one of my main theories—that there were actually three Jesse Jameses and three separate gangs. The first Jesse was who we normally refer to as Jesse the Missouri outlaw, whose birth name was Jeremiah "Jesse" Woodson James. The second "Jesse" was J. Frank Dalton, who was in fact Jesse's first cousin and close confidant. His birth name was Jesse Robert James. The third Jesse, Jeremiah Mason James, was another cousin who was a common thief and train robber. He was much shorter than the other two and had dark hair and a thick beard. This theory finally helped explain the often conflicting physical descriptions of Jesse James by the victims.

The problem was the "real" Jesse was compelled to quit the life of crime for an interesting reason, it turns out—love. He then legally became a bounty hunter, while his cousins continued in Jesse's outlaw footsteps. Jesse Frank Dalton was determined and committed to hurting the North by plundering their resources for use in the eventual resurrection of the South, pursuing his quest with a vengeance.

There was some overlap between the two different gangs while Jesse was tying up loose ends, hence the confusion of who was robbing what, where and when. There were also as many as twenty imitators during this time, getting a free ride on the James Gang's reputation.

The point is, sometime during the years 1869 through 1871, Jesse moved out of the robbery business and into bounty hunting. There are physical records of him being deputized to do this type of work.

In fact, I called the head of the records division of several police departments to do a criminal records check on Jesse. I was surprised to learn he didn't have a record, nothing. That was really strange.

Among the interesting artifacts Jesse left in his trunks was a Special Police badge. So, I decided to try a long shot and check it out too. It took a couple of weeks before I got my answer. The letter stated there was in fact a Jesse W. James employed as a policeman. And, he was on active duty until retiring in 1921.

That rascal.

The other Jesse, J. Frank Dalton, was becoming quite successful in his own illegal ventures. Soon though, they were at odds—Jesse was trying to live the straight and narrow with his wife and family. While J. Frank Dalton and the other cousin were bringing ever more attention to the outlaw Jesse James and his gang.

There were several attempts by hotshot gun toting bucks to take Jesse in. And the new federal government was also after the James Gang. Jesse and his brother Frank along with his cousin J. Frank Dalton finally had to make a fateful decision. In order to get everyone off their backs, the legendary figure needed to die. Not disappear, because then everyone would still wonder what happened to him. No, he had to die. And publicly, to leave no shred of doubt of his ultimate demise.

They formulated a plan and rounded up the gang.

It was brilliant and deceptively simple. Two of the gang members would say they shot Jesse. It would be publicized in the papers, and then after the funeral, Jesse would live out his life under an assumed name, while Frank and the boys could turn over a new leaf.

No Jesse; no gang; the heat would be off.

But there were some hitches. One, Jesse couldn't tell his Mother, lest she blow the whistle inadvertently during the ruse. Another major hitch: they needed to present a body for the funeral.

The second problem proved easiest, when another cousin of Jesse's, one Jeremiah "Mason" James, started being a little too entrepreneurial and brought a lot more heat down on the gang. They had planned on quietly disposing of him at a later date. However, this presented them the opportunity they needed.

J. Frank Dalton brought a group of fifty-two men to St. Joe, Missouri on April 1st, 1882. (April Fools' Day) The gang had staked out the home of their bandit cousin and waited for him to go out to the barn. They shot him after a fight and escape attempt by the "victim".

The only thing that differs between Dalton's account of the murder and the forensic evidence in the autopsy is the name of the victim and the time of the killing. J. Frank Dalton calls the victim Charlie Bigelow, no doubt to spare the feelings of his cousin's family. The time of death issue was that it occurred at sundown versus sunup.

After all, you wouldn't wait until the day of the ruse to come up with a body. Most certainly, they would plan ahead and have their victim in place well before "executing" a plan as important as this.

Thereafter, the two gang members, the Ford brothers told their "amazing" story of how they shot the outlaw Jesse James to the newspapers. However, it didn't go as smoothly as planned.

News accounts tell that upon seeing the body, his "supposed wife", Zee and his mother, both denied it was Jesse. The detectives assigned to the case also said they doubted it was Jesse.

Missouri's Governor Crittenden, as it turns out, was in on the ruse, having received thirty thousand dollars of campaign donation from Jesse to gain his office. This was his return favor for getting elected.

Sheriff Timberlake deputized three James Gang members to "handle" the victim's corpse. And going against orders in an armed standoff, they buried the body on the James farm.

But the real clue as to what happened was the 1882 coroner's report on the body itself. The discrepancies between the newspaper accounts of stated events and the physical pathology were glaring.

The two killers stated they used a brand new .44 caliber Smith and Wesson model 3, serial number 3677, with a six and one-half inch barrel. The Ford brothers further state they shot him from behind, the bullet exiting the left temple, and striking the wall. Yet, amazingly, there was no exit wound or blood splattered evidence on the wall.

In point of fact, the coroner pulled a .36 round ball slug from the skull of the "victim", lodged behind the left ear.

The coroner's report of scars and wounds didn't match Jesse's known injuries. One glaring difference was Jesse's tooth abscess, which was actually a groin abscess on the victim.

I also found that there never was a death certificate issued for the most notorious outlaw of all time? I suppose nobody was willing to commit such a fraud should the truth get out.

And finally, the man pictured in the coffin didn't remotely resemble Jesse. He was short, stout, with thick dark hair and a scraggly beard.

I mentioned Jesse's "supposed wife". From my research, it appears Zerelda Mims was actually the wife of the murdered cousin, Jeremiah Mason James. She went along with the scheme for fear of ending up with the same fate as her now deceased husband.

Jesse returned to a life he had created a decade earlier under an assumed name, safe now that the outlaw Jesse James had been dispatched to the great hereafter.

To add a local touch, I told the story of how Jesse influenced another famous Wild West outlaw. While Jesse was in Wichita in 1869, he dated a woman named Catherine McCarthy for about a year. He helped her out of cleaning brothels and into her own laundry business. He taught her son, Henry, how to shoot a gun and ride a horse. Henry was part of a gang of street urchins who had the run of hell town, Delano.

Catherine later married her neighbor, William Henry Antrim and they moved to New Mexico in 1871 for her health. Henry took his new stepfather's first name and went by William Henry McCarthy. He later became famous under the alias William H. Bonney or "Billy the Kid".

The group of Masons I was addressing seemed to intently absorb the depth and details of this new approach to the story.

I wanted to take a few minutes to show the group what evidence I was talking about.

First, there are the artifacts within the two camel back trunks found in his daughter's home. Many of the items were shown in photographs of Jesse and his family throughout their lives. It is considered authenticated historical material when you can match up original photographs with the jewelry item shown in the picture.

But perhaps one of the most interesting finds were the diaries containing notes written by Jesse himself—decades after his supposed death. There were also dozens of pictures and many other items including newspaper accounts and funny enough, copies of books written about him. I guess he had an ego and a sense of humor, too.

And there is the genealogical evidence. A picture of Jesse when he is twenty-five years old exactly matches a picture of Jesse V, the great grandson, at age thirty. I've even put the two halves of each man together in a split image and you still have the same person.

But what has recently come to my attention is the result of modern technology and the heightened awareness for national security within our country. Facial Recognition Software or FRS was developed to detect criminals and terrorists. A photograph of Jesse at sixteen years old and of Jere Miah James, the same man many years later, were given to the Visage Company, a division of General Electric for facial analysis. The result?

Their analysis came to a definite conclusion: the two subjects are, in every respect, the same person.

In other words, Jesse James at sixteen years old is also Jere Miah James at over eighty years old.

This is where we are today. Modern technology and good old fashioned detective work have come to the same conclusion. Jesse James faked his death in 1882 and became Jere Miah James for the next fifty years until he "supposedly" died again in 1935.

Supposedly, because of other information that recently showed up. But first, I just want to say that the new documentary for the History Channel does not share the same conclusion that I have just laid out before you. (The 2003 Bill Kurtis Documentary) It is because they made what I consider a fatal leap in logic.

They were trying to compare the DNA from our recent exhumation of the Neodesha gravesite with the DNA from the original 1995 study. I have a problem with that, and I'm sure you can see why. If you are claiming that the first grave is Jesse James, then there's no point in testing any other grave to see if it matches. The 1995 test was flawed and does not prove anything.

And suppose it did match. What would that mean—that there were two Jesse James? Twins? We know that's not the case. Cousins yes, but a genetic double is impossible!

What legal bureaucracy would allow me to exhume a body if there wasn't sufficient evidence to the contrary? And yet they did approve the exhumation.

There were other sources of DNA available for testing, but the show refused and/or ignored them, leaving the costs out of the budget.

They also declined to include the facial recognition data, in part due to time constraints of the production.

The program concludes that the lack of a match for the DNA test negates all of the other evidence. That means the second grave doesn't contain Jesse James, because the 1995 DNA doesn't match the Neodesha grave. It's idiotic!

The show left out a number of other interesting anomalies, such as the viewing glass being at the feet instead of over the face, so it would have been impossible to see who was actually in that casket when it was buried in 1935.

I mention this because there's one other piece of evidence I'd like to share. An affidavit has surfaced in which a one Joseph L. Hines confesses to being the original outlaw Jesse James. The reason he is doing this is to *confirm* that Jesse's cousin, J. Frank Dalton, was the other person masquerading as Jesse James. The affidavit has been in the custody of the former Attorney General for the state of Texas.

I wanted to point out that an obscure book had surfaced, by this same Mr. Dalton, which he wrote just before his death. In essence, the memoir confirms most of what I have presented to you today, especially that he participated in helping Jesse fake his death.

I also want to point out that this affidavit is dated after the supposed death of the man I believe was Jesse James in Neodesha.

What does this prove?

Conclusively? Nothing.

But it was possible that Jesse James outwitted the world again and faked his second death. The coincidence is too great for someone to come up with this affidavit after the second death, especially if they didn't know who the Neodesha man really was. I am currently researching this in more depth and hope to have some additional information in the near future.

If it turns out to be true, then Jesse must have buried his son in his grave. Jeremiah James Jr. died of pneumonia he developed from digging his mother's grave in January of 1935. That didn't jive since his death certificate shows him dying in 1934.

Another enigma.

I also had a handwriting expert review the samples of the various subjects. At first, he dismissed all of the samples as not being Jesse's. When I called him and pointed out that he missed the two known samples for Jesse and Tom Howard, he changed his tune. In the end, he stated that Jere Miah James' handwriting was more confident and sophisticated then Jesse's, but he wouldn't go so far as to eliminate it. We have to keep in mind he was trying not to be Jesse, so he was trying to conceal his identity as not to match. Again the "expert" was operating from a flawed premise and contrary to what he was asked to do.

APPENDIX – F

The Mysterious Joe Vaughn Manuscript

During the summer of 2003, within a thirty-day window, I received three very interesting phone calls on the same subject. The first was from an elderly man who lived about fifty miles east of Wichita. He asked me various questions about Jesse James, which then shifted toward Frank James. He asked me if I had ever heard any stories about the possibility that Frank had changed his identity and moved to Arkansas. I told the gentleman I hadn't heard such tales but was willing to believe just about anything at this point regarding the James boys.

After dancing around with him for about ten minutes, I asked point blank what he was inquiring about. He finally came forward with the information that he was the grandson of Frank James, alias Joe Vaughn. He stated that he was in possession of a manuscript written by Frank and published a few years before he died in 1928.

I told him I was always interested in hearing new stories, especially those that were not part of traditional history. So I made an appointment to drive out and see the man the following weekend. The recollection of Jesse James using the alias Tom Vaughn piqued my interest.

I arrived at the man's home on a beautiful Sunday afternoon and was warmly greeted at the door by his wife. She escorted me into the living room where Mr. Vaughn sat at the dining room table with a book in front of him.

After some small talk to learn a bit about his family history, I asked him if I could have a look at the book. The title on the cover was, "The only true story of the life of Frank James, Written by himself". We talked about the information contained within the book for about an hour while I took notes.

His story was quite compelling, and I really wanted to get a copy of the book, even though I didn't have time to take from my research to go off on this tack right now. Any sideline research on Frank James would merely be goal diffusion, and I needed to stay focused on the upcoming History Channel project.

I asked Mr. Vaughn if I could borrow his book and make a copy for my research in the future. He politely declined as it was his only copy and he had loaned out other copies of the book on previous occasions to people who had failed to return them. So, I asked if he would kindly make me a copy and send that instead. He said he was quite ill but would try if time allowed.

Within a few days, I received a second phone call from another descendant of Joe Vaughn who lived in Oklahoma, also offering to send me a copy of the manuscript. Hedging my bet, I accepted the offer figuring one of them would come through with a copy.

Several weeks went by and I did not hear from Mr. Vaughn or the other party. However, I received a call from a third man in Wichita who said there was another descendant of Frank James who worked in a local music store.

This supposed heir was completely willing to discuss the book and said he would make me a copy and bring it by the museum. True to his word, he arrived the next day with a photocopy of the Joe Vaughn manuscript.

I immediately started studying the book and found it was full of interesting information that seemed somewhat credible and related to the James family story from southeast Kansas. As I read through the manuscript, I found problems with the accuracy of the information right from the beginning. An example was at the bottom of the first page in Chapter One, where Joe Vaughn gives a brief family history.

"Father was in Lexington, Kentucky, studying to become a minister, when he met Zerelda Cole, a girl who was pregnant by Edd Reed. They were married and shortly afterwards, moved to Missouri. To them was born three children, I, William Nelson (alias Jesse James) and James Monroe. I, Frank James, was a base begotten child, and was only half brother to Jesse James and James Monroe."

This paragraph was somewhat troubling to me in that it was historically inaccurate. Not only did it contradict the traditional genealogy of the James family from Missouri, but it didn't hold up with the family history of the Kansas lineage either.

I continued reading the entire manuscript, making many notes on the backs of the preceding pages and highlighting areas of interest. It seemed Joe had so many detailed facts that there had to be some truth to his claims. But, how could he be so wrong about the names of his own brothers?

One evening, my thoughts drifted to a recent trip to Denver. My host mentioned one of his neighbors had heard I was in town doing Jesse James research. They said they had a colorful character in their family history they wanted to share with me. The neighbors pulled out a great deal of historical photographs.

Many were of a gentleman who was apparently a hired gun during the Wild West era and had been involved in the Lincoln County, New Mexico and Johnson County, Wyoming cattle wars. Although he had been known by the family under the first name of Henry, I found some of photographs actually called him Jeremiah on the back.

One of the items in the collection of historical materials was a postcard sent by this man to his wife and family. It was signed, Anna Graham. Obviously his name was not Anna Graham, but in fact information contained on the postcard must have been an anagram.

Suddenly, it struck me that the Joe Vaughn manuscript with the incorrect genealogy may also be an anagram. I pulled out my notebook and started playing around with the paragraph in question. It was actually quite simple. I took the first half of the first word and underlined it. Then I took the second half of the second word and underlined it. Then I combined the two half words and joined them together.

To my surprise a new sentence emerged. It stated Jere Miah James moved near Neodesha in Wilson County, Kansas. A rush came over me that I had just made a brilliant breakthrough. Or, I had just fabricated the James family claim out of some non sequitur paragraph of a delusional old man from Arkansas. I chose to believe the former. I found many more messages coded within the text in the form of anagrams.

What are the chances of Frank James assuming another identity after 1882, finally revealing himself in 1926? And that he also revealed his brother, Jesse's identity in Kansas via a fairly simple coded message? Traditionalists would simply say *Balderdash!* I don't think we can easily dismiss such compelling clues. Especially in light of the secret lives they were living.

APPENDIX - G

Robert Salle James
Jeremiah "Jesse" Woodson James' Father

It was the book, *Uncommon Men—A Secret Network of Jesse James Revealed*, (by Ralph Ganis) that gave me the idea of the good reverend's involvement in clandestine affairs. I never really bought the story that he had gone in search of gold. It was out of character, and he was too involved with his family, parish and seminary activities.

In light of the fact that California was a hotbed of Knights of the Golden Circle activity in the 1850s, I found it interesting to note the traveling party that went to California with Robert Sallee James.

William Woods, age 30, first cousin to the Jameses and Youngers. The Woods lived in Clay Co. Missouri, near the James' farm.

Dan Showalter, who later became a colonel in the Confederate Army.

Merriman Little, who later won a seat in the California Assembly as a Douglas Democrat siding with the South.

They went to meet with Robert's brother Drury Woodson James, a wealthy health spa owner in San Luis Obispo.

Robert James had returned to Clay County, Missouri and married Sara Mulkey under the alias of Robert Johnson.

I believe the death of Jesse's father in 1851 was an obvious ruse and that Robert is really buried with Jesse at the Ross Cemetery near Neodesha, Kansas as William Restored James.

APPENDIX - H

Jesse Frank Dalton

Some of the claims in J. Frank Dalton's memoirs are so outrageous, they hardly seem worthwhile to research. One such claim was that Dalton was the Copper King and became a senator in Montana. When I checked the congressional register, I had to wonder if it really was true. The resemblance in the Senator's photograph to Dalton was uncanny. He also claimed Jesse and one of the Youngers were masquerading as Senator Elkins and Senator Davis within the Congress of West Virginia. Again, a search of the record revealed compelling photos.

Could it be that they so thoroughly infiltrated the system that they served inside the federal government? It was a little too much for me to fathom and I'm pretty open minded. Could that be the big secret that was keeping this story from getting out?

The enigma keeps expanding.

Frank James & Annie Ralston

Frank James

APPENDIX – I

Background of Ron Pastore's Finding and Deciphering the Inquest on Jesse Woodson James

It took about three years to track down a copy of the autopsy, coroner's report and the inquest. If the post mortem was accurately performed and recorded, then it should still exist. All attempts to find it in any of the Missouri archives failed. It was as if all of the information on Jesse Woodson James the week of the killing for that matter had been sanitized from the public record and from history.

I frequently received replies from various state, county and local city officials in Missouri stating the records had been burned in the 1920s or 30s. At least all of the cases that were thirty years or older were gone. That meant everything before 1886 was destroyed and lost forever. But, didn't they film the records for archiving, like every other governmental body in America? Especially with someone as famous as Jesse James?

Finally, the Clay County prosecutor stated that films were made and stored somewhere.

I decided to revert to academic sources and found the genealogical and historical records might have the files I needed. I figured Lawrence, Kansas had played a role in Jesse's history and the KU archives might have what I sought.

I hit the anthropology department archives, the library and finally the historical archives. After searching the catalogues, I filled out dozens of document request forms. Hours later, in one of the last three items, I found it. A detailed account of the autopsy and inquest. An academic had compiled the data from the actual records before they were destroyed.

As I read through the autopsy listing the injuries present on the body, I was shocked. I thought, this was a one shot killing, boom to the back of the head and he drops and dies??? But, this guy's got major trauma. The coroner's comments read, "Entry wound in right occipital of sufficient size to fit the base of a large tea glass." Upon removal of the brain, he discovered a .36 caliber round ball lodged with bone matter inside the left occipital lobe.

A .36 caliber?!

Left lower brain area? That shot was horizontal at ninety degrees to the right, not from behind and below.

"The body was about twelve to fourteen hours rigid."

So the victim was actually shot the night before. About nine p.m. not nine a.m.

That made sense; if you were going to stage a killing in the morning, you probably ought to have a body ready to go. Why wait 'til the last minute to go shopping for a corpse. The killing had to happen the night before so "everything" was ready to go. Nothing could be left to chance under these circumstances.

But, from the injuries to the victim, he seems to have put up a lot of resistance in the last moments of his life.

"Struck in the left temple with the butt of a gun…" It was not an exit wound, and the autopsy said so. The 1995 exhumation of the victim and reconstruction of the brain vault revealed there was no exit wound in the skull. And now we find that none of the bullet wounds to the corpse matched the caliber of the assailant's .44 caliber weapon.

That confirms that the single shot fired from Bob Ford's gun was aimed and fired at the wall, and the victim was already dead.

The photo of the hole in the wall reveals only a smeared bloody hand print and no blood splatter pattern. The victim had to have been killed in the barn the night before. Ambushed and pistol whipped when the victim went for his gun, the attackers twisted it out of his hand bruising the index finger and severing the thumb with a knife to get him to let go of his weapon. Gets shot twice in the ribs and shot in the head while lying on the ground from someone standing above him. That may explain why the close range shot didn't exit the skull if it was lying on the ground. It would also explain the blood transfer stain from the temple to the left shoulder. A blood stain on the left arm on the inside of the elbow streams downward, so the hit to the temple occurred before the victim went down. So, there it was, the death photo of the whole body revealed wounds just like the autopsy said it was. Corroborated forensic evidence.

Since the chest "wounds" didn't leave blood stains on the shirt, it indicates that the victim's heart was no longer pumping blood when the bullets entered. Two final shots to make sure he was dead. Those last two shots had to be out of shear spite since there could have been little doubt in the mind of the attackers that the head shot was fatal. Head shots are a signature of J. Frank Dalton, though they were most frequently over the left eye.

The only thing that differs between the forensic evidence and the accounts of the assassination of "Jesse James" by J. Frank Dalton are the name of the victim and the time and place of the killing.

That story was surely shortened to match popular mythology. The name of the victim was changed to protect his family and close cousins who were all James family relatives. Dalton attributes the victim's name as Charlie Bigelow and says he killed Bigelow's two brothers as well. This was another half truth since the three Bigelow brothers were killed in a shootout with the Jameses during the Civil War. Fletch Taylor is credited with actually killing them. By calling their cousin (Jesse *Mason* James) Charlie Bigelow, they spared their families any public scrutiny or scorn. It's ironic they had to kill one of their own to protect the rest.

The Missouri Jesse had retired to a life of bounty hunting, horse trading and livery stables back in 1871. That's when he married Martha Jane Presgrove under the name of Jere Miah James in Oskaloosa, KS just thirty miles west of his mother's Kearney, Missouri farm.

Since Jesse's cousin was using Jesse's identity to rob trains and banks, Jesse used the cousin's identity for himself. This went on for ten years before Dalton hatched the plan to end it once and for all.

By now Jesse had settled in Neodesha and enlisted a local widow by the name of Maggie Bolton to visit the governor of Missouri, Crittenden and set up the ruse. Dalton had given Crittenden $30,000 to run for governor a few years earlier. Now it was time to collect that debt. Sheriff Timberlake of Clay County, Missouri was advised of the plan and it was executed. Three James gang members, even though were wanted on murder warrants, were deputized to baby sit the body until it could be taken back to the James farm for burial. (Robert Woodson "Wood" Hite, a James Gang member was killed by Dick Liddel at the Ford's farm on December 4, 1881.) It was interesting that legal authorities, which now include Dick Liddel, found Wood Hite's decomposed body on April 6, 1882, a mere three days after Jesse's alleged death. Hmmm.

On the morning of April 3, 1882, the dead body of Jeremiah M. James of Carter Co, Kentucky was brought into the St. Joe, Missouri home where he had live under the name Tom Howard. The James Gang laid him out in the parlor and poured fresh blood on the carpeted floor. With everyone involved in place and ready, Bob Ford fired a single .44 caliber bullet from his weapon (into the wall). The Ford brothers then scurried off to the sheriff's office and reported they killed Jesse James. The sheriff went to the house, deputized three James gang members (including Dick Liddel) and took the body to the mortuary. The next day they held a funeral, which J. Frank Dalton attended as Jim Reed; the real Deputy Reed actually died in 1874, eight years earlier.

Then, the body was taken to the train station where they encountered police commissioner Craig of Kansas City. In an armed standoff with guns drawn, Sheriff Timberlake and his "Posse" took the body to Kearny, in spite of Craig's mandate from the state militia and the U.S. Cavalry to take the body to Kansas City for positive ID.

There is little question in my mind why no one questioned the body given up as Jesse James. If the man himself is standing in front of you, you give the answers you are expected to give. "Hell yeah, that's Jesse." No doubt about it. It is Missouri, don't ya know.

Jesse James and his gang killed the man, took control of the body as deputies and buried it. And the ruse has worked ever since, until now. We have him, or should I say them, by separating the three men who form this enigmatic person.

APPENDIX – J

Narrative of the Jesse James Gang
Northfield Bank Robbery

September 5, 1876 was Jesse's thirtieth birthday. Jesse sent Bill Chadwell into Northfield, Minnesota from their camp fifteen miles west of town. Chadwell knew his way around and could case the bank to see how many tellers remained over the lunch hour. Chadwell went to the saloon across the street from the bank posing as a cattle buyer using the alias, Bill Stiles. Apparently, someone in town got wind of the name and knew Stiles was riding with the James Gang. Chadwell was none the wiser and rode back to camp with his report. The next day, the James Gang rode to town about midday, and each man went to his designated post for the holdup.

They covered the Bridge Square as Frank, Cole Younger and Jesse tied off their horses in front of the bank. Bob and Jim Younger stood outside the general store across the street from Bill Stiles and Bill Chadwell. Clell Miller dismounted in front of the hotel and tied up to the hitching post.

Frank and Cole stood to either side of Jesse as they entered the bank. Jesse commanded the bankers to stand and yield. That was when tellers A.H. Bunker and Joseph Heywood raised their guns from behind the counter. Jesse's quick reflexes delivered a shot to each, winging them both. Frank ordered Bunker to open the safe, poking him in the nose with his long barrel Colt 45. The teller said he could not comply as the safe was on a time lock and it would not open until four o'clock in the afternoon. Frank was suddenly enraged to a point of folly and shot the man in the head. Jesse screamed at him for killing the man. Frank snapped a steely gaze back and said he had an old score to settle.

The outlaws started gathering what little money they could from the cash drawers. At that moment, Jesse saw the back door open as several deputies barged in with guns drawn. The gang opened fire on the deputies to drive them back again and then ran out the front door. As they hit the boardwalk, three riders were coming down the main street at a gallop. They were deputized locals named Ross Phillips, Jim Greg and Eldon Stacy. Jesse fired, forcing them to dismount and take cover. Over the crackling gunfire, Jesse yelled for his boys to take off and ride out.

Weapons were coming out of every door and window of the Bridge Square like some kind of morbid marionette show. Clouds of gun smoke made the targets nearly invisible. Judge Streeter, Marshall Hobbs and Deputies Hyde, Manning and Wheeler were all charging on Bill Stiles and Chadwell. Frank, Cole and Jesse were still pinned down in front of the bank when they saw Clell Miller throw his hands up to surrender and run into the street. He was hit with bullets from all angles and died right then and there. Chadwell grabbed Stiles' arm and yelled for him to mount up and ride.

As Chadwell rose from behind the rain barrel, Deputy Manning shot him squarely in the back and he fell with an agonizing cry. Charlie Pitts was down and Bob Younger was wounded too badly to fight on. Jesse yelled again for the boys to run for it. They managed to get to their horses and ran the gauntlet of shooters all along the main street. Jesse kept firing his pistols, one in each hand as he had in so many guerilla charges. Somehow, they made it out of the Northfield hellfire, but a posse of fifty men was raising a dust cloud behind them.

Bill Stiles had taken a shotgun blast to his back and the blood was making the saddle too slick to ride. Frank and Jesse ordered the gang to split up, and they took off for the Clam Lake Chippewa Reservation in Wisconsin. A bullet had split in two as it hit Jesse's saddle horn, and it creased his right leg and cheek. The Indians treated them both with powerful snakeroot medicine from the purple coneflower. Cole and Jim Younger headed to Watonwan County where they were tracked for two weeks before their capture in a thicket.

History is written by the victors and is often inaccurate. The papers said the James Gang made off with one hundred thousand dollars in the Northfield robbery. The actual figure is unknown, perhaps only about two hundred dollars before the guns started blazing in the bank. The tellers told Jesse the vault was on a time lock. In reality, the men were bluffing, and there was no time lock on the vault. In fact, the vault door was merely pushed closed. The handle was not even latched, so all they would have had to do is pull it open. But the bluff worked, and Jesse was too busy to open the vault with all the shooting going on. Some other folks in the bank must have helped themselves to the money in the confusion and convenience of the moment.

APPENDIX – K

Ron Pastore's DNA Explanation for the 2003 History Channel Show

I did not expect a mitochondrial DNA match for Jere Miah James. The basic premise of the test was flawed since we were looking at two different subjects. You cannot have two of the same person, therefore only one could be Jesse James. If we used the 1995 mtDNA as a comparison sample, we were saying it was a valid test. So, there was no reason to conduct a new test if it was valid. A match could only mean the two men were brothers with the same mother. And that outcome only works if we were exhuming Frank James.

Since I contended that the subject in the 1995 test was not Jesse Woodson James, the mtDNA must be different. I was certain it would be similar since the men were cousins. But DNA was not the way to prove this case until there was a complete genetic catalogue of all the primary subjects. We would need samples from Jesse's mother, sister, brother, niece, etc.

Additionally, I knew a negative match would not negate the fact that he faked his death. The evidence was overwhelming that he did. The trunks full of artifacts and the original coroner's report laid that issue to rest.

I told Bill Kurtis unequivocally he was presenting a fatally flawed argument and the audience would see through it. He obviously didn't get it since he presented the results as he did.

I was also surprised that Orchid Cellmark's DNA lab tech did not understand this either. They are supposed to be the experts.

APPENDIX - L

Notes by Ron Pastore sent to Kurtis Productions on discrepancies in the video they sent him

- Why did the Jere Miah James we exhumed have all of the original Jesse James family artifacts in his possession?

- Why didn't they show that the physical remains of the Jere Miah James we exhumed had physical injuries consistent with the original Jesse James?

- When we examined the bone in the lab we found the following:

- The lower jaw had an abscess from when Jesse had an abscessed tooth. (The 1882 victim's autopsy showed an abscess in the left groin. That is not consistent with a dental abscess.)

- There was an arthritic first vertebra consistent with the injury Jesse sustained when he was dragged with a rope around his neck.

- The remains had an arthritic left ankle which is consistent with the injury Jesse had when he was thrown from his horse and got his foot caught in his stirrup.

- Why does the mysterious corpse laid in the 1882 grave NOT resemble Jesse James?

- Why didn't they show the photos I had provided of the man who did match the corpse, the cousin Jeremiah Mason James?
- Why didn't they include the original autopsy report with all of the trauma and rigor mortis being twelve to fourteen hours when he had allegedly only been dead two hours?
- What about the detective's report stating it was not Jesse James?
- Why had Sheriff Timberlake taken charge of the crime scene when he was out of his jurisdiction?
- What about the fact that the sheriff had deputized several James Gang members to handle the body and bury it in spite of orders to take it to Kansas City.
- And there was the ensuing armed stand-off at the train station between the sheriff and the police commissioner over the body.
- Why was the viewing window on Jeremiah James' coffin in Neodesha placed at the feet rather than over his face? Did someone not want it known who was laid to rest in 1935?
- Why does the great, great grandson, Jeremiah "Jesse" James V from Neodesha, Kansas look exactly like the historical Jesse James?

APPENDIX – M

Parody by Jesse Woodson James
(As contained in his lost diaries)

Let the Rest of the World Go By

Is this land we hold dear
Filled with cranks and near beer
Really worth while do you suppose?
I've been wishing today
I could hear some one say
Come down where the Bud-weiser flows

First Chorus

With co-cola cheer, bevo and near beer
I'd like to leave 'em all behind
And go and find
Some real old style to
Make you smile
That would hold you for a while
And bring perfect peace
Where joys never cease
In this land where we're all so dry
Give us real large beer
And let the rest of the drink go by
Is it our future lot
To drink soda pop
And bar real beer out-side
While malt and real hops
Across the great divide

<u>Second Chorus</u>

With Mexicanna hot ginger ale and soda pop
I'd like to leave 'em all behind
And go and find
A real live bunch and a
Big Dutch lunch
With Anheuser Busch
That had a punch
That kind of a feast
Would bring perfect peace
And nobody would be dry
We'd sing Baby Mine
And drink another stein
And let the rest of the world go by

APPENDIX - N

A DECK OF CARDS
By Jesse Woodson James

A well-known regiment in no man's land in 1917 visited a church. There was a soldier with them who they thought took a prayer book out of his pocket, but it was a deck of cards.

The captain who noticed them ordered the soldier to put them back in his pocket.

The soldier didn't obey the captain's order, however, but looked at the cards with pleasure.

After church, the captain took the soldier to the major. Addressing the soldier he said, "How dare you play cards in church? This is a serious offense. What have you to say for yourself?"

The soldier said, "A church is God's home and I disturbed no one."

The major replied, "You will have to explain yourself better or I will put you under arrest."

The soldier then said, "Do you see the ace? That shows there is but one God, who made heaven and earth.

"The deuce shows there are two natures, man and beast.

"The trey shows there are three persons in God, namely the Father, Son and the Holy Ghost. The four spot shows there are four evangelists whose names are St. Matthew, St. Mark, St. Luke and St. John.

"The five spot shows the five wounds of our Lord Jesus Christ.

"The six spot shows God made the world in six days.

"The seven spot shows God rested on the seventh day and we should serve him.

"The eight spot shows eight persons were kept alive on the ark, namely Noah, his wife, his three sons and their wives.

"The nine spot shows the chorus of angels, who were nine in number.

"The ten spot shows the commandments which were given on Mt. Sinai and written on two tablets of stone.

"The Jack of clubs is not honest," said the soldier, "so we'll lay it aside. The other three Jacks are the executioners of our Lord.

"The Queens are the women who anointed Christ and the Queen of Hearts is his mother.

"The three kings are the wise men who came from the East to worship the infant savior.

"The fourth, The King of Spades, shows Christ started One Church which will last until the end of time.

"The Diamond shows the pillars of the church. There are three hundred sixty-five days in the year, which denotes the three hundred sixty-five spots on the cards.

"There are fifty-two cards, which show there are fifty-two weeks in the year.

"There are four sets of cards, which denote the four seasons of the year and the four last things for all human beings namely death, judgment, heaven and hell of which everyone ought to think.

"Yes, I will tell you a deck of cards are as good to me as a prayer book in church."

The major said to him he has laid aside the Jack of Clubs and said nothing about it, only that it is not honest.

"If you will not punish me I will tell you," said the soldier.

"Speak up my son. I will not punish you," the major said.

The soldier then answered, "The Jack of Clubs is the traitor Judas, the captain who reported me to you."

The major then pulled out his pocket book and gave the soldier six dollars with the words: "Go drink to my health for you are the cleverest rascal who's ever come before me. Get out and have a hell of a good time on me."

APPENDIX-O

FOR SALE
By Si Pifkins
(Alias Jesse Woodson James)

One Ford car with piston rings

Two hind wheels and one front spring
Has no fenders, seat made of plank
Easy on gas but hard to crank
Carburetor split half way through
Engine missing, hits on two
Leaking oil and radius rod bent
Extra tire ain't worth a cent
Gasoline tank leaking gas
Good windshield but has no glass
Ten spoke twisted wheels ain't plumb
Three old tires, inner tubes on the bum
Top is gone and the body is nude
Radiator busted should be glued
Hind axel twisted in the differential gear
But the horn's got a honk
Both loud and clear
The transmission gears
Got an awful squeak
But the steering wheel
Is hard to beat
Two spark plugs
Just bought new
Won't fire any better
Then the other two
Front lights burn when

The weather is hot
Don't know if the tail
Lights working or not
She's full of carbon
Break bands no good
Brand new fan belt
Regular Ford hood
Three years old from the spring
Got shock absorbers
But there darn poor thing
Starts in low and
Stops in high
Had to let the other
Cars go by
By rights the engine
Should be re-bored
Then she'll be good
As a brand new Ford
She's got the speed
If you turn her loose
Burns gas, coal oil or tobacco juice
You can buy her right
If you've got the tin
It's a hellava good Ford for the shape she's in.

About the Authors

Ronald J. Pastore

Ron Pastore lives in rural Butler County, KS and divides his time between research projects and operating a Corporate Security Consulting firm. Upon graduating from KNC in 1994 he began exploring archaeological sites and caves throughout Kansas. As the

Director of the National Geomantic Survey, Inc. (NGS) he leads a team of ten researchers with expertise in a wide array of specialized technical fields that explore various sites throughout the world. Pastore's research was the basis for the widely viewed History Channel special *Jesse James Hidden Treasure*, as well as being the featured personality.

www.NationalGeomanticSurvey.com

John O'Melveny Woods

John O'Melveny Woods has been writing television and movie scripts, online articles and books since attending USC School of Cinematic Arts. Prior to this he was the CEO of various companies including USA Print, International. His company, indieTV, created the first interactive television show in partnership with Microsoft Corporation. His books include *10 Minute Win,* and *Return to Treasure Island,* a sequel based on the original Robert Louis Stevenson classic, *Treasure Island.* He created and Executive Produced *Jesse James Hidden Treasure,* which aired on the History Channel and is based on the information in this book.

He lives in Fairhope, Alabama.

www.JohnWoodsAuthor.com

Now Available at

The authors have made available many of the documents mentioned in this book, as well as pictures and a lot of background information and recommended reading on the web site:

www.JesseJamesSecret.com

We invite you to visit it.

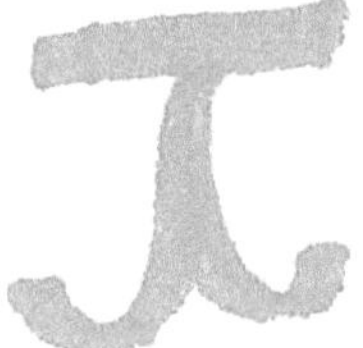

Photo Credits

Page	Photo	Credit
v	James Woodson James	No credit
1	James Gang	Steven A. Crowley
9	JJ Initials	RJ Pastore
26	Cave Spring cave	RJ Pastore
35	JWJ age 25	No credit
37	Robert Sallee James	James Family Collection
37	Zerelda James	No credit
39	Baby James	RJ Pastore
40	JWJ age 10	No credit
41	JWJ age 12	James Family Collection
43	Stonewall by JWJ	James Family Collection
46	Chief Go-Lightly	James Family Collection
48	JWJ	LOC Library of Congress
50	Quantrill hideout cave	RJ Pastore
60	Dime novel	No credit
64	A. Pinkerton	Library of Congress
66	Bullet hole in JJ house 1902	Heaton-Bowman Funeral Home
67	Corpse	Library of Congress
69	Heirlooms	James Family Collection
71	Aunt Daisy	James Family Collection
76	Heirlooms	James Family Collection
101	Treasure sign	RJ Pastore
109	KGC exposé	No credit
117	RJP	RJ Pastore
125	JWJ group	RJ Pastore
126	JFD group	RJ Pastore
127	J Mason J group	RJ Pastore
146	JJ museum	RJ Pastore
147	Treasure sign	RJ Pastore
166	Treasure sign	RJ Pastore
174	JMJ family portrait	James Family Collection
175	JMJ family portrait	James Family Collection
177	Facial recognition analysis	Bob Schmitt
197	Petroglyph	RJ Pastore

217	JMJ headstone	RJ Pastore
227	1882 corpse	Library of Congress
249	JWJ wedding photo	RJ Pastore
249	JMJ family portrait	James Family Collection
275	Frank James & Anne Ralston	No credit
275	Frank James	No credit
293	Ronald J. Pastore	No credit
293	John O'Melveny Woods	No credit

www.ingramcontent.com/pod-product-compliance
Lightning Source LLC
Chambersburg PA
CBHW030547310726
48979CB00010B/2059/J

* 9 7 8 1 9 4 5 1 9 0 1 3 1 *